The Mistmantle Chronicles
BOOK THREE

The Heir *of* Mistmantle

by

M. I. McAllister

Illustrated by

Omar Rayyan

miramax books

HYPERION BOOKS FOR CHILDREN
New York

For Brenda Mearns,
and for all of you who helped me through the darkest time

PROLOGUE

FROM THE HIGHEST TURRET of Mistmantle Tower, Urchin the pale-furred squirrel and old Brother Fir the priest leaned out to get the best view they could. They looked down on the sparkling sea, light golden sand, the treetops, the meadows, and the dark red fur of a squirrel leaping from branch to branch.

"There he is!" said Urchin.

Squirrels darted out of the way, moles jumped to a smart salute, hedgehogs hurried to open doors as King Crispin dashed through the bright summer woods to Mistmantle Tower, his paws outstretched, his tail streaming out behind him. Crispin bounded up the stairs and flew along corridors, but as he reached the doors of the royal chambers, he heard the high-pitched mewing of a newborn squirrel.

The guard mole opened the door to a room full of busy females. Mother Huggen the hedgehog beamed with satisfaction as she bent

1

over the queen. Moth the mole was washing her paws while squirrel maids whispered excitedly in a huddle. But Crispin, unbuckling his sword and flinging it into a corner, saw only Cedar, the queen, gazing at the squeaking bundle in her arms.

"A daughter," she said as Crispin came to sit beside her.

The baby squirrel's eyes were tightly shut, and her paws curled against her mouth. As Crispin touched the tiny pink ears, she opened her eyes, blinked, and, as if she saw nothing worth staying awake for, went back to sleep. But Crispin, taking the baby in his arms, felt that nothing could ever make him turn his eyes away from that small, sleepy face.

Once in his life before he had held a baby as new as this. He had been much younger then and had rescued a newly born orphan squirrel from the sea. That pale, wet little scrap, found on the shore and named after the sea urchins, had become an exceptional young animal who had resisted tyranny and faced dangers, but still liked to run up and down walls and splash in the sea with his friends. Looking down at this new infant squirrel, Crispin wondered what her future would be.

"She's a little beauty, Your Majesty," said Mother Huggen. "A right little princess. Two of you young squirrels, go and fetch Brother Fir and ask him to come and give her a blessing."

"And send for Longpaw the messenger to spread the news around the island," said Crispin, still gazing at the baby. "Tell everyone!"

"And can he tell them what her name is?" asked Mother Huggen.

So, on a summer morning, Catkin was born to Queen Cedar and King Crispin. She was born on Mistmantle, the island fairly and wisely ruled by her parents and their captains and guarded by the enchanted mists folded about it. As she grew up, she would learn about her island, and how few ships reached it through the mist, and how nobody who belonged to the island could leave by water and return by water. It was dangerous to go through the mists. Few animals left the island, and fewer returned—but most animals wouldn't dream of leaving Mistmantle, with its valiant otters, its bright-spirited squirrels, its loyal and hardworking moles and hedgehogs. There were woods and shores, burrows and tunnels, caves and waterfalls, hills and valleys, plenty to eat, good friends, and the king and queen in Mistmantle Tower high on the rocks. But for now, Catkin slept in her father's arms, her paws curled tightly against her mouth, completely unaware that she was born the Heir of Mistmantle.

CHAPTER ONE

WHEN CATKIN WAS OLD ENOUGH to look about her and her fur was growing soft and red-gold, the island began to prepare for her naming ceremony. That summer had produced an excellent harvest, and there were grains, nuts, and berries to be gathered and stored, well into the beginning of a hot, dry autumn. Otters, being shore animals, were never far away from the sea with its fresh breeze and cool salt waves, but they worked as hard as anyone, carrying heavy loads up the rocks to the tower. All over Mistmantle the work was hard and dusty, and the animals talked with yearning of the celebrations and fun of the Naming Day to come. *Soon, very soon.*

On the night before Naming Day, two events took place. The first was seen, enjoyed, and wondered at by every animal on the island. The second was not noticed at all. It was a long time before anyone knew a thing about it, and by that time the harm had begun.

Riding stars! A night of riding stars! These nights happened from time to time when the stars leaped free from their orbits, whirling and swooping across the sky, dancing and spinning so low that you could almost touch them. Brother Fir always knew when there would be riding stars, and the islanders made a great party of these nights, with bonfires on shores and high hilltops and, of course, a good supper. A night of riding stars before Princess Catkin's Naming Day was even more exciting, for something important always happened after a night of riding stars, either for good or for harm. Of course, they must be for good this time, for the princess's naming.

The squirrel grandfathers said that the stars were better when they were young squirrels, but they always said that, just as they always said that almond shells were getting harder these days. Some dismal moles and hedgehogs who grumbled about everything said that the last few nights of riding stars had all brought something good, so this time it must bring harm. The rest only laughed and told them to go away and find something useful to do. How could the stars be a warning of harm, with Catkin's Naming Day ahead of them? Times were good since Crispin had become king.

It was going to be an exceptionally good night for bonfires on hilltops and beaches, partly because of the long, dry summer, but also because Twigg, the carpenter mole, was moving his workshop. For many years, all the carpentry had been done from a cave near the tower, behind Seathrift Meadow, but there was much more work needed at the tower now—new frames were being made for Threadings, chairs for visitors, more comfortable furnishings for the tower animals and, of course, a cot, a cradle, and a coatrack. Twigg, who was always covered with sawdust, had needed to take on more apprentices. He was also an excellent boatbuilder, and was so much in demand that he'd decided he may as well work as near to the sea as possible without falling in. He was moving into a new workshop in a cave not far from the tower jetty. Of course, as Twigg and his assistants trailed back and forth from the old workshop to the new, there were scraps of wood, bark, and old branches being dropped and wood shavings to sweep up. The cry of "Can we have this for the bonfire, Master Twigg?" followed him everywhere.

Juniper the squirrel was helping Twigg. Juniper was training as a priest, but Brother Fir believed that novice priests should do some hard physical work from time to time. He also believed that it was cruel to keep a young animal in a priestly tower on such a day, so Juniper had been sent to Twigg.

In the old workshop, with its sharp, clean scent of freshly cut timber, Twigg was in a quiet conversation with his girlfriend, Moth. Juniper, not liking to interrupt, waited at the entrance. When Moth's two young nephews, Tipp and Todd, came racing to the door, he put out his paw to stop them from running straight in. Todd slowed down, but the older one, Tipp, was in his usual wild rush and didn't notice.

"Tipp!" said Moth. "Oh, hello, Todd! And Juniper! Tipp, I hope you didn't just push past Brother Juniper!"

Tipp turned and bowed so impresssively that it looked as if he meant to throw himself at Juniper's paws and beg for a blessing. Todd murmured "Morning, Brother Juniper," then "What wants doing, Twigg?"

"Yes, what wants doing?" asked Juniper.

"You lads can load up the rest of the smaller tools into a wheelbarrow for Brother Juniper to wheel around to the new place," said Twigg. "All the scrap bits of wood that might come in useful, they can go in another wheelbarrow."

"At once!" cried Tipp. He hurled himself into the task, but as every piece of wood he picked up became a sword, a shield, or a bow, he progressed slowly. Todd worked steadily.

"If you must have a sword, I'll make a couple of wooden ones," said Twigg. "Blunt ones, mind, and I'll take them off you if you do any damage with 'em. Suppose you want shields, too?"

"Yes, please!" said both moles.

"And a bit of firewood for your bonfire," said Twigg. "I wonder how I knew you wanted that?"

"Do you want the floor swept?" asked Juniper.

"I'll do that," said Moth quickly, knowing that Brother Juniper's lungs had been badly damaged in the past and fearing that clouds of sawdust would make him ill. After a few journeys wheeling wheelbarrows around the tower to the sandy new cave on the shore, with Tipp trying to help and swerving the wheelbarrows so that half the timber landed on the beach, Juniper returned to the old workshop to find it swept and clean with only a few old tools and some long timbers stacked neatly against the walls.

"They can stay there," said Twigg. He threw open a trapdoor in the floor at the back of the cave and disappeared into it. "I'll get the last of the stuff out of the storeroom, then we're all done."

"I'll go down there with you!" volunteered Tipp.

"You won't," Twigg's voice echoed back up. "I'd never get you out again."

"Are there tunnels?" asked Todd, his eyes brightening.

"Definitely not," said Twigg firmly. "Look out, now!" Hammers began to fly out of the trapdoor as if they were juggling themselves. "Put those in a wheelbarrow, and mind yourselves, they're heavy."

Juniper leaned down so that Twigg could pass the tools to him.

"I reckon there probably were tunnels down here once," muttered Twigg. "There's a locked door down here, and I'm sure there's tunnels behind that, and at least one more blocked door. I can tell by the echoes and vibrations. But we won't tell those two."

"Absolutely not," agreed Juniper, and turned his head to cough. "Come on, lads, we'll get these tools loaded up."

By evening the removal was complete, drinks had been brought down from the tower, and the young moles were armed with blunt swords and small wooden shields. Bonfires were lit. Everyone waited for sunset, watching for the first star to ride across the sky. Some of the young animals were playing their old hide-and-seek game, which began with chants of "Find the king, find the queen, find the Heir of Mistmantle." Now and again one of them would point to the tower and shout, "She's in there!" and they'd all shriek with laughter, finding it just as funny even after the first ten or twenty times. On the beach nearest to Mistmantle Tower, shore animals and those who worked in the tower gathered around a bonfire where fish was already cooking. Padra and Arran the otters, wearing their captains' gold circlets and swords, broke off steaming pieces of fish for their twins, Tide and Swanfeather. Tide ate his slowly and carefully, while Swanfeather took a large bite and presently blew out her cheeks and widened her eyes with the heat.

"You shouldn't try to eat so much at once," said Arran. Her tufty fur stuck out around her circlet. "It's not good manners. They'll bring soup down from the tower soon, so leave some room for it."

"I expect she gets her manners from me," said Padra's young brother Fingal airily. "I'm responsible for all her bad habits."

"What about mine?" asked Tide.

"You don't have any bad habits,"said Fingal; then, not wanting Tide to feel left out, he added, "You're really good at boats. As soon as I get my boat, I'll take you out in it."

Captain Padra, who had a pleasant face and always looked ready to laugh, did laugh. He looked around for Urchin, who wasn't far away.

"Urchin, I won!" he called.

"Congratulations, sir," said Urchin, coming to join them.

"Won what?" asked Fingal.

Urchin had expected to lose, and didn't mind at all. "Captain Padra said you'd be talking about your boat before they brought the soup," he said, "and I said not even you could do that."

"Oh, Urchin!" said Fingal. "I'm deeply hurt!"

"And the loser has to polish both sword belts for tomorrow," said Padra. "But I think I should do them. I've already been caught out once this evening,"

"Oh, good," said Fingal. "Who by?"

"You," said Padra. "You just said you were responsible, and I never thought I'd hear that."

"I only said I was responsible for . . ."

"Swanfeather's bad habits, I know," said Padra. "Fortunately, she doesn't have many. We have another big day to come after Naming Day, so we'll all be feasted to exhaustion."

"Oh," said Fingal innocently. "Is something happening, then?"

Of course, he knew perfectly well what was happening. Urchin and his oldest friend, a very sharp-spined girl hedgehog called Needle, were soon to be admitted to the Circle, the group of senior animals closest to the king. Neither of them were very senior, but they were both Companions to the King and did much of the work of Circle animals already, and the king had decided to make it official. This meant that Needle's mother polished Needle's spines every third night to make them gleam, and Apple, Urchin's foster mother, had given him a pot of deep red paste for the tips of his tails and ears, which were

11

the only truly squirrel-red parts of him. (He had thanked her very much, but he didn't use it.)

Urchin could see Twigg farther along the beach. Wanting to ask how work was progressing on the boat Twigg was building for Fingal, he hopped toward him, but he hesitated when he saw his old friend Captain Lugg the mole and his wife, Cott, coming to talk to him.

"Here's Urchin!" called Lugg. He was looking whiter than ever around the muzzle, walked a little stiffly, and carried a frothing mug of nettle beer in his paw.

"Twigg here says he wants to marry our Moth," said Lugg, beaming. "Mind, I've told him he'll never see her, she'll always be looking after Princess Catkin, like she is now." He nodded at Tipp and Todd, jumping waves on the shore. "There's our Wing's two little lads, and our Wren's just got wed, and now Moth and Twigg are sorted. One of these days I'll put my paws up and play with my grandchildren."

The sky grew darker, and the air cooled. They were glad of the bonfires with their fierce heat and smell of wood smoke, and the soup that made you unbearably hungry when you smelled it and warm all the way down inside when you drank it. Lanterns were lit.

"Star!" shouted Todd.

"Up there!" yelled Tipp, hoping it would sound as if he'd seen it first.

There were cries of "ooh!" from the crowd, and "Where, please?" from Hope, the shortsighted little hedgehog who greatly admired Urchin. Then there was an "ouch" from Urchin as Needle, who was looking up at the stars and not watching where she was going, walked into him.

"Sorry," she said. "I suppose I should stand still when I'm watching the stars."

Hope's mother, Thripple, came to take him up to Fir's turret. They were always welcome there, and it gave the best view of riding stars. A little group of their friends gathered around Needle and Urchin as they gazed upward. Fingal joined them, suddenly quiet and awed as a large star spun from the sky, swooped, and rose again. Crackle, the squirrel who worked in the tower bakery, had taken off her blue-and-white pastry cook's apron and joined her friends on the beach, enjoying their company as much as the stars. Sepia of the Songs, a squirrel who sang far more than she spoke and would rather watch beauty than talk about it, drank in every detail of the way the stars danced in and out and changed places, reflecting on the sea. The moon cast a rippling of light across the sea as if it invited her to walk across it.

Juniper, limping as usual, came to Urchin's side. His dark fur still had a pleasant smell of freshly cut wood and sawdust about it. Beside him was Whittle, the squirrel pupil of Brother Fir, and Tay, the otter lawyer. Whittle was learning the history and law of the island, and worked at it intensely. As he joined them, he was muttering his latest lesson under his breath: ". . . a bird for freedom, a cockle shell for a priest, an archway for a home . . ."

"Never mind your lessons now, Whittle," said Juniper. "Enjoy the stars while they're here."

13

"Oh, er, yes, sorry, yes, good!" said Whittle and directed his face earnestly to the sky.

The last to join them was Scatter the squirrel, gazing upward with her eyes bright and her mouth open. "Ooh!" she breathed slowly. Fingal laughed and put his arm around her.

Scatter hadn't always lived on Mistmantle. She had arrived as part of a plot against the island, but when she'd discovered what Mistmantle and its animals were like, she had wanted to stay forever. The way she had been forgiven, loved, and accepted still amazed and delighted her even more than the riding stars did. She had become particularly friendly with the otters, and was making herself a cozy new home in a cave near the shore where she could be near them.

"Ooh!" This time they all said it at once. A storm of stars hurled themselves tumbling across the sky and whirled upward. They turned to watch them circle the tower like a flock of birds and sweep away into the night.

"Doesn't it mean something when the stars do that?" asked Crackle. "Do you know, Whittle?"

"Um, sorry, what?" said Whittle. "Sorry, I wasn't listening. I was going over the Threadings Code again. Sorry."

"What's the Threadings Code?" asked Scatter.

"You know about the Threadings," said Needle, who worked on those Threadings, the painted, woven, and stitched pictures of the island's stories. "Well, the details in the Threadings all mean something. Flowers and things, they all stand for something."

"'Angelica for holiness, wormwood for bitterness,'" said Whittle. "I'm up to that bit."

"Don't worry, Scatter," said Fingal. "Ordinary animals like us don't have to know it all. So, does anybody know what it does mean when the stars do that thing—that once-around-the-tower thing that they did just now?"

"My granny used to say that you have to look at them and think of all your hopes and dreams and ambitions," said Needle. "You sort of keep looking at the stars and looking at your dreams as if the two go together. It's because, when the stars go around the tower, they go out of sight and come back again, and that's the way it can be with your hopes and dreams."

"Look at the riding stars, look at your dreams," said Sepia, stretching her paws to the fire. "I remember now."

"All I dream of is having my own boat," said Fingal. "Get looking and get dreaming, everyone!"

They smiled, but their hearts were with the stars. Urchin and Needle thought of the new life before them as full members of the Circle with all its responsibilities and demands. Urchin thought, too, of the parents he had never known. He folded his paw over the squirrel hair bracelet that was all he had of them.

Juniper gazed up steadily. There were two hopes and dreams for him. One was to serve the Heart and the island as the best priest he could be. The other was to find out who he really was.

Like Urchin, he was a foundling. Damson the squirrel had found him as a baby and brought him up in secrecy in the days when any animal with a twisted paw, like his, was put to death. He was sure that Damson knew more about him and who he really was than she had ever told him.

Brother Fir had called him "Juniper of the Journeyings," and he knew it wasn't just because of his journey to the Isle of Whitewings. On Whitewings, Urchin had discovered who his parents were. That was what Juniper wanted for himself, too.

A star twirled down, so fast and bright that the flash of it made Juniper turn and squeeze his eyes shut. Suddenly he shuddered, swallowed hard, and pressed a paw against his stomach to keep himself from feeling sick.

"Are you all right?" asked Urchin.

"I don't know," he whispered.

Behind his closed eyes, with the imprint of the star still before him, he had seen with intense clarity. For a split second he had seen claws: very white, outstretched claws. There had been something blue, something that he felt he should have recognized—then the silver flash of a knife.

"I'm fine," he said to Urchin. There was no claw anymore, no flash of blue, no knife. But he had seen them.

Nobody noticed the gull that flew over the island that night with a fish in its beak. It meant to land and gobble it down; but the fish was diseased and foul-tasting, so the gull dropped it and flew on, beyond the mists, without anyone seeing it at all.

CHAPTER TWO

A FTER DAYS OF SWEATING IN THE SUN, the animals were glad of a cool breeze on the morning of Catkin's naming. It was really still too warm to wear cloaks and hats, but many of the animals—especially the older ones—felt that you shouldn't go to a tower celebration without them, so there was a great flapping of cloaks and holding on of hats as squirrels, hedgehogs, moles, and otters struggled against the wind to Mistmantle Tower. Urchin's foster mother, Apple, a well-rounded squirrel, lumbered to the doorway at the top of the tower stairs where she dusted a few stray leaves from her cloak, identified the ones that belonged on her hat, and shoved them back into place. Seeing her friend Damson, Juniper's foster mother, puffing and plodding her way up the stairs, she waited.

"Well, what a day!" exclaimed Apple as Damson reached her and paused for breath. "What a day for a naming, a right proper do and all, and there they'll all be, all up at the front, your Juniper and my Urchin, up there beside the Circle and the captains and all, won't we be proud!"

"And Needle will be at the front, too!" squeaked a very small hedgehog from somewhere near her hind paws.

"Oh!" said Apple, peering down. "It's little Scufflen. Yes, Scufflen, your big sister Needle, she'll be there too, mind you always did find those two in the same place, Urchin and Needle, where you found one, you found the other, ever since they were little. Now, little Scufflen, you make sure you get to the front row, you get a good view, if I were you, pet, I'd just stick them spines out, except you shouldn't, 'cos it's naughty. . . ."

But by now Scufflen had found his sister Needle and had moved out of earshot. Apple and Damson joined the throng of animals swarming to the Gathering Chamber.

The bay window in the Gathering Chamber reached nearly to the floor and looked out onto a breezy sea of dancing white wave tips. Threadings made the walls bright with color. Sills and ledges were decorated with gold and yellow autumn leaves, late flowers in deep, dark red and orange, clustered seed heads, and shells and pebbles from the beach. The Circle was taking their places around the dais, where a scallop shell lay by a silver bowl of water. Whittle had placed leaves in an arc, each one scratched with the clawmark of a Circle animal, to make it clear who was to stand where. Rather nervously, he announced each one as they processed in.

"Docken the hedgehog . . . Mother Huggen the hedgehog . . . Russet the squirrel . . . Heath the squirrel . . ." He mustn't forget Captain Lugg's youngest daughter, who was in the Circle now . . . and that other new Circle mole, whose name was something to do with digging . . . oh, yes . . .

"Moth the mole . . . Spade the mole . . ." Just in time he remembered not to announce the captains yet, nor Mistress Tay and Brother Fir, who would arrive later. In the anteroom adjoining the chamber, the Captains of Mistmantle—Padra, Arran, and Lugg—were putting on their robes. Urchin had been helping Padra to robe ever since he first became his page, and lifted the turquoise-and-silver otter mantle from the sandalwood-smelling chest as he had so many times before.

"You don't still have to do all that," said Padra. "In no time you'll be a member of the Circle yourself, not a page anymore."

"But I want to do it, sir," said Urchin. "And this will probably be the last time."

"You could even stop calling me sir," said Padra.

"I don't think I can, sir," said Urchin, lifting the heavy robe onto Padra's shoulders. When he himself became a member of the Circle, a whole stage of his life would be behind him. A pity, in a way.

"Don't look like that, Urchin," said Arran, adjusting her circlet. "You won't have to be all dignified all of a sudden. Even the king still runs up the tower walls if he feels like it. Hello, Needle!"

19

Needle, having found good seats for her parents and Scufflen, had a message to deliver to the anteroom. She usually wore a blue hat in autumn, but had replaced it with an elegant gold cap for this occasion.

"The royal party is ready," she said. "We can begin as soon as they're all in. The queen says the baby's in a lovely mood, so we need to get on with things before she gets hungry or falls asleep."

"Absolutely," agreed Captain Arran firmly, as Padra adjusted her circlet for her. "We're all ready. Tell the squirrel trumpeters to play the fanfare."

"Tail tip, Urchin," advised Padra quietly, and Urchin smoothed down his tail tip. A high and commanding call of silver trumpets silenced the chattering of the excited animals crammed into the Gathering Chamber. They stretched their necks, the animals at the back standing on clawtips to see over the heads of the others.

"Off you go, then," whispered Padra to Urchin and Needle. Side by side, heads high, they stepped through the Gathering Chamber, not looking from side to side as heads turned to watch them, and took their places at either side of the main door.

Mistress Tay the otter came first, the island's lawyer and historian, her dark whiskers set in a grim straight line. It was said that nobody had ever seen her laugh. She looked, thought Urchin, as if she'd trample down any animal who got under her paws. Whittle followed her in the procession, looking solemn, as he was concentrating so hard on getting everything absolutely right that he even counted his steps. He wouldn't dare to annoy Mistress Tay.

Brother Fir came next, and the very sight of the priest lifted Urchin's heart, but Fir's limp seemed worse this morning. As always, his dark eyes had a depth of joy that Urchin had never seen in anyone else, but there was a furrow on his brow as if he might be in pain, and the gap between Fir and Whittle seemed to widen, as if Fir couldn't quite keep up.

Then Juniper, slight and dark in his priest's tunic, stepped to Fir's side and slipped the priest's paw through his arm, and Urchin smiled. Through the dangers they had faced together, he and Juniper had become like brothers. Steadily, patiently, Juniper helped Brother Fir to his seat.

Padra, Arran, and Lugg had taken their places behind the two high-backed carved chairs on the dais, but nobody was watching them. Ears and whiskers twitched, eyes were bright, parents held up their children to see, and little gasps of admiration rose from the crowd as King Crispin and Queen Cedar in their gold-and-green court robes appeared in the doorway. There were cheers, there was applause, and some of the very young ones jumped up and down in excitement and had to be calmed down as the tide of joy surged through the chamber.

Crispin and Cedar took their places on the dais. A real king and queen to be proud of, thought Urchin. Then, as the king and queen looked toward the door and their faces lit up with happiness, everyone turned to watch the entrance of Princess Catkin in the arms of Thripple the squirrel.

Thripple had a hunched back and a strangely squashed, lopsided look that should have been ugly, but the kindness in her eyes made her beautiful. Holding the baby very carefully against her shoulder, because it wouldn't do to prickle the princess, she walked to the dais.

Princess Catkin was, as the queen had said, in a lovely mood. Watching wide-eyed over Thripple's shoulder, she seemed fascinated by all those faces—or perhaps, thought Urchin, it was the hats. Thripple placed the baby in the queen's arms, the singing began, and Catkin giggled. Prayers of praise and thanks were offered to the Heart. Autumn garlands, trailing with deep scarlet leaves and berries, were carried to the king and queen. Otters brought nets of pebbles and seashells to lay before the princess, and from the workrooms came two hedgehogs and two squirrels carrying, spread out between them, the baby's naming shawl.

The workmanship of the shawl was so intricate and so beautiful that a long, low whisper of "oooh!" rose from the chamber. Star-shaped and as fine as a spiderweb, it was threaded through with gold, blue, purple, and green, and shimmered with color as they wrapped it around the princess. Touching all four paws and her face with water from the silver bowl, Fir pronounced the blessing over her in a voice that sounded just a little thin and croaky.

"Child of Crispin, child of Cedar,
May your heart beat as one with the Heart that made you.

22

May you walk and dance
pray and speak
laugh and weep
with the beating of the Heart.
May the love of the Heart and of all creatures fill you.
May you find love in all seasons,
all places,
all creatures.
Grow strong, grow kind.
Be a star in darkness,
Be warmth in winter,
Be the sea breeze in summer,
Be the breath of spring,
Be Catkin of Mistmantle."

Sepia of the Songs, the sweetest voice on the island, sang. The choir joined her, their voices blending so skillfully that it seemed they couldn't be animal voices at all, but something entrancing from far beyond or above the mists. Then Urchin noticed a nod of the head from a Circle squirrel toward the gallery, where a mole pulled on a cord.

Autumn leaves and rose petals tumbled from the ceiling, twirling softly, landing on hats, on ears, on cloaks, on shoulders as animals looked up and laughed with delight. Petals fell on Mistress Tay's whiskers, and she twitched them away in irritation. Oak leaves settled gently on the king's shoulders. A rose petal landed on Catkin's nose and made her laugh. They drifted onto her soft fur. At last, to applause and more music, the royal family left the chamber and made its way through the corridors of Threadings to their own apartments with Urchin and Needle attending them. Needle was so intent on making the baby laugh that she tripped on a step, and if Urchin hadn't caught her she would have disappeared from sight. She had recovered her dignity by the time they entered the royal chambers.

"Excuse me, Your Majesties," said Needle, removing a rose petal which had impaled itself on her spines, "when we have the party tonight, it's a shame if the nursery maids miss it. I don't mind taking a turn at looking after Catkin."

"And I'll keep her company," said Urchin.

"That's very kind of you," said Cedar, "but we have a rotation of nursemaids on duty this evening, so they all have a chance to go to the party. Jig and Fig the mole maids are first, then Moth and Mother Huggen, of course, and there are two squirrels . . ." but at that moment, Moth the mole maid, a little out of breath, hurried toward them and curtsied. She held Tipp and Todd by the paws. Todd, who, like his grandfather Captain Lugg, was a solid, down-to-earth mole, marched steadily beside her. Tipp waved an imaginary sword and pulled on her paw as he lunged at invisible enemies.

"Please, Your Majesties," said Moth, "there's a message from the two squirrels who were on the rotation. They're neither of them feeling well, and they want to go home. They didn't want to look after the princess in case they've got something catching."

"Quite right," said Crispin. "I'll send two of the guards to escort them home."

"Give them our love, and we hope they feel better soon," said Cedar.

"Take care what you're doing with that sword, Tipp," said Crispin, "you nearly took Urchin's head off." Tipp looked down at his paw in astonishment. Crispin took a little time to talk to the young moles, and to ask Moth about her engagement to Twigg, and Lugg's health, while Cedar turned to Urchin and Needle.

"I'll take up your offer to babysit Catkin," she said. "And there's another squirrel we can ask. Catkin should sleep right through."

"I hope she doesn't," said Needle.

The Gathering Chamber that evening was bright with lights and alive with music. Animals danced, watched entertainments, sang, and feasted. On hilltops and shores, beacons were lit to celebrate the princess's naming. Princess Catkin herself, in the little room adjoining Crispin and Cedar's bedchamber, slept soundly in her cradle. Needle and Urchin took their turn and were disappointed that she lay contentedly wrapped in a white blanket embroidered with catkins, her eyes tightly shut and her thumb in her mouth, a cream-colored blanket beneath her, and didn't wake up once. The rose petals from the naming ceremony had been spread about her so that she lay in a nest of them. Needle rocked the cradle while singing the lullaby that all babies in Mistmantle heard, from their earliest days.

> *"Waves of the seas*
> *Wind in the trees*
> *Spring scented breeze*
> *For your sleeping, sleeping*
> *Sleep while I pray*
> *Peace for your day*
> *Heart hold your way*
> *In its keeping, keeping . . ."*

She was still singing when the queen tiptoed in.

"We've had word of another squirrel being taken ill, and a hedge-hog," she said quietly. "Feverish and aching, being sick. I hope it's nothing serious."

By the next evening, more animals were reported to be ill, and the first two squirrels were worse. The queen, a wise and skilled healer, gave instructions about care of patients and supervised the making of medicines herself, but Crispin and Fir urged her not to visit the sufferers. Urchin stood on duty by the door.

"You can't risk bringing infection back to Catkin," said Crispin. "And she mustn't be attended by anyone who's been in contact with the illness."

"His Majesty is right," said Fir. "Dear Queen Cedar, simply train the island's healers, make the medicines, and leave the rest to us. If, while you do so, this crisis has left you without enough baby-minders, I'm sure plenty of animals will rush to your aid. Urchin and Needle, perhaps?"

"Yes, Brother Fir!" said Urchin.

"Thank you, Urchin," said Crispin. "You and Needle can take the second watch with Catkin tonight."

Another squirrel came to the tower to join the nursery team that evening, a squirrel widow called Linty. Urchin met her at the main door and carried her bag as he escorted her to the royal chambers. Dimly he recalled seeing her somewhere before—it must have been at some event in the Gathering Chamber—but she didn't come from his own colony in Anemone Wood. There was a sort of faded prettiness in her pointed face and large, dark eyes, and she had a nervous, wary way of glancing around her as if she expected something frightening to leap from behind the Threadings. She said little, and her voice was soft and shy, but already she was humming the Mistmantle lullaby under her breath. Urchin left Linty, giving her instructions—*Here's her cup, here's her porridge if she wants it, and she likes being sung*

to—and went back to his chambers at the Spring Gate where Padra and Fingal greeted him. Tide and Swanfeather were rolling over each other on the floor, and sawdust clung to Fingal's fur.

"Twigg's been helping me with my boat!" he said eagerly. "It just needs a coat of paint and the sail rigging up. It's going to be red with an orange border and a pattern of green leaves, and I want to call it after someone, but I don't know who. It was going to be Princess Catkin, then Swanfeather, then Tide and Swanfeather."

"Are Tide and Swanfeather all right, sir?" Urchin asked Padra.

"They look all right to me," said Padra. "Oh, you mean this wretched disease. Otters don't seem to be catching it. Are you all ready to be admitted to the Circle?"

"I don't really think so, sir," admitted Urchin.

They drank cordial, put the babies to bed, polished their swords, and talked about joining the Circle, until it was time for Urchin and Needle to take over from Linty.

"I'll go a bit early, sir," he said. "I don't want to keep Linty waiting. She looked as if she'd be scared of anything, even the baby."

"Linty?" repeated Padra, and Urchin left him gazing thoughtfully at nothing as if he were searching for an old memory.

"All quiet tonight," said the guard mole, grinning as Urchin and Needle arrived outside the chamber. "Not a squeak out of the princess. Better go in quietly."

"Mistress Linty?" called Urchin softly as they tiptoed into the chamber, dim with lamplight. There was no answer, and he bent over the cradle. It was empty. Linty must be rocking the baby in a chair, or pacing the floor with her. They searched, they asked the guards. Anxiety grew and tingled in their paws.

There was no trace of Linty, nor of little Catkin. There was only the rumpled catkin blanket, lying cold in the bottom of the cradle, and an open window.

CHAPTER THREE

URCHIN FLEW FROM THE CHAMBER, yelled to the guards, dashed back into the nursery, and leaped from the open window to run down the wall. From every direction, guards ran to search the chambers. A squirrel dashed to find the king and queen, and soon Crispin and Cedar were rushing to the chambers, their eyes sharp with attention and bright with fear. Fir was summoned, Padra and Lugg were sent for, Crispin ordered Circle animals to organize search parties. Urchin scrambled back through the window, gasping for breath.

"No sign, Your Majesties," he panted, "the ground's too dry for pawprints."

"Any signs of struggle in here?" asked Crispin. "Marks of dragging, claws digging in, anything like that?"

"I didn't see any, Your Majesty," said Urchin, noticing that Crispin hadn't used the words "blood" and "fur." It was bad enough for the queen without that.

"How was the room when you found it?" demanded Cedar. Her voice was urgent and intense. "Was that window open already?"

"Yes, Your Majesty," said Urchin. "I jumped out without touching it."

"The naming shawl and the blanket with catkins on it are still here," said Crispin, examining the cradle. "The other blanket's missing."

"No signs of struggle," said Cedar, examining the floor. "No paw prints in here, either. The bowl of porridge is gone, and her cup."

Urchin remembered a terrible day, long ago now. He had tried not to think of that day when the last Heir of Mistmantle, Prince Tumble, had been found murdered by a single stab wound. Nobody was talking about that, but he knew they were all thinking of it. With every scrabble of paws on the stair, heads whisked round. Circle animals arrived, and Needle hurried in bristling with anxiety, but nobody brought news of Linty and the princess.

"We've sent out search parties," said Crispin, pulling out a chair as Fir hobbled stiffly into the chamber. "Sit down, Brother Fir."

"So the child and the nursemaid are missing," said Fir. He sighed, and tipped his head to one side. "I don't suppose she's just taken the baby for some fresh air on a warm evening?"

"The only way out was the window," said Crispin, "and she didn't tell anyone she was going."

31

"Which nursemaid?" inquired Fir.

"Mistress Linty," said Cedar.

"Linty?" said Fir thoughtfully.

"The possibilities," said Crispin, "are that something happened to alarm Linty and she's run away, taking the baby with her, or that somebody got in through the window and forced them away. That's unlikely because nobody heard anything and there's no sign of a struggle. And the very worst . . ." He glanced at Cedar.

"I know," she said firmly. "The worst is that Linty is a traitor and she's"—she took a deep breath—"she's taken Catkin . . . and she . . . she means . . ."

Urchin tried not to look at the picture in his head, but he had to. Prince Tumble, lying dead and cold on the floor, so small. Death had come so quickly, and so easily. It could happen to Catkin too.

". . . perhaps," continued the queen, and he heard her struggling to keep her voice steady, "Linty has already . . ."

Fir had been quiet since Linty's name had first been mentioned. Now he held up a paw.

"Dear Queen," he said calmly, "I very much doubt that Linty intends to harm your baby, but I do think she will be easily frightened. If your search parties find her, it is most important, *most* important, that they don't send her into a panic. If she's alarmed, she will do anything to keep the princess to herself."

"What is it about Linty, Fir?" asked Crispin.

"What is it?" repeated Fir. "Hm. What is it? We must all search our memories, and I will speak to those who have known her longest."

Crispin dismissed the guards. Cedar, Mother Huggen, and all available members of the Circle remained with him in the chamber. Longpaw, the squirrel messenger, and Juniper were sent for. Padra arrived, saying that Arran and Fingal were setting a watch on the shores. Urchin and Needle waited to see if they'd be dismissed, but the queen herself cleared a space for them in the window seat. Captain Lugg appeared, a bit out of breath, his face grim and set as he bowed.

"We'll find her, Queen Cedar," he said gruffly. "I've set guards on all the tunnels."

"But Linty must not be alarmed," insisted Fir. "She must be spoken to gently."

"But you're sure she won't harm Catkin," said Crispin urgently.

There was a moment's pause. "I'm quite certain she won't *mean* to," said Fir. His voice was becoming an uneven croak, and Urchin offered him a mug of water. "Thank you, Urchin. Spring Gate water. Very good. But, you know—I don't wish to alarm you, Your Majesties, but you must fully understand the situation—we are dealing with an animal whose mind has been damaged. She is intensely loving, and for that reason I am sure she'll protect the baby . . ." He paused, and added quietly, ". . . as if it were her own. As I said, if she feels threatened she may panic, and by panicking, she could do something very dangerous."

"She mustn't leave the island," said Crispin.

"She can't," said Padra. "We're patrolling the shores, and Lugg's moles are watching the tunnels."

"If she's on the island, we'll find her," said the queen firmly. "We must increase the search parties."

"Small search parties will be best, if we don't want to alarm her," said Crispin. "No more than four at most in each. Every party to include at least one animal with a good sense of smell. And get the young ones involved. She might be scared of guards and the senior members of the Circle, but not someone like Urchin and Needle and their friends."

"We really want to help," said Needle. "And little Hope's very young, but he's good at finding his way by scent. We'll find her."

"Longpaw, we'll need you to summon animals to the Gathering Chamber," said Crispin. "We'll instruct them about what to do and what not to do. And there must be a senior animal here all the time, so they have someone to report back to."

"Excuse me, Your Majesties," said Captain Lugg, "I don't like to speak out of turn. I have three daughters myself, and I know how precious the princess is. But there's still a fair old heap of harvest to bring in, and we don't know how long this weather will last."

Urchin glimpsed a frown of irritation on Crispin's face, but it was gone in an instant. "You're right," said Crispin. "We mustn't neglect the harvest. It would have serious consequences for the whole island, and life has to go on. I've lived through dangerous times, and it's doing the ordinary things that helps you to cope."

"Harvest and all the everyday things will have to go on," said Cedar as firmly as she could. "Nobody should be forced to leave harvesting and search for Catkin, but . . ."

"We *will* find her," said Crispin fiercely, "because we have to. We'll find her, if I have to dig up the whole island with my own claws."

"And," Padra pointed out gently, "we have two new members of the Circle to admit in a few days."

Urchin and Needle looked at each other. They were ready to join the Circle. Their special new cloaks were waiting for them. They had prepared for the great day, practiced for it, dreamed of it, talked of it, and agreed that the best thing about joining the Circle was that Crispin, Cedar, and the captains believed that they were worthy of it. But it wouldn't be right, not now. Nothing mattered now, except getting Catkin back.

They understood each other without having to speak. Needle stood up and curtsied.

"We'd like to wait, please," she said. "It wouldn't be right to be admitted to the Circle with all this going on."

"It would be very hard for you to wait," said Crispin gently.

"We wouldn't enjoy the ceremony," insisted Needle. "Nobody would, not while the baby's missing."

"And it would take time when we should be out looking for her," said Urchin. "Your Majesty, you wouldn't be crowned until the Heartstone was found and I came home."

"Excuse me," said Cedar in a tight, crisp voice as if she were keeping herself sternly controlled, "but you're all assuming that the princess will still be missing tomorrow. We agreed that she's still on the island, and the search parties are out. Wherever can Linty take her that she won't be found?" She opened a chest and pulled out a belted sword, then a cloak. "I'm going out to look for her myself."

"Russet, go with the queen," ordered Crispin. "And you too, Spade. Brother Fir, do you need Juniper?"

"I need to speak to the animals who know Linty best," said Fir. "They will speak more freely without a youngster present. May I go now, Your Majesty?"

Fir hobbled away, and more search parties and messengers were sent in every direction. Soon, only Urchin and Juniper were left waiting for orders.

"Now," said Crispin briskly, "you two are to go down to the Chamber of Candles. Juniper, you must have visited it with Fir?"

"Yes, Your Majesty," said Juniper.

"And Urchin's been there before, too," said Crispin. "Good. You two, go down there with Docken and search the chamber and all around it."

"Certainly, sir," said Urchin promptly. The Chamber of Candles held so many unpleasant memories for him that it wouldn't be an easy thing to do, but it seemed that Crispin knew that, and was offering him a challenge. He wanted to show he was up to it. So, with Juniper and Docken of the Circle, he slipped through the Gathering Chamber to a small door and took a sharp turn through an entrance that you wouldn't even see unless you knew it was there.

36

"Good thing I brought a lantern," muttered Docken. "My eyes aren't as good as yours, you being squirrels, and young ones."

The narrow stairway led to deep, damp tunnels, and in spite of Docken's lantern, Urchin's fur bristled as he walked farther underground. His first memories of this place still held their power.

"You still find it creepy down here, don't you?" said Juniper.

"It's all right," said Urchin. These tunnels had been cleaned and changed since he had first come this way. Lamps shone softly on the walls. There were no nameless creatures anymore, scuffling about where you couldn't quite see them. But water still ran down the walls, leaving green patches and, here and there, a strange-colored puddle. He strained to listen for any shuffle of paws, or the squeak of a baby.

Long ago Lord Husk used to come this way to a hidden chamber with a history so terrible that it had been left locked for hundreds of years, and never spoken of, but Husk had found it. Its clinging air of ancient, creeping horror had drawn him and fed the evil inside him. It had been a place of nightmare.

Since Husk's downfall, Brother Fir had quietly and sensibly taken control of the situation. He had told the islanders of the long ago time when a squirrel king had committed murder and sacrifice in that chamber. He had opened it, blessed it, filled it with candlelight, watched, prayed, and sung in it, night and day, cleansing it of its past. It was now the Chamber of Candles, a place of prayer and peace.

"Sh!" said Juniper sharply. Urchin twitched his ears to listen and heard nothing.

"Not sure," said Juniper, but as soon as they started walking again Urchin heard the quick pattering of paws from somewhere in the tunnels.

"It's to the left of us," whispered Docken.

"There must be a passageway parallel to this one," said Urchin. The paw steps stopped again, and it occurred to Urchin that they didn't have a sword between the three of them. That was all right if you were dealing with a frightened squirrel who mustn't be alarmed. It was a bit unsettling if you were wedged underground with an unknown animal running about just out of sight. The paws grew louder.

"It's ahead of us," muttered Docken and stepped forward, but Juniper laid a paw on his arm. Urchin had already seen what Juniper had seen. His eyes were on a small cleft in the rock a little way ahead of them.

Something was moving. Urchin, stretching out a paw to the others for silence, crept forward. Whatever animal was wriggling through that tight cleft it must be a small one, and unarmed. He was about to ask who was there when a small voice said, "Oof! I'm squashed!" A small hedgehog pushed its nose forward, sniffed, and peered short-sightedly about. "Hello, Urchin!" He wrinkled his nose to sniff again. "Hello, Daddy!"

"What are you doing down here?" demanded Docken.

"Hello, Hope!" said Urchin. Irritated as he was at the scare the little hedgehog had given them, he was more relieved than anything else. And nobody could ever mind Hope. He was the son of Docken, and Thripple, the hedgehog who had carried Catkin at her naming. Hope was always so eager to please that he frequently ended up in danger, but somehow, he had always emerged in one piece.

"Hello, Brother Juniper, sir," said Hope. "I didn't have any orders so I thought I'd come after you, and I found a tunnel to explore so I explored it."

"Well, you shouldn't," said Docken. "It's dangerous, you're on your own, and what's more you nearly scared the spines right off me. Does Mummy know where you are?"

"I said I was going to look for the princess and she said to stay in the tower so I did and I have and I am," said Hope.

"I know you're good at tunnels, Hope," said Urchin gently, "but it's dangerous for you to come down here alone. There must be all sorts of tunnels we don't know about."

"Yes, I just found one," said Hope. "And there's a whole other layer under this one, I think, I can tell from the echoes and the way it feels."

"Well, don't go looking for it," said Docken. "We've already got one youngster missing."

"That's why I'm here," said Hope, pattering busily along beside them. "I want to look for the princess, because now we've got Mopple, that's my baby sister, Brother Juniper, now we've got her I thought wouldn't it be awful if she went missing and we didn't know where to look for her and if she was all right or anything, and it's the same with the princess. But I don't think the princess has been down here. It doesn't smell of baby."

"He's probably right," said Docken. "He has a very good sense of smell, haven't you, Hope? But we'll go on to the Chamber of Candles, as that's our orders."

Stopping now and again while the squirrels listened and Hope sniffed, they reached the Chamber of Candles. The sight of that door still made Urchin bristle—but as Docken pushed it open, the glow of soft yellow light met him, soothed him, and welcomed him into the warmth.

Candles flickered on the floor, on shelves, and in crevices in the walls—long candles and short ones, creamy wax candles with curls of wax rippling down their sides. They cast circles of light on the damp rock, making it glisten. The draft from the door set the flames swaying, and the patterns on the walls looked like laughter.

"No sign of anyone," said Urchin. "But we have to search."

He took a deep breath, filling himself with the atmosphere of the chamber. Soaked in prayer and self-giving, it fed him with its deep peace.

"It feels so different," said Urchin. "I couldn't have believed it possible."

"It feels good," said Juniper. "But it isn't finished yet."

"Not finished?" said Urchin.

"Yes, but I'm not sure what I mean by that," said Juniper. "It just feels as if something still needs to be done."

"Finished or not, we'll have a good hunt around and report back to the king," said Docken. "There's a good chance the princess will be back safe and sound by the time we get there."

Urchin hoped so. As he left the chamber, he took one last look behind him. Juniper was still there, shaking his ears as if he'd got them wet.

A knife. Claws. Blue.

Juniper had almost forgotten that, but somehow, vividly, it had come back to him as he lingered in the Chamber of Candles. Urchin was waiting. Juniper shook his ears and limped hurriedly to the door, finding there were words in his head which nobody had put there—something about a paw and hills. He didn't understand it at all. But it was something to do with Catkin, and to do with this place, and the feeling that it was still unfinished.

CHAPTER FOUR

MOTH AND THE OTHER MAIDS left the nursery curtains open so that lamplight would welcome Queen Cedar when she came home. Brother Fir returned first, and stood, thoughtful and quiet, warming his paws at the nursery fire, but night had grown dark before the queen appeared in the doorway with her paws and face scratched, blood and leaves clinging to her fur, and her eyes wide with hope and fear. "Is she . . . ?" she began—but the empty cradle with its rumpled blankets lay before her, and the anxious maids saw the hope vanish from her face. Helplessly, they hurt for her. "Where's Crispin?" she demanded.

Brother Fir rose slowly, holding out his paws to lead her to the hearth where the log fire flickered. "He is still out searching, dear Queen," he said. "Please warm yourself. Are you injured?"

"There's water heating and I'll get the bath filled for you, Your

Majesty," whispered Moth, and led the curtsying maids from the chamber. The queen didn't appear to notice.

"I went all the way to the Tangletwigs," she said. "I went as far as I could, but the undergrowth is so dense, we'll need guards to hack their way into it, and I don't see how Linty could have got through there with the baby. Could she, do you think? It's all very well saying she mustn't be alarmed, but we have to find Catkin, quickly!"

"Linty will know all the ways through the Tangletwigs," said Fir. "She grew up in a colony on the far side. Those squirrels had all sorts of secret ways over and under the ground."

"I only tried over ground," said the queen. "Those thornbushes are everywhere, and . . ." She hid her face in her paws. "What if Catkin got scratched the way I did? She's only a baby!"

"Linty would not take her that way," said Fir, with a paw on her shoulder. "She knows the Tangletwigs far better than you do, and she will not let any harm come to Catkin."

With a flash of anger, she shook off his paw. "She's already abducted her!" she cried. "Isn't that harm enough? I just want her back!" She knelt on the hearth to lick blood from a deep cut on her arm, then sprang up suddenly, darted to the window, and gazed out, watching the lights of the search parties. The firelight glow of torches and pale lantern beams moved slowly, too slowly, through the darkness. "I can't stay here. I'm going out again."

"Is that wise?" said Fir. "The chances of somebody arriving at any moment with Catkin safe and sound are very good, you know. I've

43

remembered something about Linty. When she was young, she was a dancer and was often among the dancers at our festivals. Many of our best dancers and acrobats came from the Tangletwigs. Living in such a place made them quick and nimble, you know. Linty could carry a baby all the way through the Tangletwigs and back again without a scratch. The Tangletwigs have torn at you, but they will not have touched your daughter."

There was a gentle tapping at the door, and Fir limped to open it. Two mole maids stood in white aprons, carrying fluffy white towels across their paws. They glanced shyly toward the queen, their faces grave and concerned.

"Your bath's ready, Your Majesty," said one, with a curtsy. "Moth's put that lovely lavender oil in it."

"Then I will go back to my prayers," said Fir, and hobbled away. The maids pattered back to the bedchamber where wreaths of lavender-scented steam rose softly from the round oak bathtub.

"We're very sorry about the baby, Your Majesty," said a maid softly.

"We're all going to say prayers for her," said the other.

"And we're all thinking about you," said Moth. "All of us in the tower and all our families." From a table she lifted a large basket overflowing with posies of autumn flowers, shells, biscuits, clawmarked leaves, and bottles of cordial.

"What's this?" asked Cedar, as if she wasn't interested.

"Animals have been sending presents to the tower, madam," said Moth, "because they want to help and they don't know how, apart

44

from joining the search—and they're doing that, too. It's just their way of showing how much they care, madam."

The smaller of the mole maids, overcoming her shyness, wriggled forward and reached up to hug Cedar. The other maid followed and hugged her, too, wiping her eyes on her apron. "Thank you, bless you," said the queen, her voice growing lower and shakier until they had gone, and only Moth remained with her. Moved unbearably by their kindness, the Queen of Mistmantle broke down and wept.

Urchin, Juniper, Hope, and Docken emerged from a long, thorough, cold, and cobwebby exploration of the Chamber of Candles and the tunnels around it. There was not a trace of the baby, nor of Linty. Not a paw print.

As moonlight danced on a dark sea, Padra left his cloak at his chambers and loped down to the shore, feeling annoyed with himself. *Linty, Linty . . .* somewhere there was a memory about Linty, if only he could drag it to the front of his mind. Perhaps it would come to him. He swam to his boat, where Fingal sat at the oars.

"I'll take next watch, Fingal," he said. "You've done long enough."

"Can't I stay a bit longer?" said Fingal. "I'm not cold, and, I mean, I know it's captain's orders and all that, but . . ."

"Oh, move up, then," said Padra, and flipped himself dripping into the boat. He would be glad of the company. His heart was at the Spring Gate with Arran and his children, who had never seemed more precious, nor more vulnerable.

Linty. Children. Did Linty ever have children?

Fires were lit on the beach, to warm the shore patrols. Crackle and Scatter crouched to blow on the smoldering twigs until autumn leaves glowed, curled, and sent flames licking along dead branches. Coughing, turning their faces from the smoke, they stretched their paws to the fire.

They said nothing, because there was nothing much to be said. Crackle was wishing that she could be the one to find the princess. But, she thought as she prodded the flames with a stick, it wouldn't matter who found the baby as long as she *was* found. Scatter, too, wished she could do something wonderful for the island, but she didn't want it to be this. She didn't want to do something brave to rescue the princess because she simply hoped that, by morning, Princess Catkin would have turned up safe and sound, and it would be as if this had never happened.

She huddled closer to Crackle. This long, slow night made her imagine things she would rather not think of.

"You know," she said, "you know there was a prince before, and he—"

"Prince Tumble," interrupted Crackle quickly. "Don't talk about that."

"But it's almost as if—" persisted Scatter.

"I said, don't!" snapped Crackle, so neither of them said, *It's as if there were a curse on the Heir of Mistmantle.* But they could hear each other thinking it.

In her tree-root home, Damson was busily packing a satchel and singing the lullaby under her breath. Neatly she packed bread, apples, hazelnuts, a flask of milk, and a shawl—the things she would want for a journey, the things that might be needed by a squirrel running away with a baby. All through Juniper's childhood she had kept him secretly, with the help of the otters who lived near the waterfall. She knew about keeping a baby hidden. What would the king's guards and the Circle know about it? If anyone could find Linty, she could, and Linty would trust her. At sunrise, she'd go out on her search. Young Sepia might help. Sepia was gentle and trustworthy, but also young and small, and would be better at wriggling through tunnels and climbing trees and cliffs than she was herself.

In the Gathering Chamber, Sepia was helping Thripple to tidy up. There wouldn't yet be any great ceremony to admit Urchin and Needle to the Circle. All the draperies and garlands could come down, robes could be brushed and put away. None of that would be needed now. Hope and the new baby, Mopple, had fallen asleep in a makeshift nest of scraps of old fabric and leftover garlands.

Crispin balanced on the highest branch of the highest tree in a copse near the Tangletwigs, turning right and left, gazing as far as the night would let him see. He had climbed in and out of every hollow in every tree in this copse. The sensible thing to do would be to go back to the tower and find out if there was any news, though his heart urged him to keep searching.

"Heart keep her," he prayed. "Heart bring her safely home."

He was King Crispin the Swanrider, but his own child was missing, and he was unable to help her. On his swaying treetop perch in the deep, dark night, he was utterly alone.

"Back to the tower, find out what's happening, then get out again," he muttered as he sprang down. "Hold on, Catkin. We'll find you."

He would not give in. He would hunt, he would use every power of thought and strength, knowledge and courage, until he dropped with exhaustion, and when he woke, he would go on searching though the sun burned him, and the Tangletwigs tore him to shreds. He would not stop to imagine Catkin crying for her mother and father in the dark, and wondering why they didn't come. He could bear hardship, but not that.

The night brought a brief, thin drizzle of rain. Three animals—a mole, a squirrel, and a young hedgehog—straggling back from the search, grumbled and huddled against the tower walls. Hobb the mole was a short, sturdily built, and very smooth animal—his head looked polished. He had a habit of folding his arms and rocking back and forth on his hind paws, and a tendency to waddle. (He claimed that this was because of stiffness in his joints, but he was heavy, for a mole.) Yarrow the squirrel had a strong, square jaw, angular shoulders, shaggy fur, and a way of jerking his head in indignation. His normal tone of voice suggested that he was used to complaining a lot.

The third animal, Quill the hedgehog, was younger than the other two. He was still young enough for his mother to insist on smartening his spines in the morning, so that he had to roll in leaves as soon as he was out of her sight so as not to be embarrassingly tidy. He was so much in the company of Hobb and Yarrow that he copied their mannerisms without realizing it.

"May as well go home and get a few hours' sleep," muttered Hobb, pulling his coat about him and scowling up at the rain. "There'll not be many of us in a fit state to bring in the harvest after this. There's a lot of animals not at all well, and that means more work for the rest of us. And if that wasn't bad enough, all the athletic ones and the bright sparks will be off looking for the princess."

"Let's hope they find her tonight," said Yarrow, in a dismal voice as if he didn't expect her to be found at all. "It's bad enough, this happening, without it happening at harvest. Hazelnuts won't gather themselves, you know."

"My dad," said Quill, drawing himself up, "my dad says it's a pity the queen didn't take better care of the princess."

"Nobody should speak ill of the queen. . . ." began Hobb.

"Sorry," whispered Quill, but he felt, rather than heard, Hobb glaring at him through the darkness.

"As I was saying," said Hobb firmly, "nobody likes to speak ill of the

queen, but the fact is, she doesn't come from here. That place she comes from, I don't think they know how to do things right. They don't know how to look after their young. Nice enough squirrel, I'll give her that, but she doesn't know how to look after her baby. If we'd had one of our own, a proper Mistmantle queen, this wouldn't have happened."

"Wouldn't have happened, exactly," agreed Yarrow with a sniff and a jerk. "I suppose the king knew what he was doing when he chose her, but . . ."

"But did he?" argued Hobb, leaning against the wall with his arms folded. "I'm sure falling tail over ear tips in love is very nice, but we're talking kings and queens, here. Of course, he's not proper royalty, is he, he was just a captain."

"He would have known where he was if he'd married a sensible Mistmantle lass," said Yarrow. "We thought he might have taken to our Thrippia, her having such clever ways, but nothing came of it. And there's my sister's lass, our Gleaner. Too young for him, I know, but he could have waited for her to grow up. She's very grown-up for her age already."

"Here comes Docken of the Circle," said Quill. He elbowed the others and straightened up as he called out to the bedraggled hedgehog marching past. "Good evening, Master Docken. Any news of the baby?"

"There'd be lights on all over the tower if she were home, Heart protect her," called Docken wearily. "Away you go, home to your beds and get a good night's sleep, for it'll be all paws to work tomorrow."

50

Hobb scowled in the darkness. "Don't hurry," he whispered. "He thinks he can order us all about, now he's in the Circle."

"And I wouldn't stand so near that window," said Docken. "You're right under the queen's window there, and . . ."

"Don't move," muttered Hobb to the others, and raised his voice to Docken. "Why shouldn't we stand under the queen's window? Got as much right as anyone."

"We were on this island long before she was," said Yarrow, and wriggled indignantly. "Who does she think she is? Aren't we good enough to stand under her window?"

"My dad says . . ." began Quill, but they never found out what his dad said because at that moment the window opened and Moth and the maids tipped out the queen's bathwater. Spluttering and cursing they glared up at the window, just in time for the next soaking.

"Tried to warn you," said Docken. "Lavender. You'll smell beautiful."

"*Bathwater!*" growled Yarrow, rubbing his wet fur with his even wetter cloak and making it worse. "What's she want *baths* for? Can't she wash her face in a stream like anyone else?" And they hurried crossly home, though Quill did take the long way around to roll in a weedy rock pool. He couldn't go around smelling of lavender.

It seemed longer than a single night before a pale gold dawn spread across the sky. Catkin was still missing. Search parties went on hunting as the sun rose higher. The brief rain had soon stopped, and animals talked about whether they had ever had such a hot autumn as they worked on in the sun, gathering rushes, cones, nuts, and berries, sweating into their fur and gulping down water. The animals search-ing for Catkin labored and struggled under the hot sun. The land grew dry. Streams ran slowly.

The harvesting was harder, too, because there were fewer animals to do it. More and more were becoming too ill to leave their burrows. Healers were sent for. Urchin, hunting in hollow trees for Catkin and Linty, remembered the riding stars and did not like to wonder too much about what they meant this time.

Juniper opened his eyes with words of prophecy clear and true in his mind. When he thought of what they might mean, he covered his face with his paws in fear.

Brother Fir met with squirrels and hedgehogs who were keen to dis-cuss the past, and others who would much rather not. Many were more concerned about their neighbors falling ill—and please, Brother Fir, can we collect some feverfew from the tower? But as Fir patiently listened and talked and listened again, they began to talk of the terri-ble time when Lord Husk controlled the island, and any animals born weak or even a little deformed had been put to death. Some could hardly bear to talk about it, and some, when they had started, could not stop talking.

Old friends of Linty told how she had kept to herself for years. She never talked about the past. Poor Linty, she could hardly bring herself to speak of what happened to her.

CHAPTER FIVE

COVER THE DOOR, *COVER THE DOOR*. Linty gritted her teeth with effort as she heaved an old tree root back into place to hide the entrance over her head. Using the blanket as a sling, she had wound the baby to her, keeping her safe from the thorns as she wove her way through the Tangletwigs. She had run through deep streams, lifting the baby high out of the water, and rolled them both in white wild garlic to lose their scent. More ramsons grew around this tree. Nobody would scent them down. No busybody digging mole would find them.

The tower was no place for a baby. Long ago, with hard work and ingenuity, she had made this hiding place, and another, nearer to the shore, furnished with all she would need to keep a baby hidden. They were so cleverly concealed underground, with deeply hidden overgrown entrances and confused scent trails, that they were impossible to find. She would have lost track of them herself if she hadn't returned every spring and autumn to clean them and bring in fresh food and bedding. She never knew when she might need them.

There were two ways out of this deep refuge. One led into undergrowth and the other to a cave near the shore, both through concealed tunnels. She could slip out to fetch provisions if she had to, though it would be risky. She had left places above the entrance where rain could run down through the moss, so there was no need to fetch fresh water. In the meantime, in case it didn't rain, she'd brought spring water. She'd thought of everything.

She couldn't remember clearly what had happened at the tower. She had been looking after this baby. *Catkin.* That was the baby's name. She had been rocking the baby in her lap, yes, she could remember that. The warm, bath-smelling baby had cuddled against her and sucked a corner of a blanket—and unspeakable terror had struck hard into Linty's heart, shaking her from her ear tips to her claws. That wave of horror had left her so sick and shaking with fear that she had thought she would pass out.

Tower! Quick, get her out!

She would keep this baby safe. No animal on Mistmantle would outwit her.

Wide-awake and bright-eyed, Catkin was sitting up and looking at her.

"You'll be safe with me," Linty said, and smiled with love as Catkin stretched out both front paws to her. She picked her up, cradling the soft baby fur against her cheek. "You'll be safe with Linty, little . . ." what was the baby's name? Daisy? No, this one was Catkin.

"You'll be safe with me, little Catkin," she said. "They can search all autumn and winter. They won't find you."

In the Throne Room, the windows had been thrown open because of the unseasonable heat. Many of the Circle were out searching for Catkin, harvesting, or caring for the sick, but as many as possible had been summoned, including Arran. Urchin, Needle, and Juniper were there, to hear what Brother Fir had to say. There was no brightness in his eyes today.

"I should have remembered," said Fir sadly, "but so many babies were killed when Captain Husk was in power. Linty had a daughter, born small and before her time. She might have lived. But Captain Husk swooped, had the baby brought to the tower, and killed her himself. Nothing could be done to save her. Later, when Linty's little boy was also born early and very small, we tried to save him."

"There were so many," said Arran, frowning as she tried to remember. "But I remember dashing to collect a baby and take it to the secret nursery and finding I was too late. I couldn't forgive myself for not getting there in time."

"Think of all the babies you did save, Arran," said Fir. "Linty has never been the same since—of course she isn't, how could she be?

But none of us had realized how badly damaged she was. I fear her mind must have been breaking. The night of the Naming Ceremony she found herself in the tower with a baby squirrel."

"But her babies were taken to the tower to be . . ." cried Cedar.

"Exactly," said Fir. "All Linty could think of was that she had to rescue the baby from the tower."

Cedar covered her face with her paws.

"I must speak the truth to you, Your Majesty," said Fir. "Catkin is in the care of a squirrel who wants to guard and protect her, but whose mind is fragile."

Crispin's voice suddenly sounded much older than it ever had before.

"What do we do?" he asked.

"We carry on," said Fir firmly. "We search. We encourage the young to help with the search, because Linty will not be afraid of the young. She will be very afraid of captains. We pray, we search, we keep vigilant, we go on."

All the next day, and the next, the search went on, up hills, in caves, through woods. The queen's eyes grew red with sleeplessness. She hardly ate, and her face became gaunt. When she did sleep she would cry out and wake suddenly, convinced that she had heard Catkin crying.

Apart from a few brief showers, the hot weather continued, a heavy heat as if all the air had been sucked out of it. Every hollow tree was hunted through. Waterways were watched. On Queen Cedar's orders, female animals were sent, two or three times each day and night, to stand in tunnels and caves, in woods and beside streams, to talk to Linty in case she was near enough to hear.

"Talk to her gently," she said, though her paws were curled tightly around the yellow-and-white catkin blanket. "Thank her for looking after my baby. Tell her no babies are . . ." she stopped suddenly, and listened. "Did you hear that?"

"There's nothing, Your Majesty," said Thripple the hedgehog. "Just the sounds of the little ones playing outside. It's just because you . . ."

"Yes, I know," said the queen. "Tell Linty it's safe to bring her back. Tell her the baby needs me."

Silent and sympathetic, they went their different ways to search. Thripple, hunchbacked and lopsided, took the queen's paw gently.

"My little lad was taken for the cull," she said, "and your husband and Captain Padra saved him, and took him to the secret nursery. But I missed him so much, I used to hear him crying even when he wasn't there, just like you did, Your Majesty, just now. Do you hear her in your sleep, too?"

"Oh, yes," replied the queen, and it was as if she were about to say something else, but she only pressed Thripple's paw and added, "Thripple, try and call me by my own name. Call me Cedar."

She needed friends who would use her own name. But even with Thripple, she would not talk of what she saw in her nightmares.

57

Damson trudged up and down hills. Needle tried searching in a place where she had once been trapped by one of Husk's moles. The ancient Mole Palace, a wide arched hall, dry and earthy under tree roots, was investigated by Padra and Urchin. The old routes to it had been blocked and new ones made, and few animals knew how find it, but Padra and Urchin had learned its secrets. They found it empty.

Hot, airless days dragged on and on. Harvesters, sweating and aching with effort, took long drafts of water from the streams and sluiced themselves from the buckets that were kept filled for them. Hobb, Yarrow, and Quill were loading wheelbarrows with fat blackberries.

"Not natural, this weather," grumbled Hobb before plunging his head into a bucket. He emerged sleek, wet, and looking more polished than ever.

"Maybe not," said Russet of the Circle, who was nearby, "but it's given us a good harvest." (Russet and his brother Heath were very similar, but Russet was slightly taller, and the tip of his left ear was missing.)

"Blooming berries," said Hobb. "Can't move for blooming berries. Juice gets everywhere. Except," he muttered quietly to Quill, "the queen's paws. Bet she doesn't get berry juice on her precious paws."

"I expect she does," said Quill, though he didn't like to argue with

Hobb, who seemed to know everything. "She's a healer, so she must use all kinds of plants and things. They say since there's been so much sickness about, she's been making medicines herself."

"Then she can come and heal my knees," grumbled Hobb. "Can't hardly walk some mornings, let alone heave all these blooming berries about."

Yarrow grunted, and muttered something about how the queen's foreign medicines might do more harm than good as far as anyone knew, and a good honest Mistmantle squirrel like our Tippy wouldn't have minded getting berry juice on her paws. Quill was about to say that the queen didn't mind either, then he remembered that Yarrow was older than he was and said nothing at all.

"I hope the king remembers to give us a feast when the harvest's all in," grumbled Yarrow. "We always have a harvest feast. Fair enough, we might have to wait till the princess gets found."

"Two feasts, then, otherwise we've been had," said Hobb. He folded his arms, squinting against the sun. "We should have two, one for harvest and one for when they find the littl' 'un. Mind you, I don't feel much like a feast just now. We shouldn't have to work in this heat, it's making my head ache."

He waddled back to the water buckets. Yarrow, seeing his brother nearby, wheeled a wheelbarrow of berries toward him and jerked his head in a way that was meant to look significant. Nearby, a cluster of young animals, who had been having a wonderful time making blackberry-stained paw prints on a rock, began to play Find the Heir of Mistmantle, but before they had the chance to run and hide, their parents or grandparents seemed to appear from nowhere.

"It's not suitable, not now, playing that," said one hedgehog mother.

"And one little one missing is enough," said her friend. "If the king's own baby can vanish, it makes you wonder about the rest."

"It certainly does make you wonder," said Yarrow, with what was meant to be an air of wisdom, "if they're telling us everything about this baby. I reckon that lot at the tower know more than they're saying."

Other animals stopped or slowed down to listen. Adults held the children's paws tightly. Quill trundled over to join them. "Why?" said Yarrow's brother. "What do you think?"

"I think someone put Mistress Linty up to it," said Yarrow knowingly. "She couldn't have done this all by herself. Someone's helping her."

"Oh, come on!" said a mole. "Who'd do a thing like that?"

Yarrow hadn't thought of that, and it was difficult. Faced with a bunch of inquisitive animals waiting for him to say something, he tried to think of a suitable villain and was suddenly inspired.

"We all know about Captain Husk, don't we?" he said mysteriously.

"But he's dead!" said someone."

"We've been *told* he's dead," said Yarrow, "but who saw him die? Not many, and they only said they saw him fall. Never found a body, did they?"

Hobb surfaced from a bucket and folded his arms. "That's exactly what I've been thinking," he said. "It's Captain Husk. He's back, and they daren't tell us."

Gleaner scurried to the tower. You could always find a length of muslin if you knew where to look. The kitchens used them for wrapping food and straining jam, and those fussy needle animals used swathes of it to protect their unfinished Threadings. She took a length of white muslin, folded it carefully, filled it with bits of the herbs that were supposed to keep sickness away, made it into a bundle, and hurried to the Tangletwigs.

In a clearing, deep in the Tangletwigs, was a cairn of stones decorated with a polished bracelet and a few scattered wildflowers which were now faded. Gleaner, hot and uncomfortable on such a day, scratched by thorns and irritated by midges, trotted on sore paws to the cairn and pressed her face against the cool stones.

Whatever they said about Lady Aspen, she wouldn't believe it. *She was my lady. She should never have died, not my lovely Lady Aspen.* She crumpled the dead flowers and disposed of them in the bushes.

"The flowers aren't lasting these days, my lady," she said. "It's too hot. I've brought you some muslin to keep the sun off you. And there's some nasty disease about, so I've brought the right herbs to keep it off, for I don't want it coming anywhere near you."

Gleaner knew that Lady Aspen, in her grave, could not suffer from any sickness, but she couldn't bear the thought of harm coming near her. So she spread the muslin and scattered the strewing herbs. *It's for my Lady Aspen. I can still do something to look after my lady.*

Urchin and Juniper trudged back to the tower after a long, hot day of failed searching. They had no heart to run up the walls and shook their heads at the guards as they climbed the stairs to the Throne Room.

"I can't help imagining the worst that could happen," muttered Juniper.

"Try not to even think of it in front of the queen," said Urchin. "Juniper, are you all right?"

"Yes, I'm just tired, the same as everybody else," said Juniper, because he couldn't tell Urchin what worried him.

The words of prophecy he had received were nagging and prodding at him. He could not understand it and was afraid of what it might mean. The only person he could discuss it with was Brother Fir, and Fir was already worn out.

"Go to bed, Juniper," said Urchin. "I'll report to the king for both of us."

By the morning, Urchin hardly felt he'd rested. He, Needle, and Juniper climbed to a hilltop where they scrabbled, scratched, dug, sniffed, and listened until their ears and noses were so confused that they couldn't distinguish anything clearly, and they stopped for a rest. Urchin had soil dust in his eyes and ears, and a catching in his throat.

"Are we far from the stream?" he asked hoarsely.

"Sorry?" said Juniper, and when Urchin repeated it, he hopped away to find his satchel. "I brought flasks of Spring Gate water," he said. "You see that row of trees on the skyline?"

Urchin twisted around to look. "Do you think we should look there next?"

"We should, if nobody else has," said Needle. She had found a useful supply of earwigs and popped one into her mouth.

"The thing about those trees," said Juniper, "is that beyond and below them there's a sheer drop to Tangle Bay. Damson found me near there."

Urchin turned to him with sudden interest. As Juniper had been in a world of his own all day, it was a relief to hear him talk about Damson.

"Has Damson told you anything more?" he asked.

"No," said Juniper with a shrug, as if it weren't important anymore. "She might not know much about who I am, but she knows more than she's telling me."

Needle sprang up. "It's her!" she called. Urchin and Juniper leaped up, scattering crumbs and gulping down chunks of apple.

"Sorry," said Needle, "I didn't mean Linty, I meant Damson." She waved with both paws. "Damson, we're here!"

Damson lumbered stiffly up the hill. "I'm getting too old for this," she panted. She put down her basket, sat down beside Needle, and rubbed her hind paws. "But I reckon Linty's got a place well down, all carved out, all in and out the tree roots, and well covered. I had places like that where I kept you, Juniper, before I found our home behind the waterfall. Excuse me asking, Needle, but where did you find those earwigs?"

"Just here," said Needle, clearing a space with her claws around the heather roots. She was about to add, "There's plenty," when she remembered that, of course, squirrels don't eat earwigs. Didn't know what they were missing.

"That'll do," said Damson, and sprawled face down on the heather. Juniper and Urchin exchanged puzzled glances.

"Mistress Linty," she called gently, "no need to be alarmed, now, it's only Damson. Are you still looking after little Catkin?"

Juniper, Urchin, and Needle looked at each other and back at Damson. Had she really found Linty, or should they be worried about her?

"I'm sure you're taking good care of her," Damson went on, "and King Crispin's most grateful, but he and the queen are missing her very much and they want her back. It's time she had a sleep in her own cradle. Brother Fir said he thought you might be afraid of Lord Husk. Well, Husk's dead and gone, Mistress Linty. King Crispin and Queen Cedar are good animals and don't have culling. So my dear, you bring little Catkin back to the tower. They'll be happy to see you both." She got up slowly, brushing dust from her fur.

"Have you found her?" gasped Needle. "Is she really down there?"

"I've no idea," said Damson. "I might just be a silly old squirrel talking into the ground. But where there's a lot of creepy crawly things about, like earwigs, there are insect runs, and where the insects can get through, so can the sound. When I was in hiding, I heard a great deal of what was said aboveground. Linty might be able to hear voices. It wouldn't hurt if you all tried talking into the ground for her, especially you, my dear." She nodded at Needle. "She might be more willing to trust a girl." She looked up at the hills above them. "I've come this far, I may as well go on."

"We'll do the uphill bit," said Juniper, "but you're worn out, so I'll take you home first."

"You will not!" said Damson. "You'll go on searching for the princess as King Crispin told you to! Do as you're told. I'm going downhill and you're going up."

Juniper and Urchin leaped up the hill. Around them mothers took children back to their nests and burrows, holding their paws firmly, casting sharp, worried glances over their shoulders. Needle followed more slowly. She'd do anything to rescue Catkin. She would go through fire and water, place herself in any danger, and risk her life. But she hadn't imagined having to sprawl across the heather, whispering kind words into tree roots. Danger was one thing, but looking ridiculous, really. . . .

She saw a gathering of wood lice, lay down, and began talking. She'd do anything for Catkin, even this. She'd better tell the queen about it, in case she wanted to try it herself.

Dusk settled. Animals worked on, searching for Catkin and gathering the harvest, though heads ached and limbs were stiff with effort and heavy with tiredness. Only the otters, smoking and salting fish and drying seaweed, seemed to keep up the pace of the day's work. Even squirrels trudged to their nests instead of running.

"But the harvest's almost in," said Padra to Captain Lugg as they met on the shore. "It'll all be under cover when the weather breaks."

"Can't break soon enough," said Lugg. "We need rain. Streams are running slow. Sluggish water isn't good. No wonder animals are falling sick. How are Crispin and the queen?"

"Keeping very busy," said Padra, "searching, organizing, and doing whatever they're needed for. It's the only thing that makes life bearable. I don't know how they can stand it." Nearby, two moles hurried home, their heads bowed and close together in conversation. When their children ran ahead, they were sharply called back.

"What's going on?" asked Padra. "Suddenly there's a lot of whispering going on. And the children—ever since Catkin disappeared, the animals have been very watchful of their young, but now it seems they don't want them to go out to play at all."

"Something's up," agreed Lugg. "Better ask a few questions, find out what it is. Missus might know. And that lot in Anemone Wood hear everything. I'll see what I can find out."

Underground, Linty rocked herself. She had heard paw steps above, up and down, coming, going, searching, not leaving her alone. But then she had heard a kind voice, speaking her name—*Mistress Linty . . . they're most grateful . . . they want her back . . . he's gone . . .*

Linty remembered that voice. That was Damson. She had admired and envied Damson, who had managed to keep a young one safe through the bad times. If Damson said it was safe to take this baby to King Crispin, it was safe. Good King Crispin. She remembered Crispin. He was a nice young squirrel.

A terrible thought struck her. What if that wasn't really Damson? What if . . . she turned hot and sick with fear when she thought of this—what if it were a bad animal playing a trick, putting on Damson's voice? Or what if Damson were wrong, or couldn't be trusted? In these strange days, who could you trust? If she were lured into a trap, Catkin would be killed, and it would be her fault.

She hugged herself and rocked. What was the best thing to do for the baby?

Stay here, dig farther in, move to another refuge, and hope they don't find us, or take the baby back. Just take her back to her own mother.

She couldn't hide forever. She could trust Damson. She'd take the baby back to King Crispin and the queen, maybe tomorrow. Tomorrow, she'd go to the tower. Or would she?

A snuffle and a squeak from the cradle made her jump up to look at the baby, but Catkin was only stirring in her sleep and looked more adorable than ever. Her paw, wrapped in the cream-colored blanket, was in her mouth.

Suddenly and bitterly, Linty remembered her own sorrows. The queen must be broken with grief over this baby, and Linty knew how terrible that was. No mother should endure that. She'd go now, before she could change her mind.

Quickly and methodically, she packed up the food, the clothes, and the toys. She lifted Catkin from the cradle, wrapping her warmly with her rose petals still around her. At the sound of paws close by she stopped and tilted her head, listening, but it was only the sound of moles pattering along a tunnel nearby. She caught a few words.

"You know what they were saying, today, at the berry-picking?" a mole was saying. "Someone's saying Husk's about again. Nobody ever saw him dead."

Linty began to shiver uncontrollably. She told herself not to be silly. How could Husk be back? It was only some loudmouth making trouble. Husk was dead. We had good King Crispin. Damson said so.

She laid Catkin back in her cradle and yearned for the days when life had seemed so simple, when she had been young and full of life, when her future lay before her, and she held her first baby in her arms. Miserably she rocked Catkin, weeping softly with her head turned to one side because she must not wake the baby.

CHAPTER SIX

URCHIN RAN UP THE STAIRS TO FIR'S TURRET, and knocked at the door. Fir's voice sounded reassuringly calm, but tired, and quieter than usual.

"Urchin's knock," he said. "In you come, Urchin."

Urchin stepped into the round, simple chamber where curtains wafted gently from open windows. Fir and Juniper were at the windows, their backs to him, but Fir turned with a small watering can in his paws.

"My little garden needs water, these hot days," he said. "We have to look after the window boxes. Herbs are much needed at present. Is it time to go the Throne Room, Urchin?"

At the sight of Juniper, Urchin had to bite his lip to keep from letting his shock show on his face. His face was gaunt, his fur was dull and spiky, and the pain in his eyes was the worst thing of all. He looked like a trapped creature desperate for rescue. As Brother Fir dried his paws on his tunic, Urchin hopped to Juniper's side.

"Whatever it is, Juniper, tell me!" he whispered. "Or tell Brother Fir. But tell someone!"

Juniper, offering his arm to Brother Fir on the stairs, made no sign that he had heard, but Urchin was sure he had. He was sure Brother Fir had, too.

No sunlight fell on Crispin and Cedar's thrones. The king and queen sat upright as birches. Their faces looked hollow, and there was a sharp alertness about them both as if they were constantly watching and listening. Looking at them, Urchin knew that eating and sleeping were no longer important to them. The queen clutched Catkin's remaining blanket in one tight paw.

Captain Lugg stood beside them, his feet planted firmly apart, his claws in his sword belt, his face grim. Padra and Arran were silent and solemn. Docken the hedgehog was there, and Sepia, though she couldn't imagine why she had been summoned. Tay the otter arrived, looking disdainfully at the young animals. She clearly felt they shouldn't be there but knew better than to argue with Crispin about it.

A chair had been provided for Brother Fir. Juniper and Whittle took their places at either side of him, as Urchin bowed to the king and glanced at Padra for guidance.

"No news of Catkin," said Padra. "The search goes on."

"Firstly," said Crispin, "Sepia. The queen and I would like you to sing for Linty and the baby."

"Excuse me?" said Sepia.

"Music can be healing," explained the queen. "If Linty hears you and the choirs singing, it might help her to calm down and think clearly. It could bring her to the state of mind where she'll be reasonable and bring Catkin back."

"Of course I'll sing, Your Majesty," said Sepia. "Thank you for asking me."

"Now we'll hear Captain Lugg's report," said Crispin.

"Your Majesties and friends," began Lugg, with a neat and rather stiff bow to the thrones, "there are some very silly things being said by very silly animals who like exercising their mouths without troubling their brains first. A lot of troublemakers, Your Majesties."

"And what are they saying?" inquired Brother Fir mildly.

"They've got it into their heads," said Lugg, "that Linty didn't take the baby just because she's crazed with grief. They reckon she couldn't have kept her hidden all this time without help, and there must be someone backing her up. And they say"—he glanced uncomfortably at the queen, and Urchin could see how awkward this was for him—"they say that"—he squared his shoulders, put a paw to his sword hilt, and took a long deep breath—"that Husk's come back."

Urchin felt his fur prickle. Needle gasped—she couldn't help it—then looked at the floor and pretended she hadn't made a sound. Sepia bit her lip hard.

"Can't be, of course," said Lugg, "but there's animals saying it."

71

"That's ridiculous!" exclaimed Urchin. "Even if Husk were still around, Linty wouldn't work with him! She'd want to kill him!"

"Exactly what I said," replied Lugg, "but they're saying she's so frightened of him that she'll do what he says, or else she's mad enough to do anything, or he's killed her and hidden the body and took the baby; and as far as I'm concerned they might as well say moles are all taking wing and flying, and the rain falls down as best beer. This weather's getting to their brains. But Linty or no Linty, they've got this idea that Husk's back and it's got stuck in their little skulls like an otter down a mole hole, if you captains will pardon the expression." Tay raised her eyebrows alarmingly. "And you, Mistress Tay."

"But we know Husk's dead," said Padra. "Some of us were there when he fell. Do they think they've seen or heard anything?"

"Well, some of them are saying it's his ghost," said Lugg, "but it beats me how a ghost can handle a real live fur-and-claws baby. There are—you know how it is—there are those who think they've seen him, but . . ."

Needle's paw flew to her mouth.

"I shouldn't worry, miss," said Lugg. "Couple of moss-brained hedgehogs at dusk, last night. They say they saw a squirrel on the ridge near them steep cliffs. Saw him against the skyline. Swore it was Husk, but I daresay they'd swear to anything."

"Didn't they go nearer to find out?" asked Needle.

"Too scared, miss," said Lugg, "and too drunk. I'm surprised they only saw one of him. Didn't have the sense or the guts to check what they'd seen, as you would have done yourself. Ran off and told every-one who'd listen."

"So now," said Padra, "the island is wriggling with rumors that Husk has come back for revenge. Rumors like this are dangerous. They spread fear of old horrors returning. They'll always be looking over their shoulders now. They'll become frightened to go anywhere, do anything, or trust anyone, so it's important to sweep these rumors away. Mostly, that must be up to those of us who witnessed Husk's"—he hesitated for a moment—"Husk's fall."

"His fall, yes," said Crispin firmly. "*That's* the point. You were going to say, 'his death.' Let's face this. None of us actually saw him die, we only saw him fall, and heard him. Does anybody doubt that he's dead?"

"I have no doubt at all," said Fir.

"He's dead," said Padra.

"Good," said Crispin, "because we have to be absolutely sure of what we saw and heard that day. Animals who hear these rumors will be coming to ask us about it, trying to find out if he's really dead. Examine your memories. Be sure that you're sticking to the truth. If you have doubts about it, tell me now."

Urchin imagined himself back in the dark tunnel leading to the dungeon, with Hope holding his paw and eating berries. Husk had retreated in terror, his paws shaking—had inched back into the dungeon—then there was the long cry, growing fainter and fainter, a wild laugh from far away—then nothing.

"He must be dead," said Urchin.

"Excuse me," said Needle, "I don't like having to say this, but when Brother Fir first told us about the pit, he said that hundreds of years ago, when animals were thrown down there, some of them survived and dug tunnels to get out. That was how the moles came to build their palace. So it's possible for an animal to survive that fall." She looked down at her paws. "Sorry."

Urchin put a paw on her shoulder, and she looked up with gratitude. Urchin wanted her to be wrong, but he knew that, unfortunately, she was right. Husk might have survived that fall.

"You're quite right to remind us of it, Needle," said Crispin. "Thank you."

"But a squirrel's heavier than a mole and falls harder," said Padra. "And we don't know what the ground is like underneath. It may have dried out and hardened since then."

"Well, sir," said Lugg, "I'm getting the moles unblocking as many old tunnels as possible as part of the search for Catkin. If, while we're at it, we find Husk's body, I'll be delighted to let you know. If I find a door with a squirrel-shaped hole in it, Your Majesty, it would be a pleasure to go after him and give him what he's been asking for, but I think it's most unlikely. I'd be glad to find his body myself and know that he's as dead as a pickled walnut. And then those troublemakers will have to find something else to talk about."

"They will," said Arran.

"Still," said Crispin, "let's face this. It's possible, just possible, that

Husk is still alive. It's most unlikely, but possible. But this time he hasn't taken over the island, and we're not going to let him. Brother Fir, you had something to say?"

Everyone looked at the priest. He looked so old and tired that Urchin hurt for him.

"Oh, dear," said Brother Fir, quietly, as if he were talking to himself. "Oh dear, yes. Hm. Sometimes I find it hard to understand why the Heart allows things as it does." Then he straightened himself up to address them all. Urchin saw the depth and love in the dark brown eyes that held the attention of the whole room, and the suffering in those eyes. He saw it more clearly than ever before, and felt it in his own heart.

"A number of animals have been unwell lately," said Brother Fir. "At first it seemed to be nothing that couldn't be put down to hot weather and some minor infection, the kind of thing that's easily shaken off. By last night I feared that it might be something worse, and this very morning I was sent for as a matter of some urgency. More and more animals are falling ill, and the symptoms are getting far worse—severe headaches, high fever, vomiting, aching and swollen limbs—some are having convulsions. There is sometimes a red and yellowish rash on the paws."

"All the symptoms of fouldrought," said Crispin.

"Fouldrought!" said Juniper, and his eyes widened.

"I'm afraid so," said Fir. "The otters don't appear to be catching it, only the land animals."

75

"Juniper," said Queen Cedar, "are you ill?"

"No, Your Majesty," answered Juniper quickly. "Just—just alarmed. I've learned about fouldrought."

"Is fouldrought all over the island, Brother Fir?" asked Padra. There was a sharply focused look about him—Urchin remembered him looking like that when he rallied the islanders against Husk. He couldn't remember the last outbreak of fouldrought, but he had heard of it.

"In the past day or two I have been to Falls Cliffs, to the edges of the Tangletwigs, to Anemone Wood, and to the west and north shores," said Fir. "There are clusters of it everywhere. The woods around Falls Cliffs appear to have the most cases. But not one animal living in the tower, nor the ones who work here and live elsewhere."

Every animal in the room was silent. Each one thought of some friend or relative. Urchin's foster mother, Apple, lived in Anemone Wood, and so did Needle's family and the friends they had grown up with. Damson lived near Falls Cliffs. Lugg's two married daughters, Wing and Wren, and their families lived not far from the north shore. Above all, they thought of Catkin. The Heart alone knew where she was now.

Urchin glanced nervously up at the queen, not wanting to intrude on her grief. Her paws were clenched tightly, but she looked as she did when they were in danger on Whitewings. She was very still, concentrating, planning the next step. The same expression was on Crispin's face, too, and tension in his voice.

"How serious will it become, Brother Fir?" he asked.

"That," said Fir, "is something we have yet to find out. It's many years since we had a violent epidemic of anything. For that reason, I fear this one might take us badly. We haven't been building up our resistance to contagion, you see. Usually with these things, those who are generally fit and healthy recover. But those who have less to fight with—those who are already unwell, the very old and the very young—they are in greatest danger."

"I have seen something similar on Whitewings," said Cedar. "May the Heart keep Catkin and Linty. All my skill as a healer is at your service." In the silence that followed, Urchin wanted to kneel at her paws, stunned by her calm strength. Crispin stood up, and those animals who were seated—all except Queen Cedar—rose too.

"Animals are to stay in their home areas except by permission of a member of the Circle," ordered Crispin. "The Circle will be assigned different areas of the island, their own areas as far as possible. They are to help the healers, send messengers when healing is needed, comfort those in need, and keep animals from traveling to areas of infection. They may grant animals permission to leave their home areas only when there is the greatest reason or the lowest risk. Those Circle animals who have young children are excused from this service. You mustn't bring disease back to them."

"Otters don't catch it, Your Majesty," Padra pointed out.

"Otters haven't caught it up to now," corrected Crispin. "You can continue to lead the search for Catkin. Urchin, Needle, and Sepia can help you."

"Thank you, Your Majesty!" said Urchin, with Needle and Sepia joining in. "But," added Urchin, "we'll have to leave the tower to do that, and we mustn't bring infection back."

"I'll show you how to use a mixture of herbs and vinegar to keep disease away," said the queen. "You must rub it into your fur, every time you go out and come in."

"Juniper," said Crispin, "your orders will be from Brother Fir, not from me."

Juniper did not respond. A shudder shook him from ears to claw tips.

"Juniper!" said Crispin. "If you're ill, it's most important that you tell us!"

"I'm perfectly well," replied Juniper, his voice shaking. "I'm just anxious, and it . . ."

"We understand, Juniper," said the queen. Urchin caught her eye and gave a twitch of his ears. There was something Juniper needed to tell, but perhaps he'd tell it later to Urchin, when they were alone.

"And Whittle must learn and memorize every detail of this disease," said Tay. "The symptoms, the duration, the various treatments, and the result. And he must commit all the names of the dead to memory."

Whittle nodded earnestly. He had memorized the symptoms of fouldrought as soon as Fir listed them, and looked forward to learning every single remedy.

"Cedar," said Crispin, "please gather the healers together and get them to work, but not Mother Huggen, nor Moth. We may need to send the very young into a place of safety, and those two are the best animals to put in charge of looking after them. And it'll keep Moth safe," he added with a glance at Lugg. "All animals are to keep their paws and fur scrupulously clean. And don't eat or drink anything unless you know where it comes from. Brother Fir, is there any chance of finding the source of the infection?"

"I am only a priest and a healer, Your Majesty," said Fir. "Mistress Tay may know of a case like this in the past where a source has been identified. And the queen, who has protected islands from all kinds of catastrophes, may understand such things."

Tay's whiskers set into a hard, dark line. She clearly felt that they could manage perfectly well with her own expert knowledge without consulting the queen, but she didn't dare say so.

"I'll come with you, Brother Fir," said Cedar. "We'll go around the island together, until I've seen the whole situation for myself."

Crispin seized her paw. "You mustn't become ill," he said.

Just now, Urchin had hurt for Brother Fir. Now, he hurt for Crispin. He had lost his first wife, lovely young Whisper, his child was missing, and he couldn't bear to lose Cedar. The queen took a deep breath.

"I have nursed young and old through plagues, skin diseases, rare contagions, and common sicknesses," she said, "none of them have harmed me yet. I'll have infusions of rosemary, sage, thyme, and all the purifying herbs made up, for washing in. And we need angelica, pennyjohn, feverfew, borage, lavender, and lemon balm. Don't fear for me, Crispin. Fir, I'll come with you now."

Urchin hopped to the door to open it for them, reached out for her paw, and pressed it gently. He and Juniper owed their lives to Cedar.

"We'll find your baby," he said. "She'll come back to you." Then he darted as close to the throne as he could, bowed, and whispered, "Please, sir, may I go with Juniper now?"

Crispin gave the slightest nod of his head, and Urchin saw that he understood. "You two may go," he said.

Urchin and Juniper bowed and left the Throne Room together. That moment of shared understanding with Crispin the King, Crispin the hero of his childhood, lifted Urchin's spirits. They both knew that there was something Juniper needed to tell, and Urchin might be the only one he could open his heart to. They walked a little way along the corridor, but at the first window seat, they sat down.

"We can't stop and sit about," protested Juniper. "There's Catkin to find, and I have to—well, pick herbs and things. Or go to Brother Fir, or . . ."

"You're no use to Brother Fir or anybody else when you're like this," said Urchin. "Can't you tell me?" And when Juniper didn't answer, but didn't walk away either, he went on, "I've been nearly shipwrecked, abducted, put in prison, and spent half my life falling off things and out of things, so whatever's the matter, I won't be surprised. And you were there to help me when I needed it, so it's my turn."

"And there were prophecies about you," said Juniper thoughtfully.

"Well, yes, but . . ."

"I wasn't going to tell you this." Juniper straightened his back and lifted his chin as if he were gathering himself up to a great effort. "All right, if you want to listen, listen, and don't interrupt at all, because if I stop I might not be able to get going again. It's a prophecy."

Urchin's eyes lit up. He nearly spoke, but remembered in time that he mustn't.

"Do you think that's wonderful and exciting?" demanded Juniper. "Well, it isn't. I hoped and hoped that it wasn't the real thing, but I'm sure now that it is. It was just a few pictures at first, so quick that I could hardly see them—outstretched claws. Something blue." His voice faltered. "A knife. And then the words came."

He took a deep breath and closed his eyes. For the first time, slowly and reluctantly he pronounced the words of his prophecy.

> *"The fatherless will find a father*
> *The hills will fall into earth*
> *The dead paw will stretch out to the living*
> *There will be a pathway in the sea,*
> *Then the Heir of Mistmantle will come home."*

With a sigh, he slumped back in the window seat. His eyes closed. "Do you understand it?" asked Urchin.

"I hope not," said Juniper miserably. "The fatherless finds a father, the hills fall to earth—a path in the sea! Don't you see what that could mean? It could mean that it's impossible! That she'll never come home! How am I supposed to tell them that?"

Urchin put a paw on his shoulder, but he said nothing, because there was nothing to be said. Nothing that would help, anyway.

CHAPTER SEVEN

F INGAL SPLASHED ABOUT in the shallows with Tide and
Swanfeather while Scatter watched anxiously from the shore.
She wasn't at all convinced that Fingal knew anything about looking
after little children, and felt that she ought to stand guard. Fingal's
boat, finished at last and freshly painted in red with its border of
orange and green leaves, lay upside down on the shore to dry.

"She's been underwater for a long time!" called Scatter.

"She's an otter!" shrugged Fingal as Swanfeather bobbed to the surface. "And it's not enough!"

"Not long enough?" asked Scatter in horror.

"No, I mean this isn't enough," said Fingal. "I'm looking after
Padra's children while he does the dangerous things. Any otter could
do the baby-minding. You and Needle are always telling me how
to do it, and you're not even otters." He looked past them at a young

squirrel hurrying down from the tower, wearing the pale blue-and-white apron of a pastry cook. "Here's Crackle," he said. "She's always good for a biscuit or something at this time in the morning."

Crackle looked flustered and anxious as she joined them at the shore. "We've had orders about asking permission to go in and out," she said. "We mustn't risk catching anything. But I'm allowed to come down here."

"Biscuits don't catch diseases," said Fingal hopefully. Crackle fished in her apron pocket for broken biscuits, and they sat down on the jetty to eat. From the waves, two small otter heads bobbed up beside Fingal, and he slipped bits of biscuit to them.

"It's all a bit difficult, really," said Crackle. "All the captains and the Circle are busy, and we don't know how many to cook for." She lowered her voice. "The poor queen hardly eats a thing these days. Fingal, are you all right?"

"Don't I look all right?" asked Fingal in surprise. "Oh, you mean, 'have I caught anything nasty?' Otters don't get it, and anyway, I'm indestructible. Padra says he doesn't know how I've survived this long." He bent to heave Tide onto the jetty and nudged Swanfeather to the shallows. "Isn't that right, little Swanfeather? I'm indestructible."

"But you're not," said Crackle unhappily. "None of us are. Any of us could catch fouldrought, or . . ." she didn't finish. The thought of being caught by Lord Husk, or his ghost, was too horrible to put into words.

Another squirrel was bustling toward them, and, shading her eyes against the sun, Crackle saw that it was Gleaner. Gleaner, who seemed to blame everyone for the death of Lady Aspen, was always in a bad temper.

"Have you got nothing to do all day?" demanded Gleaner. "In case you hadn't noticed, the rest of us are very busy. Haven't you been listening to orders? We need thyme, sage, and rosemary; angelica, borage, and . . . and all that sort of thing. Mother Huggen says the queen needs them for stopping diseases. You're not going to find them in the sea."

Glad to be useful, Scatter and Crackle sprang away. Gleaner was pleasantly surprised. Animals didn't usually obey her this quickly. But this disease was going to make far too much work for her, and it wasn't fair.

She only hoped the queen knew what she was doing, letting Scatter help. She didn't know much about Scatter's past, but from what she'd heard it wasn't at all ladylike. Scatter and the queen were both foreigners from the same island, and not a very nice one, from all she could gather. There you are, then. The foreigners are sticking together.

Swanfeather lolloped happily from the water, shut her eyes tightly, and gave herself a thorough shaking before Gleaner got out of the way. Gleaner seethed with annoyance. Fingal was teaching that child bad habits already.

Dusk fell with a pleasant twilight, the sky turning to violet and gray as the first stars appeared, but Juniper was too tired to care and too anxious to enjoy it. He yawned enormously. Usually, he had to slow down to keep Brother Fir company. Tonight, Brother Fir was slower than ever, and Juniper was glad to keep pace with him. He felt he wouldn't care if Lord Husk really did appear. He wouldn't have the energy to run away. It was marvelous that Brother Fir was still able to walk, but he limped on ahead, sometimes leaning on Juniper's paw, sometimes on Whittle's or Cedar's. Whittle and Juniper had been told to help each other memorize the symptoms of disease and the treatments, but there was no need anymore. They both knew them all by heart. They had spent all day observing them.

That was the thing that had worn Juniper out, more than the long day climbing all over the island to visit the sick. With muslin masks tied over their noses and mouths to protect them, the four of them had entered dimly lit burrows, climbed into neat dry tree nests, and crept into cool sandy caves to care for the sick, though Fir and Cedar had done most of the caring while Juniper and Whittle watched and learned. At least it helped him to forget the prophecy for a little while, until the sight of the hills or a flicker of something blue brought it back to mind.

Juniper had watched a young mole whimpering and shivering until his teeth chattered. He was his parents' eldest child, just learning the skills of tunneling and trying to impress his family when he first became ill. He had heard a hedgehog crying out in pain and delirium, and had known that this was an old hedgehog, already suffering from aching limbs, who had always been kind to the young and who had fought valiantly in the battle against Husk. The constant watching of animals in fever, distress, and pain, and the anxiety of their families, had drained him. But it made him desperate to stop the suffering and eager to learn.

He had learned which infusions Cedar used to bring down fever, to fight infections, and to cleanse and sweeten the burrows and bedding. He had borne with the smell of vomit and had cleaned it up. He had washed his paws repeatedly, because Cedar said it was important not to carry disease from sick animals to healthy ones. He knew, too, that there were more infusions to make tonight before they went to bed. The queen never seemed to want to go to bed at all. There were stretches of the northeast of the island they had hardly visited at all, and the thought of doing all this again tomorrow made him almost too exhausted to walk.

"Look," said Whittle. In the half-light, squirrels and hedgehogs were scurrying from all directions toward the far-off tower, Crackle and Scatter among them, their arms full of flowers, leaves, and branches. "They're bringing in the plants we need for the medicines."

More work, thought Juniper, but he felt he shouldn't say so. The queen had worked harder than anyone today, and she'd probably supervise all the making of medicines herself. His breathing was beginning to hurt as they trudged uphill, and he was so tired he almost walked into the back of Brother Fir, not realizing that he and the queen had stopped.

"Take a little rest," said Fir, and Juniper flopped gratefully onto the heather even though he knew how hard it would be to get up and go on afterward. Cedar spread herself facedown on the ground, singing softly into the earth.

It didn't seem respectful to watch her. Juniper looked past her to the sea as it went on swishing softly to the shore and back, forward and back, not knowing anything of what was happening on the island, just being the sea. It was calming. A figure wrapped in shawls was hobbling slowly toward him—it looked like Damson, and he had risen to meet her when the sweetest sound met him and made him turn to look where it came from, wide-eyed at the beauty of it.

That sweet, true voice could only be Sepia. Somewhere, she was singing, and it was as if the air around her turned to silver. Other voices wove with hers, blending and harmonizing, and the song wafted like fragrance. Fir's ears twitched toward it.

Lanterns nodded and waved in an unsteady line. The choir, cloaked and carrying lights, were climbing the hill as they sang.

"Peace in your breathing,

Sleep as the stars keep you, deep as the sea and its quiet . . ."

It was almost unbearably beautiful. The animals carrying herbs to the tower stopped to listen. The queen sat up and brushed her eyes with both paws. Damson, weary and alone, put down her basket and knelt in the heather to listen.

The singing stopped, hanging in the air, and the silence that followed was holy. Nobody wanted to move. But the choir turned and wound its way downhill, and all the animals began to scramble to their paws and stretch and shake their limbs as they realized it was growing cold. And Juniper did what his heart told him to do, and hurried to help Damson to her feet.

"Have you been out searching for Catkin all day?" he asked. "You're so far from home, and it's late!"

"There's nothing more important to be done," said Damson. Her voice was low and weary. "And I'm old enough to look after myself. No sign of the princess yet, but we'll find her. We'll get her back." She hobbled stiffly to the queen and laid a wrinkled paw on her shoulder. "We'll find her, Your Majesty. Don't you ever lose hope."

Cedar pressed her paw and couldn't speak. Juniper reached for Damson's basket.

"I'll take you home," he said.

Damson's paw tightened on the basket as she straightened up. "I can take myself home," she said. "You've got your duties to attend to. You're nearly a proper priest now, and we need priests at a time like this. Poor old Fir, he can't do everything himself."

"Juniper," called Whittle, "are you coming?"

"Off you go, and don't keep them waiting," said Damson.

"I'll come after you," called Juniper to Whittle. He pulled Damson's shawl more closely around her and tucked her paw firmly into the crook of his arm. "I'm not leaving you, Damson."

Damson frowned. "Disobedient young whippersnapper," she muttered. "Now you're a tower squirrel, there's no telling you anything."

But she let him carry the basket, and seemed glad of his arm as they began the long walk to the waterfall.

"If you won't do as you're told, then I'll make the most of your company," she said. "You'll be that busy helping Brother Fir. I've some thyme hanging up, I'll let you have some to take back, for the queen will be wanting it."

They talked about remedies, and Damson told him of plagues she had lived through, and the ways of treating them, and the time it took to recover, and how to prevent them spreading. She told him again the stories she had often told him about the years when she kept him hidden behind the waterfall, and Juniper let her talk and didn't tell her that he had heard these stories many times, and that the story he really wanted to know was the one she had never told him. Finally, as they heard the murmur of the waterfall, slow in the hot weather, she said, "I'm proud of you, you being a priest. Maybe I've no right to be, for all I did was look after you, I didn't make you a priest. But I am, Juniper, I'm proud of you."

Juniper pressed her paw. "I'm not a priest yet," he said. "I'm only a novice."

"Nearly a priest, and you will be a priest," she said. "Never thought, when I found you . . ." She stopped, and looked up at the sky. "Not a bad night tonight, all things considered."

They talked about the hunt for Catkin and told each other that she'd be found safely. At last they reached the ancient tree roots where Damson had her nest, and she filled his arms with bunches of fragrant thyme.

In spite of everything, peace filled Juniper. Catkin was still missing, disease and unrest troubled the island, but in this time and place he found he could not be worried, even if he tried. Even his prophecy could not dismay him. There was only the warm night, the scent of thyme, and Damson.

"Now, you take care," she said firmly. "Don't get sick. Use plenty of rosemary to keep the fever away, and keep washing." She placed her paws over his. "Don't know what I would have done all these years without you," she said. "You've been my son, even more than you could have been if I'd birthed you myself."

"You take care too, Mum," said Juniper. Something in his heart swelled and overcame him, and he hugged her tightly. "Thanks for everything."

It was so good just to hug her and be hugged. At last he stepped back and said, "Good night, Mum. Heart bless you." And it struck him as strange, because mostly he didn't call her "Mum," only "Damson."

"Heart bless you," she muttered back, and she watched until he blended into the night. Then she wiped her eyes, stifled a cough, and ducked into her home. She had important sewing to finish.

Before the queen and Fir went out the next morning, Padra arrived at the gathering of the Circle with news of the first deaths from disease. Urchin, standing with Juniper and Whittle at the Throne Room door, wondered how much worse it could get. Catkin was still missing; the island was riddled with fouldrought and rumor. The heat was still sticky and oppressive. Perhaps that shouldn't seem important, but it did. At this time of year everything should smell of wood smoke and cinnamon. Today, he could only smell sweat and vinegar.

"We need to have the old Mole Palace ready for use as a nursery again," Crispin was saying. "If this goes on we'll have to move the very young in there, to keep them safe from disease. Mother Huggen will be in charge."

"And we must use water only from underground springs," said the queen. "All animals should be warned to use the springs, not streams."

"Is there something the matter with the streams?" asked Arran.

"Maybe not," said Cedar, "but I've seen something like this before, on Whitewings. It was a hot summer and we found there was something rotting in a slow stream. So until we've found the source of the infection, we should only use water we know to be pure, and keep everything very clean. Meanwhile, we'll be investigating the streams and rivers."

"Otters can do that, Your Majesty," said Padra.

"But they'll have to keep out of the waterways while they do," Cedar pointed out. "It may be that the reason we haven't had any sick otters is because they mostly use the springs for their fresh water."

"In that case, Padra," said Crispin, "take some good sniffers with you when you go to search the streams. Animals who can pick up a bad smell at a great distance."

It occurred to Urchin that there were more than enough bad

smells on the island in this weather, but it wasn't his place to say so. Fingal probably would have done.

"And pray, everyone," said Crispin. "Now."

They prayed silently, then went on their ways. Fir was the last to leave, walking very slowly. His lame leg seemed to be troubling him these days.

"Shall I take you back to the turret, sir?" asked Whittle anxiously.

"It's been hard," admitted Brother Fir in a voice so weak with exhaustion that Urchin was alarmed. "I'm not a young squirrel. You young ones can manage without me, if I've taught you anything worth knowing. Hm."

He took the arm Whittle offered, and stood in silence with his head down, breathing deeply, seeming too tired even to move. Urchin and Crispin had both darted forward to bring him a chair when he raised his head, lowered his shoulders, and in a suddenly commanding voice, said, "Juniper!"

Juniper drew himself up, hopped to the priest, and, without any order, knelt before him.

"Much will be demanded of you, Juniper," said Fir. "I think I am to be put to one side for a short while. Juniper, attend the dying. Give them your blessing. Take my place until I am well. Urchin, support him, help him." He raised a paw, prayed a blessing over Juniper, then, gathering all his strength, went on, "The island faces the greatest enemy it can ever face, and you must find out for yourselves what it is. This enemy will turn paw against paw, mind against mind, heart against Heart. Now, Juniper."

Juniper felt the warmth of the priest's paw on his head. He felt as if the presence before him was wise, strong, and all-surrounding, all-protecting. But when he looked up it was only Brother Fir, trembling with weakness, his wise, kind eyes heavily weary, and so physically drained that he needed both Urchin and Juniper to escort him back to the turret. Urchin waited as Juniper helped the old priest to bed, and Whittle hurried after them.

"I'll look after him," said Whittle, eager to be useful. "We should all take turns, all of us who can, because he shouldn't be left alone, should he?"

Urchin and Juniper hurried down the stairs together.

"Can you cope without him?" asked Urchin.

"Have to," said Juniper, and after a moment of indecision, added, "You know how busy it's been."

"Silly question," said Urchin.

"Yes, I know," said Juniper, "but what I'm trying to tell you is, with both of us being so busy, and not always together, I never told Fir about my prophecy. I can't very well tell him now, can I?"

No, he couldn't tell him now, and Urchin didn't feel that it was the right time to ask Juniper what was meant by the greatest enemy the island would ever face. What was the worst thing there could be? A curse on the Heir of Mistmantle?

He wished he hadn't thought of that.

CHAPTER EIGHT

A FLASH OF RED FUR SPRANG from the tower, and the little knot of animals leaning against the walls ducked as Longpaw flew over their heads. He had landed, whisked round, and leaped onto a rock before all the animals in sight had gathered to hear him.

"Drink only from the springs and the rainwater pools, not from the streams and rivers, until told otherwise," he announced, "by order of the king. If any of your colony are sick, report it to your nearest member of the Circle. Healers are out doing all they can."

"Please, sir," asked Quill the hedgehog, "my mum wants to know, how long is it going to go on?"

"Nobody knows," said Longpaw, "but the queen knows what she's doing. She's seen something like this before, and she thinks it might be to do with the streams, that's why we're not to use them. Those with the best noses, report to Captain Padra."

Longpaw leaped away to spread a team of messengers across the island. Keen hedgehogs and moles ran off to find Padra, arguing about who had the best nose. Hobb, Quill, and a few of their friends returned to leaning against the tower walls.

"Typical tower animal," remarked Hobb. "Thinks he can give us all orders. Where's Yarrow today?"

"He's not well," said Gleaner in a high, worried voice that might have been a touch too dramatic. "I didn't sleep at all last night, worrying about him."

"The queen knows what she's doing," said Quill. "That's what I heard."

"The queen?" said Hobb. He scratched his polished head and folded his arms. "Her, know what she's doing? Didn't you know? It's sad, really. She's gone mad as the wind. She goes round whispering down wormholes now. Haven't you seen her? And where's this sickness come from? She says herself that she's seen it before, and there you are, then. We never had it before she came here." (Quill had a feeling that they had, but he didn't like to argue with Hobb.) "Animals are dropping dead all over the island, but the queen hasn't caught it. Neither has that one." He nodded at Scatter, who was running off to join Fingal. "Stands to reason. They're immune. That Whitewings place must be riddled with it, and they've brought it here. And now the queen's off her head; we're all going sick and likely to die and running after lost squirrels because Her Majesty can't keep her own baby safe; Lord Husk's planning something horrible and roaming the island, and if he hasn't got the baby, sure enough he will get her. But try telling any of this to that lot in the tower. They won't have it. It's no good expecting the king to do anything."

"Maybe it's Lord Husk that's been poisoning the water," said Quill, and felt very pleased with himself for having an idea of his own.

"Could be, son," said Hobb. "Could be. Whatever it is, the king isn't doing a thing about it."

"The king?" said a passing squirrel. "Are you having a go at the king?"

"Pity," said Hobb. "He was the best captain we had in a long time. I always said so. But a king? He can't handle it."

A large, muscular hedgehog put down a box of berries and came to join them. "It's not the king!" argued the hedgehog. "It's her! There was never any trouble before she came!" He twisted awkwardly to look over his shoulder. "We should get organized. We should call a meeting!"

"I was just doing that," said Hobb firmly, tipping back his head to look the hedgehog in the eyes. If there was any organizing to be done, he was going to do it, not some lumbering, jumped-up hearth brush.

Crackle hadn't heard about Longpaw's announcement. She rubbed infusions of herbs and vinegar into every inch of her fur until, she decided, she smelled like a pickle barrel; then she added more vinegar. Her eyes watered. She had spent long enough making biscuits, and it was time somebody found the princess. What's it like, she wondered, when everyone admires you, loves you, and thanks you?

She wanted so much to find out—but far more than that, she wanted the princess home.

Under the ground, Linty curled up with Catkin in her arms. It was time the baby had some fresh air. When she had climbed up nearer to the surface, she had heard the most beautiful singing, lovely voices that soothed the baby. She had heard a soft female voice, too, calling for Catkin, claiming to be the queen. Catkin had heard it, too, and whimpered, so that Linty had been ready to scramble straight out and take her back to the surface, deliver her to her mother—*but it might be a trick. Maybe it wasn't really the queen at all.* She had hustled the baby far under the ground again, where the singing would not reach them.

Besides, she had heard other whispers. Stories that sent her hunting for a stone to sharpen her knife. Stories of disease. Stories of Lord Husk! She drew the knife viciously across the sharpening stone. The island aboveground wasn't a safe place anymore, so what was she to do for Daisy now?

Catkin. The baby was Catkin, not Daisy. But she was very like Daisy.

A movement above made her whip around so quickly that the knife blade swept across her arm and left a trail of blood springing along the wound. Be more careful, she told herself. You'll hurt Daisy if you're not careful.

Gleaner wriggled through the Tangletwigs, hugging the bunch of mauve daisies she had brought for Lady Aspen's grave. Perhaps the muslin would be damp by now, and she would have to hang it on the trees to dry. The daisies would look so pretty against the muslin, and Lady Aspen had always liked pretty things.

The cairn stood bare. There was no muslin. Gleaner stared and shivered.

Who would take the muslin from Lady Aspen's grave? Gleaner could think of only one name, the name that was already being whispered with fear all over the island. *Husk.* She ran to the bushes, pulling at thorns with her paws. Not a shred of muslin remained. Around the cairn, she pressed close to the ground to search for paw prints. The ground was very dry, but—yes, that was a squirrel print. Definitely a squirrel print. She pressed her own paw beside it. It wasn't hers. Fearfully, she glanced over her shoulder and all around her.

She should tell someone. Really, she should tell them at the tower, but they wouldn't listen to her. And she didn't want other animals knowing about Lady Aspen's grave, crowding about it, gawping and touching things. They'd spoil it.

"Scatter!" called Fingal. "Is your nose any good? I've got really important work to do!"

Scatter's ears twitched with interest.

"Streams need investigating," said Fingal. "That might be where the fouldrought's coming from. But if anything smells, it must be a long way up in the hilltops, because nobody's found it yet, even in this weather. You can come if you like, but it won't be much fun."

"Fun!" said Scatter, and drew herself up in indignation. *"Fun!"*

"Come on, then!" said Fingal. "We may as well go at once."

They chose a stream that, as far as they could tell, wasn't being inspected by anyone else and set out to follow it uphill to its source. On these hot autumn days, leaves were falling and dancing around the island so that Scatter, who longed to play with them, had to make a great effort to concentrate on what she was meant to be doing. As they climbed, Fingal said the scents were confusing. Farther uphill, he paused.

"There's a whiff of some strong pong, but I can't tell where from," he said. "With all these animals catching diseases, there's every sort of unpleasant whiff around." He sniffed again. "Can't smell a thing in this wind, can you? We'll keep going farther up. How do you fancy a long trek? All the way up to the top?"

"I'll do anything for Mistmantle!" said Scatter earnestly. Looking for polluted streams wasn't as exciting as saving a baby, but at least she was doing something useful. So she scampered on uphill, chatting to Fingal, pausing to raise her head and sniff the air. They climbed farther up and farther north, where trees were sparser.

"Hang on," said Fingal, and stopped. His nose twitched.

"Something nasty. This way, I think. Farther up, and follow this stream." A waft of south wind cooled their faces, and he turned his head in disgust. "Fire and flood, something's deader than it ought to be! Are you sure you want to come with me?"

"Yes, please!" said Scatter. It was getting exciting now. And her nose wasn't as sensitive as Fingal's.

Crackle was tired, dispirited, and lonely. She hadn't meant to come this far. She had just meant to go to the top of the next ridge—then she'd thought she'd go on to the trees—then she'd decided she may as well go to the rock, which didn't look far, and would give her such a good view—now she was tired, hot, thirsty, and a long way from home. She'd rationed the water in her flask, but even so, climbing uphill on a hot day, she'd finished every last drop.

She flopped down in the heather. She hadn't found a trace of Linty and the baby. She wasn't the rescuing heroine who would bring the baby home. She was a long way from home and alone, with a wasted morning behind her. With both paws she pulled up a stalk of bracken and fanned herself.

A pleasant, musical sound of water reached her, making her ears twitch. She must be near a stream, which was exactly what she needed. The sound of water dancing over stone made her thirstier than ever. She was tired, but not too tired to look for it. Clambering uphill and over rocks, struggling through tall brackens, coughing as dust and pollen tickled her dry throat, she came at last within sight of the stream. In the hot weather it ran slowly and was shallower than it might have been, but sunlight sparkled on it as it rippled over the stones. It seemed to call her.

She hurried to it, scenting the heathery air. She sniffed as she bent over it, but smelled only the overpowering scent of thyme, rosemary, and vinegar on her own fur. The water must be all right. Crackle bent down to drink.

Something hit her across the shoulder so hard that it knocked the breath out of her and hurled her sideways. Rolling over, shocked by pain, she struggled to her paws and found her voice as somebody caught her from behind and held her tightly.

"Help help help help help help help!" she yelled, and stretched out her claws as she fought, kicked, and tried to bite the paws that held her. "Get off me!" She stopped thrashing to tip back her head and take a good look at her attacker. *"You!"*

"Yes, only me, sorry," said Fingal, "I didn't mean to hurt you, I just had to stop you touching that water. Couldn't you smell it? Farther upstream it stinks something disgusting. Didn't you know we're not supposed to drink from the streams?" He helped her to her paws, and she dusted herself down.

"Nobody told me," she said plaintively.

"You're covered in that pongy stuff that the queen's been giving out," observed Fingal. "I don't suppose you could smell a thing. Good thing we were here. Aren't you supposed to be in the tower? Who's baking the biscuits if you're not there? And you've set out uphill on your own."

Crackle's lip trembled. She was shaking.

"Leave her alone," said Scatter, and put her paws protectively around Crackle. "She was probably looking for Catkin, weren't you, Crackle? And she's upset."

"I didn't mean . . ." began Fingal, but Crackle was sobbing violently into Scatter's shoulder.

"I only . . . I only wanted"—she gulped—"to help." She stopped sobbing, pouted, and hiccupped. "And I nearly . . . I could have been *poisoned*!"

"Yes, but you weren't," said Scatter, hugging her. "Fingal stopped you in time. You're all right. Fingal, she's had a very nasty fright!"

"Oh, I'm sorry," said Fingal. "Sorry to be a very nasty fright. The fact is, Crackle, I saw you bending over that stream, and it scared the whiskers off me, because I'm pretty certain that water's polluted. It smells worse farther upstream, so we need to keep climbing uphill to find the source. You can come with us if you like, but it'll be pretty unpleasant."

Crackle dried her eyes on the back of her paw. "I'll come," she said.

The steep uphill climb led them through a pine wood (which, as Fingal observed, smelled a lot better than the water did) until the trees grew thinner and they stood on almost level ground near the thin trickle of a stream, which fell halfheartedly into a pool. Crackle and Scatter took a few steps back when they saw the pool, and Crackle couldn't help turning her face away. Even Fingal held his breath.

Something thick and gray-green floated on the top of the water, something that might have been mold, or decayed flesh, or rotting plants, or perhaps all of those, thick and spreading enough to obscure whatever might lie in the water beneath. From the pool, the water overflowed into the course of the stream. Crackle and Scatter pressed their paws over their mouths and noses, and Fingal pulled a face.

"Whatever died in that, it died a lot," he muttered through clenched teeth. He retreated to the trees and scratched about in the undergrowth.

"Whatty lookyfor?" asked Scatter, through her paws.

"A stick," called Fingal. "And more sticks. We need something long to prod in the water, find out what's making the smell and the—whatever that scummy stuff is—and get it out. But before that, we need to get a fire going, because whatever it is, it should be burned."

"That's brilliant!" said Scatter.

"It won't burn," said Crackle. "It'll be wet."

"Then we'll make it a really good fire," said Fingal with confidence, dragging a branch clear of the woods, "and a long way from the trees. We've got enough trouble without setting the hillside alight." He stopped, thought for a moment, and turned to Crackle.

"You're quick, Crackle," he said. "A lot quicker than I am. Get down to the shore. There are otters on watch all around the island. Get a message to the king, and everybody else, and let them know this stream is the bad one, and nobody's to go near it. Fast as you can. Follow the path of the stream so you don't get lost, but mind you don't get a paw wet."

Crackle nodded. It wasn't quite the same as rescuing the baby, but it was doing something to save the island. And she'd get away from that awful stench at the same time. She turned and bolted down the hill.

"Scatter," said Fingal, "go with her. She might get lost."

Scatter hesitated. She didn't want to get any nearer to that water than she absolutely had to. But she couldn't leave Fingal to manage this on his own.

"She won't get lost," she said. "I'm staying with you."

"Scatter," said Fingal, suddenly sounding grown-up. "Go with her. I won't catch anything. Squirrels aren't immune, but otters are."

"No, you're not," argued Scatter, scraping up an armful of twigs to add to Fingal's heap of branches. "I think the otters don't catch it because they don't drink from places like this. If you get anywhere near that water—and whatever's in it . . ."

"Bit of rotting fish, I think," said Fingal.

"Whatever it is, it could make you ill," said Scatter.

"Then it could do the same to you," said Fingal, rather shortly, as he was dragging a heavy branch at the time.

"I'm from Whitewings," said Scatter, building the sticks into a bonfire. "The queen thinks we may be immune to it, and she's been out healing, and she hasn't caught it, and anyway the queen should know, because she . . ."

"Just *go*, Scatter!" snapped Fingal, and turned his back on her to face the pool. Scatter didn't say another word. He heard a scampering of paws running downhill.

That was better. He hadn't liked sending Scatter away, and pretending to be cross with her had been very hard, but he couldn't put her at risk. It was up to him now. One animal in danger, not two. It would be better that way.

He bunched together the kindling and struck dry sticks until a spark flew into the brittle leaves. Cupping his paws around the smoldering heap, he blew softly, coaxing the flame into life. The fire must become a powerful blaze before he could leave it long enough to retrieve the blockage from the pool. When the flames leaped and roared and the smoke blurred his eyes, he took the longest and sturdiest branch he had found and, warily, carrying it at arm's length, approached the pool.

Cautiously, holding his breath, he used the branch to nudge the thick covering of decay onto the rocks. He could see something now, lodged against a stone, green and black and bloated. He couldn't see what it was and didn't want to know, but he guessed that it was an old and diseased fish. Standing as far back as he could, he poked at it with the branch until the corrupted body floated free. Lumps of rotting flesh dripped from it as he lifted it on the branch's end from the water and dropped it into the heart of the fire, pushing it in as far as possible. It spat sparks and twisted. Acrid gray smoke curled from it.

"Done," he said.

A sudden breeze caught the flames so that they flared, roared, and blew smoke into his eyes, but he leaned closer to push the foul thing deeper into the fire, making sparks shower up. The rotten fish sputtered as it burned, and Fingal pushed it in farther, narrowing his eyes as it blackened and crumpled, and he threw the branch in after it. The smoke was still blowing toward him, and his eyes stung. Admiring his bonfire, he walked around to the other side of it, careful to avoid the stream, pleased with his work, forgetting just for an instant to sniff the air, not noticing the change in the wind until a sudden gust sent hungry flames roaring toward him.

The bitter smell of singeing fur was in his nose and filled his mouth as he staggered backward, beating at his fur with paws and tail, grabbing at his whiskers—he couldn't feel burning, but only a terrible stinging. With smoldering fur, he flung himself on the ground, rolling, thrashing, and beating furiously at himself to quench the fire. Then small, cool paws were beating out the sparks, dragging and rolling him farther from the fire. He tried to speak, but the smoke in his throat made him cough till his eyes streamed.

He sat up at last, rubbing sore eyes with sore paws, coughing and confused, wondering where the burning was coming from, and who was hitting him, and why. His eyes and his mind cleared slowly. It was Scatter, her face set and determined, as she beat on his fur. She stepped back, coughing hoarsely, and walked all around him, inspecting him for any more signs of smoke.

"You're all right now," she croaked. "It's a good thing I stayed to look after you. Shall we go now?"

Fingal tried to answer, but his voice was rough in his throat. "We should stay till the fire"—he tried to take a breath, and coughed violently—"burns down. Can't use that water to put it out. Wouldn't be safe to leave it. You all right?"

Scatter looked down at her paws, noticing for the first time that they hurt. Of course, she couldn't have put out Fingal's fur without getting burns herself. She licked at her paws to take out the heat, but she felt proud of those burns.

"Of course I'm all right," she said. "What about you? You were the one who was on fire."

Now that the shock was over, Fingal's burns were becoming painful. He grinned down at her.

"Nothing that I can't put right with a soak in the sea," he said. He put an arm around her, and they both winced. "I might have been as dead as a smoked herring, you know, if not for you."

Scatter only smiled with happiness, though the hug hurt her. She took a deep breath of satisfaction. She hadn't saved the baby. She hadn't found the source of the bad water, either. Fingal could have done it all without her. But she'd done something. She'd saved Fingal. That felt so good.

When the fire was nothing but hot ash, they piled damp earth on it and left.

"All that fuss for a bit of bad fish," said Fingal, and suddenly looked up. "It's raining!"

"Clean water, *and* rain!" said Scatter in delight. They lifted their faces to it gladly as they began the long journey downhill in the fading light, catching raindrops on their tongues, holding out burned paws to the soothing coolness. Scatter longed to run ahead to her friends, but instead she slowed down. It was hard for Fingal to keep up when he was hurting so much, and he was trying not to limp.

CHAPTER NINE

R AIN!" PADRA AND ARRAN LAUGHED and hugged each other, raising their heads to catch the rainfall on their faces.

"Rain!" cried Apple, as she ran for cover. "Oh, Heart be thanked!"

"Rain!" whispered Crispin on a hilltop, and closed his eyes. It felt as if a great weight was washing away from him.

Rain hammered on rocks and bounced from leaves, waking scents of wet grass, wet moors, wet trees, wet rock. It filled the rivers, churned the waterfall, and cleansed the streams as Fingal and Scatter stumbled down the hill. On a hillside, Urchin and Needle hugged each other and held out their paws to the rain. Juniper, on the rocks by the tower, threw back his head and gave thanks. Hobb the mole waddled, shivering, to the shelter of a burrow with a damp huddle of muttering hedgehogs and moles hurrying after him. He was coughing violently, but at last he found a voice.

"Haven't we got enough?" he spat out bitterly. "The queen's off her whiskers and can't look after her own littl' 'un, we're riddled with disease . . ."

". . . queen's fault," put in someone.

". . . said that, didn't I?" he growled with a glare. "First the waters are poisoned, and now it's blooming pouring. We'll get floods now. And Husk's about to strike. If he's waiting to take his revenge, this is just the sort of opportunity he'll take. Chaos. Chaos! There's a lot of that under this king."

"He made a lot of trouble coming back," said Gleaner's mother, shaking water from her ears. "A lot of trouble. He should have left Lord Husk alone." She sighed dramatically. "At least that sweet Lady Aspen would still be alive."

"Do you really think that Husk might still be here?" asked Quill. He couldn't help glancing warily over his shoulder as if he feared Husk might be creeping along a tunnel as they spoke. When a squirrel leaped into the burrow, he had to stifle a squeal.

"Hello, our Gleaner!" said Gleaner's mother, but Gleaner, wild-eyed and gasping for breath, ignored her.

"He's back! He's back!" she panted, and struggled to get her breath back. "The things I put on Lady Aspen's grave have gone!"

"That doesn't mean . . ." began a hedgehog, but Gleaner glared at him with fury.

"Who else would take them?" she demanded.

Hobb coughed noisily. Gleaner retreated a few steps, as did Quill.

"Nobody ever saw him dead, did they?" He shivered, and hugged himself. "Can't even get a decent warm burrow these days."

"You're not well," said Quill, and took another step back. "I'll get a healer."

"Don't you go anywhere," wheezed Hobb. "If I'm ill, it's the fault of the queen bringing her Whitewings pestilence here. Crispin should have turned her around and sent her back through the mists, not married her. Poor chap was mistaken in her. We should all help to rule this island by telling him how to do it." He sounded less sure of himself and added, "Or something."

"Excuse me!" said a hedgehog from farther back in the burrow. "How can you talk like that? Can you remember what life was like before Crispin was king."

"But he wasn't brought up to be a king," insisted Hobb, and coughed harshly. "He needs sensible animals like us to tell him what—to advise him." He coughed again, and animals began to retreat. "Where are you all going? I might be really ill. I might die. So it's important that you hear what I've got to say. We need some new ideas about how this island is run."

Gleaner and Quill hurried out of the burrow and scurried home against the rain. Quill reported to his parents that Master Hobb was coughing and shivering and perhaps they should find a healer, and by the way, Master Hobb said that Husk was back and he'd take over the island any time now, and we should all help the king rule the island by doing it for him, or something like that.

A lamp burned dimly in a burrow where cloaks lay in a straggly heap on the floor, a jug of water balanced on a lopsided stool, and a sprinkling of pennyjohn and rosemary covered everything. The air was sour and stale. In an untidy nest lay Yarrow, thirsty and aching, with his eyes closed because the effort to keep them open was too great. There were whispers of conversation at the entrance, but he was too ill to care what they said, until they came closer.

"The healer's arrived," said Hammily, his wife. With an immense effort he rolled over and opened one eye a little. Then, in a lower voice, she said, "It's really very good of you, Your Majesty, and you with all your sorrow, too."

Yarrow tried to sit up and failed. "Not *her*!" he argued hoarsely, though speech felt like a sharp knife through his throat. "I don't want *her*!"

"Yarrow!" cried his wife. "I'm very sorry, Your Majesty."

"Don't worry, Mistress Hammily," said Cedar, and raised her voice so that Yarrow could hear her clearly. "Yarrow, if you don't want me to help you, I won't. But all the other healers on the island are busy, and we all have long lists of animals to visit. So it's me or nobody, I'm afraid."

Yarrow looked up through aching eyes. Everyone said the queen was mad.

"Just leave medicine," he croaked.

"*Yarrow!*" said his wife.

"Not until I've examined you and know what's best to give you," said Cedar.

With a great effort, Yarrow raised his head from the nest.

"I'm getting better," he whispered.

"Yarrow!" said Hammily again. She was a tall, gaunt squirrel with a stern look about her. "You are not!"

"If he doesn't want to see me, I can't insist," said Cedar. "There are more animals who need me, and they may be near death. Send for me if he changes his mind."

"His friend Hobb hasn't been too well, please, Your Majesty," said Hammily timidly.

The queen rubbed her eyes, which were aching with tiredness and tears, and stifled a yawn. "I'll go to see him," she said.

Urchin and Needle, with rain soaking through fur and spines, had gone on searching for Linty's hiding place long after the rain began to fall. Only the failing light made them turn back to the tower, and Sepia was already darting through the trees.

"I've just been to see Damson," she gasped. "She's very ill. Really very ill, and I'm worried. She wants Juniper *and* Brother Fir, but the way things are, she'll have to settle for one or the other."

"Brother Fir's too ill to get out of bed," said Urchin, "but I can go ahead and tell Juniper."

"Oh, please!" said Sepia. "You're faster than I am."

Urchin, suddenly realizing how weary he was, gathered himself together and leaped away toward the tower. Sepia, adjusting to the poor light, peered down from the treetops at Needle.

"What's that stuck on your spines?" she asked. "A flower or something?"

Needle twisted to look. Something pink had impaled itself on the spines near her left hind paw.

"It looks like a—yes, it is," said Sepia curiously. "It's a rose petal. It's wet now, but it's still pink—it must have dried out in the sun." Gently, she pulled it free. "I've seen one like this somewhere—oh!"

In the same moment, they both remembered where they had seen petals like these before. A few days before, though it seemed a lifetime, hundreds of them had cascaded around the Gathering Chamber.

In tunnels and under tree roots, there were squeaks of excitement from small moles and hedgehogs, each holding tightly to the paw of a grown-up, or a nearly grown-up, as they pattered down to the old Mole Palace. There were blankets to be carried down, satchels over shoulders, and lanterns in paws as little ones gabbled out their questions, and parents tried to explain that it wasn't really a palace any more, and yes, they would sleep there tonight, and no, they didn't know when it would be time to come home. Some were shy and fearful, some were eagerly pulling on their mothers' paws, and some wanted to know where their squirrel and otter friends were. Parents, leaving their children in the nursery, glanced anxiously over their shoulders, reluctant to leave—but, as Mother Huggen had explained, there wasn't room for all the young and their parents as well. The parents whispered to each other that of course they understood, but all the same, you didn't like to take your eyes off them, did you, not while Princess Catkin's missing and—they lowered their voices—*Husk might be about.* A few remarked that Hobb the mole and his friends had some good ideas about running the island, if they lived long enough to tell us, poor things.

"Otters are staying on the shores, where they like to be," said Captain Lugg, marching ahead with a lantern. "And the squirrels are coming later. It's us moles and hedgehogs that are at home in tunnels. Can't expect squirrels to go first."

Linty scrabbled earth into place over her new hiding place, then pulled, pushed, and wove the tree roots into place. It hadn't been easy getting here. She had wanted to take the baby over ground and had crawled through the undergrowth with Catkin wrapped up in her arms, but there had been animals about, and she had retreated into the nearest tunnel. Even in the tunnel there had been voices close by—why couldn't they leave her alone?—and she had needed to dig out a new route to her refuge. At least Catkin had been aboveground long enough to get a little fresh air into her lungs.

Now they were here; this was a better hiding place. She had managed to bring the piece of muslin she had found on a cairn in the Tangletwigs. It would be so useful for lining nests and for straining the pips out of berries for Catkin. When Catkin was settled into her cradle and was sitting up looking about at her new surroundings, Linty lay with her ear to the ground. She heard hurrying little paws and the chatter of young voices, more and more of them. Why were all the little ones moving? What did this mean? Not more danger, oh, please, no, not more danger. It was so hard to know which way to turn. She held Daisy—*no, Catkin, this one is Catkin*—very tightly.

Rain slashed against the windows of the dimly lit turret where Brother Fir lay in bed, propped up on pillows. Juniper, kneeling with paws outstretched to the fire as steam rose from his fur, reflected that this must be the best place on the whole island tonight. It was worth getting wet and cold to come back here. All day he had tramped in and out of caves, burrows, and tree homes, administering drinks and medicines, soothing the sick, calming distressed families, caring for the dying. Whenever he had felt exhausted he had thought of the queen, who seemed to work twice as hard as anyone else. Finally he had staggered home through the rain, stumbling with tiredness, until he reached this haven in the sky. Here he was safe from the storm slashing against the windows, safe where the firelight warmed him through, the saucepan of hot cordial sat on the hearth, and candles glowed softly. Perhaps he should turn his mind to the prophecy, but he was too tired to think, and gratefully, he soaked up the warmth. Brother Fir's eyes were closed, so that Juniper wasn't sure if he were awake or not.

He picked up the saucepan carefully, poured cordial into two mugs, and carried one to the bed. "Brother Fir?" he said softly.

Brother Fir's eyes opened. "I wasn't asleep, you know," he said in a voice that was still low with weakness. "Only resting. I feel very rested. Cordial! Hm! Thank you so much, young Juniper."

He tried to sit up a little further, but Juniper could see what a huge effort it was. He put an arm round Fir to help him up and pushed the pillows into place around him.

"I shall be well soon," said Fir. "However, I'm sure the island runs very well without me." He sipped the cordial. "Very good, Juniper. You are an excellent novice, and the king and queen surpass all our hopes. If I must be ill, this isn't such a bad time for it."

Juniper nearly told him to be quiet, knowing that talking hurt his throat, but it seemed disrespectful to speak like that to the priest. He returned to the hearth, aware that the smell of herbs and vinegar lingered about him. It was the smell of all the healers now, but it was a smell that reminded him of sickness and death, and he longed to wash it off.

"Fingal and his friends have cleansed the waters," said Fir. "So it will soon be over."

"Don't hurt yourself speaking, please, Brother Fir," said Juniper.

"Hm," said Fir. When he had finished his drink and seemed to be drifting into sleep, Juniper pulled the blankets over him. He could go down to the kitchens to help make yet more infusions, but he didn't like to leave Brother Fir alone. It was so good just to be here and rest at last. *Prophecy.* Could "the fatherless" mean a young animal orphaned by fouldrought? And what was this about a pathway in the sea? Was that the jetty? He had put another branch on the fire when a sharp knocking at the door made him drag himself resentfully from the hearth.

"Don't wake Brother Fir!" he whispered, then saw who it was. "Urchin!"

Urchin's pale fur looked darker and coarse with rain, and he was shivering. Juniper pulled him to the fireside. "Do you have a headache?" he demanded. "Or a cough? Do you feel . . ."

"I'm all right," said Urchin quickly. "I'm only wet." Taking in the gentle warmth and peace of the turret room, the fire and the half-finished drink on the hearth, he saw that Juniper hadn't been back for long. Now he had to send him out again, and he hated himself for it.

"Have you heard?" said Juniper, fetching another mug. "They've found the source!"

"Yes, I heard all about that," said Urchin. "Listen, Juniper. Sepia came to meet me with a message for you. It's Damson."

Juniper stopped scurrying about with drinks. He stood completely still, ready for what Urchin would say next.

"She's very ill," said Urchin. Brother Fir's eyes had opened. "She says she wants you and a priest, but . . ."

"I'll do for both," said Juniper, and reached for a cloak.

"I must . . ." croaked Brother Fir, and took a wheezy breath, "I must go. You . . ." He tried to climb out of bed, but as he put both hind paws on the floor, he swayed, and Urchin caught him.

"You have to stay here, Brother Fir," said Juniper. "You'll end up worse if you try to go out."

"I'll go with Juniper," said Urchin. "And I'll ask Whittle to stay with you, Brother Fir."

As Urchin found someone to fetch Whittle, Juniper checked the contents of his satchel and added more feverfew, rosemary, and pennyjohn. He knelt for Fir's blessing, then side by side, Juniper and Urchin pattered down the turret stair, not speaking, hearing the beat of rain as they passed the window. As they reached the work-room landing a small mole was running up the stairs toward them, a bit out of breath.

"The king and queen want Urchin in the Throne Room at once," he gabbled earnestly.

"You have to go to them, I have to go to Damson," said Juniper as Urchin hesitated. "It's that simple."

"Then don't go alone," said Urchin. "Get someone to go with you, Fingal or someone."

"There isn't time," said Juniper.

Urchin wanted to promise to come after him later, or to send someone else—but how could he promise that? He didn't know what the king and queen would ask of him. It had hurt him to drag Juniper away from his warm turret, and it hurt even more to see him running into the storm alone. Feeling the tug at his heart, he turned his steps to the Throne Room where he found Crispin, Cedar, Needle, and Sepia in great excitement, talking about a rose petal, one of the dried rose petals from Catkin's naming ceremony, and a new search.

Juniper huddled his cloak around him, running against battering wind and rain to the waterfall. He had grown up here. He knew every track and cave, even without the otter raising a storm-buffeted lantern.

"Is that Brother Juniper?" the otter called. "She's still asking for you. Mistress Apple's with her."

So she was still alive. *Apple mustn't catch it*, thought Juniper, ducking under a tree root. If his own foster mother was dangerously ill, he didn't want Urchin's to catch fouldrought, too. He wriggled between twisted old roots, knotted a muslin mask around his face, and saw Apple, leaning in candlelight over the shrunken figure propped up in the nest.

"Here's your Juniper, Mistress Damson, you're all right now, your Juniper's here," said Apple. She rose stiffly and waddled to Juniper's side, lowering her voice to a murmur. "It's not at all good, my dear, I'm sorry for you with all my heart, but it's not good."

"Thank you for staying with her, Apple," he whispered back

through the muslin. "You'd better go. We don't want anything to . . ."

"Oh, don't you worry about me, I never catch anything," she said, patting his paw. "I reckon it's my cordial, I drink it every day, if we all drank it there'd not be a cough or a sneeze anywhere on the island. I'll stay awhile, if that's all right with you, I'll keep out of your way, you being like a son to her and nearly a priest and a healer and all. And I'll make up the fire."

Juniper took off his wet cloak, knelt at Damson's side, and saw the signs he had dreaded. It wasn't just the labored breathing, or the swollen wrist and rash on her paw as he lifted it. It was something in her face, as if she knew that the struggle was over and had given in, that laid a cloud over his heart. He uncorked a bottle of Spring Gate water, poured it onto a pawful of moss, and held it to her lips.

"That's good," she said, and turned her head, narrowing her eyes. "That's not you, is it, Apple?"

So her sight was failing, too. "No, it's Juniper," he said. He leaned closer to her as Apple brought the candle closer, and they looked clearly into each other's faces.

"My Juniper!" Damson cried, and reached out her arms to him. Juniper held her tightly, feeling how thin her shoulders were and how coarse her fur had become. Then he laid her gently back in the nest and held her paw.

"Don't you get ill," she whispered.

"I won't," he said. "Are you in pain?"

"No, no pain nor anything," she said, and sighed. "I've got you. That's all. But for a priest, I need the priest."

"I'm afraid you'll have to make do with me," he said. Damson frowned.

"I need Brother Fir," she insisted. "Will he come?"

"He's not well," said Juniper.

Her eyes widened, anxious and afraid. "Is he . . . ?"

"It's not disease," he said.

"But will he come?"

Juniper didn't want to disappoint her, but he mustn't give her false hope.

"We'll see," he said. As Apple nursed the fire into life and the warmth spread, Damson seemed to drift into a light sleep; but when Juniper moved to make himself more comfortable, she opened her eyes and smiled weakly at him.

"You're still here," she whispered.

"I won't leave you, Mum," he said, and she smiled again with contentment.

"You've always been like a real son to me," she said. "Never had none of my own, but you were my son from the night I found you. Can't bear to think how lonely I'd have been without you. Brightest thing in my life, all these years."

He held tightly to her paw. That settled it, then. This could have been the last chance to find out anything she knew about who he really was. But he couldn't ask her after this. And, for the first time,

123

he felt he didn't need to know. She had been all the mother he needed. Holding her paw in his as she lay dying, he wanted them both to forget that he was adopted, and simply be mother and son.

"And you've been my real mum," he said, and gave her the moss so she could drink again.

She drank the water, talked a little, muttered something about having sewing to finish, and slept again. Juniper tucked the blanket round her, held her paw, and waited. It would be a long night.

Apple brought him a warm drink and wrapped a cloak round his shoulders, and as the night cooled, he was glad of it. Damson's paw still rested in his. Now and again Apple would prod the fire and add more wood, and the crackling of stirring flame and sticks spoke out clearly in the surrounding silence.

Still unable to concentrate on his prophecy, he thought of what Brother Fir had said just before he became ill. The island would face its greatest enemy, setting paw against paw, mind against mind, heart against the Heart.

Was this the real enemy behind Catkin's kidnapping? Was Linty being controlled by some evil power, and if so, what terrible things could happen to Catkin? Was everything, Catkin's disappearance and disease too, really the work of Lord Husk, or of his ghost? Husk had murdered the last Heir of Mistmantle. Had he come for the next?

His imagination wandered into dark and confused places, searching for what the worst might be. Was there a curse on the Heir of Mistmantle, or even on all of them? Would fouldrought claim them all?

Behind him, something was moving. He could hear it scuffle. It was coming nearer. The terror of seeing it made him rigid with fear. Sweat ran down his neck. He must not move. Whatever—whoever— was in the cave must not notice him. But the greater terror of not seeing it made him turn, stiffly, cautiously, to look.

From the gloom in the back of the cave, something darted forward. Juniper flinched, bit his lip to stifle a gasp, and froze. Then with sheer relief, he laughed.

A tiny frog crouched on the floor, looking up at him with wary, bulging eyes. It looked much more afraid than he was. It stayed, its throat pulsing, then sprang for safety into a cleft into the wall. Damson, disturbed by the movement, turned and muttered in her sleep.

Juniper felt the tension fall away from him. He had imagined a grim specter and found a small frog. He felt sorry for it. The reality was this quietness, the fire, Damson's paw in his, and the patient love surrounding her death. And this death was not something to dread. It was gentle. Then Juniper understood, and he realized why Fir had told them they must understand for themselves what the island's worst enemy was. It wasn't disease, death, or even Husk, living or dead.

Juniper understood now.

CHAPTER TEN

C APTAIN LUGG AND A TEAM OF MOLES marched up the muddy
hillside, bending their heads against the storm. Already,
cloaked squirrels and hedgehogs stood about with lanterns, while others scrabbled and sniffed. Urchin and Needle, Cedar and Crispin,
knelt around the spot where Needle had found the petal.

"But we searched here before," said Urchin. "I'm sure it wasn't
there then, or we would have seen it. It must have been dropped since
then."

"And there were lots of those petals," Needle pointed out. "They
were falling into hats and everything. This one might not be anything
to do with Catkin."

"I think we're onto something, Your Majesty," shouted a mole. A
small squirrel, one of the dancers, was squeezing her way through
a gap in a tree root. Her voice, muffled in the earth, called back

to them as they crouched on the soaked ground and strained to hear her.

"The roots have been blocked up," she was saying. "But the moles think it's not all the same thickness. There might be a way through, where it's thinnest. We need a mole to hear vibrations and things."

"It'll have to be a littl' 'un," said Lugg. "Go on then, young Ninn." A small dark female mole slipped deftly into a tunnel as Lugg and Cedar pressed their ears to the wet moss, trying to hear every creak and every pawstep through the pounding of rain. There was more scrabbling and muttering from the animals underground as Lugg listened intently—then he sprang up with a spray of rain from his cloak.

"Over there!" he cried. "That patch of heather! Get scrabbling!" he yelled. The animals dashed through the scratching heather and fell to their knees, clawing furiously at the earth.

"Goes a long way down," said Lugg. "Need a couple more good small moles in through the nearest tunnel—you and you, in you get." Moles dived underground as Cedar tore wildly at the heather.

"There's a space!" she gasped. Urchin narrowed his eyes to look and saw only tightly packed earth, but there were no roots twisted through it. It was not a natural thing. Somebody had made it like that.

More scrabbling came from beneath them, then with a soft falling of earth, Cedar had slipped down through the gap with Crispin after her. Urchin, holding the lantern, followed them down.

He found himself in a tunnel so tight and twisting that he was sure he or the lantern would get stuck, but within seconds he had wriggled

127

his way through and joined Cedar and Crispin in an arched chamber, pulling the lantern after him. He had already caught his paw on a sharp stone and cut it by then, but at least the lantern had stayed alight. The chamber appeared clean, dry, and perfectly empty except for some shreds of turf and candle ends on the floor. Sandy soil irritated his eyes, and he rubbed them with his free paw.

"They were here," she whispered. "They were here, and we're too late." She sat on the ground and hugged her knees.

Urchin called back up the tunnel.

"They've gone," he shouted, then sat down beside the queen with his paw across her shoulders. He remembered how she had cared for him when he had been a prisoner. He desperately wanted to find Catkin for her.

"They must have been all right when they left here," he said. "That must be when the petal fell, in the last day or two."

"There are dozens of tunnels," said Crispin, "some of them blocked, none of them used recently as far as I can tell. They must have gone over ground, but I don't see how they managed that without being seen."

Cedar raised her head. "There won't be a trail," she said wretchedly. "All this rain will have washed it away."

"She can't have stayed aboveground for long," said Urchin, trying to think one step ahead. "Too dangerous. There must be another of these places somewhere."

"It could be anywhere," said Cedar. With her voice on the edge of tears, she rubbed her paw across her eyes. "What do we do now? Start all over again? I'm sorry to whine, but I don't know how much more disappointment I can bear."

"You're not whining," said Crispin, coming to sit beside her. "You have the strongest spirit I've ever known."

Urchin thought hard. "You led the resistance on Whitewings," he said. "You had to keep secrets. You kept Larch and Flame alive and let everyone think they were dead. If you were Linty, what would you do?"

Cedar stared ahead of her with deep concentration on her face. At last, slowly and thoughtfully, she said, "We missed this place for so long because it's ingeniously well-hidden and a long way down, and seemed impossible. Impossible to make, let alone to get to. She's gone somewhere else impossible. So we have to look in impossible places. And if I were doing what Linty's doing," she said slowly, thinking aloud, "I think—I think—I'd try to get down to the shore, in case I needed to take Catkin off the island!"

She sprang up, then stopped as if she had been frozen to the spot. Her eyes were on something on the floor. Urchin had never seen such horror on her face before. He and Crispin both followed her gaze to a small, dark patch on the floor.

"Blood!" she whispered.

"That's me," said Urchin. "I cut my paw on a stone."

The queen knelt and examined the stain. Then she raised her eyes to him.

"This isn't fresh blood," she said. "It can't be yours. It's dried."

Crispin took her paw. "It's only a little," he said. "It could be anything. Linty might have cut herself. Don't lose hope."

"It's all I have," she said. "I don't know what to do next."

"Please, Your Majesty, I wish you could sleep," said Urchin. "The rest of us can keep searching."

She raised her eyes to him. "If you knew my nightmares," she whispered, "you wouldn't say that."

All the long night and the next day, in driving rain, the search for Catkin went on. In the Mole Palace the little ones squealed and chased each other, played at having picnics, ate porridge while listening wide-eyed to Moth and Mother Huggen telling them stories, and slept cuddled together in warm nests. Twigg made toys out of scraps of timber and polished them with vinegar before sending them to the little ones. Shadows lengthened, the streams ran clear, and Catkin was not found.

Sepia arrived at Damson's tree root, and Apple went home. As it grew late, Damson turned her head restlessly. From the way she grasped about for his paw, Juniper understood that her sight had failed completely, and she struggled to raise her head when he spoke to her, as if she found it hard to hear his voice.

She muttered, whimpered, and whispered, and though Juniper laid his ear as close as he could to her lips, he could not understand a word. He straightened up, rubbing his eyes and wondering when he had last slept properly, when a sudden sob and a gasp from Damson startled him bolt upright.

"I need a priest!" she wailed. "Bring me the priest!"

"I'm here," said Juniper. He stroked the top of her head and took her paw. "I'm a novice priest now."

"I mean the proper priest!" cried Damson. "Brother Fir!"

"Sh," said Juniper gently. "Sleep now." It was no good trying to tell her that Brother Fir could not come. She drifted into sleep, but each time she woke, her cries were more pleading and urgent. "Where's the priest? When is Brother Fir coming! I need Brother Fir! Tell him I'm dying! Please! Please! Before I die!"

She became calmer at last and lay with her head in Juniper's lap. Perhaps she would slip away quietly now, like this. That would be best. There was a quietness that came with dying. He had learned about that over these last few days, and he recognized it now. All he could do was wait with her while she died, however long it took. She opened her eyes at last, wept silently, and pressed his paw.

"That's the priest, isn't it?" she whispered calmly. "I so wanted you before I died. I knew you'd come. I was afraid you'd be too late. Sepia, is that the priest?"

Juniper looked across at Sepia, and she came to sit beside them. If Damson had said, "Is that Brother Fir?" it would have been much more difficult. But she had said, "That's the priest, isn't it?"

He was nearly a priest, and only a priest could comfort her now. So he made the decision that would change his life.

"Yes," he said. "The priest's here." He felt the soft letting-go as Damson relaxed in his lap. There was a quiet sigh.

"Then I can tell the truth," she said.

CHAPTER ELEVEN

EPIA STOOD UP AND TOOK A STEP BACK. She was looking intently down at Juniper, who met her gaze. She gave a tiny shake of her head, but Juniper still looked back at her without flinching.

Sepia spoke so softly that she barely said the words at all, only framed them.

"You're not meant to hear this."

"It's too late," Juniper whispered back. "She has to say it. She won't die in peace if she doesn't."

Damson had to believe he was Brother Fir. It wasn't only because he wanted to hear what she had to say. She had to believe she had spoken to Brother Fir, or she would die in distress. He held the moss to her lips. She managed her words slowly, stopping now and again to gather her strength.

"I never told it before," she said. "Long ago, I was living higher up than here, up on the north side, near where the ridge stands up, with the larch trees, and far below it there's that little bay. Animals keep themselves to themselves there. My husband had died in the last bad storms. We'd had no little ones of our own, and that was our great sorrow. There was a young squirrel lass there, a pretty, dark-furred young thing, sweet-natured. Always had time for a chat. Helpful. Her people had died in the storm, too."

She paused for breath, then went on, her voice low as she struggled with the words. "Too trusting. Too willing. Called Spindrift."

There was another long pause and a wheezy breath. "Told me lots of things, but not what mattered most. Never told me she was with young. I noticed it, but she said nothing till her baby was in her arms. He was a beautiful baby, very like his mother. She said she'd been wed, and it was a secret, and her husband was coming to take her somewhere special. I wasn't to speak of the baby. He was secret, too. I doubted all that, Brother Fir. I reckoned it was somebody from the ships, and he might never come back for her."

Juniper gave her a drink, and presently she dozed while he watched over her, stroking her head. His legs grew stiff and painful, but he stayed still, not wanting to disturb her. The fire was burning low. Sepia fed it with more branches, then brought him a cloak to warm him, wrapping it around his shoulders so he would not have to move. She placed the candle nearer to him. In her sleep, Damson murmured phrases of song, and Juniper thought he recognized

134

the Mistmantle lullaby. There was nothing to do but to wait until she woke again. When her eyes did open she looked about her, seeing nothing.

"It's dark in here," she said. "You still there?"

"I'm here," said Juniper. "Did Spindrift's husband come for her?"

"Oh, he came," she said, and her voice was almost a moan. "Dead of night, he came for her."

Juniper's skin turned cold under his fur. He began to think he would rather not hear this. But he no longer had any choice. The words of his prophecy whirred in the back of his head like something far away, heard dimly, but not seen.

"She told me one evening," said Damson. "She told me he was coming that very night. I woke in the night—heard the baby crying— I could hear something moving on the cliff top, high up over the shore. I heard a voice—remembered that voice, Brother Fir, all these years! I wish I could forget it. 'This way, my love.' That was what he said. That voice sank into my mind. Stayed there.

"To this day, Brother Fir, I don't know for certain what I saw. Night was pitch black, no moon, and my night sight was never good. I heard a scream. Even then, I didn't know, didn't know what to do! I muddle easily, sir. Sometimes a scream is just a few young ones larking about, but it sounded like a proper scream—I scurried off to look. I'll tell you now . . . never told before." There was a long pause. "Should have. Didn't."

She took a deep breath. Juniper felt the pulse in her wrist.

"Peace, Damson," he said. "Take your time."

"There was a boat near the water. I saw a squirrel put something in that boat—it was all bundled up, couldn't tell what it was. He did something to the boat. Came back. Saw the white on his chest. He was walking about the shore, stopping, starting, like searching for something. You still listening?"

"Yes, I'm listening," said Juniper.

"Lost sight of him," she said, "then there was that bit of white again, and something in the air—he'd thrown something. Heard a splash. He pushed the boat out.

"I was so scared I didn't want to move, but I had a terrible feeling, terrible, about what he'd thrown into the sea. I waited till there was no sign of him, and I ran . . . I ran to the shore."

There was another long wait while she gathered her strength again. Juniper stayed very still. He had guessed what she would say next.

"I was right!" she wailed. "Couldn't believe it! Bobbing on the water, kicking enough just to stay afloat. He'd tried to drown the baby! Little Juniper!"

At last, thought Juniper, at last, I know what she tried to hide from me. My father tried to kill me. He had always known that there was some dark secret in his past, and he knew at last what it was. He could understand why Damson had kept it from him, and felt grateful to her. It was terrible, but the uncertainty was over.

Sepia slipped closer, wanting to take Juniper's free paw, and

136

found she couldn't touch him. The moment was for Damson and Juniper. She was an outsider.

Damson closed her eyes again, and when she drifted into sleep, Sepia did hurry to Juniper's side, putting a paw tightly round his shoulders, but he didn't move. It was as if he had no idea that she was there.

Damson still slept. The fire burned down again, and Sepia fed it with twigs and heated a cordial. She would have liked to offer some to Juniper, but she knew he wouldn't drink it. She huddled by the fire, sipping the hot drink and wishing somebody else were there with them—Mother Huggen, or Moth, Arran, or Padra. Somebody who would know what to do. She was growing drowsy by the fire when she heard a low moan from the bed. When Damson slowly opened her eyes and stirred, her voice was weaker than ever.

"Got him out of the water," she moaned. "Took him back. I should have gone to the tower. I should have told King Brushen, but I was shy of him. I should have told a captain, or someone. I should have told them what happened to Spindrift, and how that squirrel tried to kill Juniper, too. I should have told!" She gave a little cry of distress. "I was that scared! I didn't know who that squirrel was! I couldn't name him! If they couldn't find out who he was, he'd still be free! He'd have come for me, and what's more, he'd know the baby was still alive. He'd have come for Juniper! He would!"

Juniper smoothed her fur, and hushed her gently. "Sh, now, Damson. You've done nothing wrong. You saved the baby, didn't you?"

"I was scared, Brother Fir! Didn't know what to do! Just took

Juniper and loved him. His foot had got twisted, must have been when that squirrel threw him, but he wasn't seriously hurt. He thinks he was born that way. Sometimes, I thought—tomorrow I'll go to the king. But I was that scared! I kept putting it off. There weren't many knew about Juniper, and when the culling law came in they all kept quiet on account of his paw. When I went to the Gathering Chamber for anything I stayed at the back, ready to get away quickly and go home to Juniper. Didn't mind if I couldn't see or hear much. Never did see or hear much, not even that day when we did the clawmarks and cast lots, not until . . ."

She paused, taking deep breaths. Finally, with an effort, she said, ". . . until that wedding."

Juniper wrapped both of his paws over hers. He wanted her to stop, but whatever she had to say, he had to hear it now. He felt the hard, fast beating of his heart.

"I saw him then," she said. "I heard his voice and saw the turn of his head. And I recognized him!" She clutched his paw more tightly, and her voice grew higher and trembling. "That was him, Brother Fir! After all those years, I knew the voice, and the turn of his head, like when he was on the shore . . . I knew, and I ran for my life."

Juniper's own voice was unsteady. He fought to keep it under control.

"Who . . ." he began, but Damson broke in again, fearful and distressed.

"I should have denounced him! I was afraid! Who would have believed me? Who'd believe me against him?"

Juniper's stomach churned, and he struggled to take deep breaths. He could feel Sepia's gaze as if she wanted to strengthen him.

Damson let out a deep, long sigh. After so many years, it must be too hard for her to say. The whisper was quiet, but Juniper and Sepia heard it in terrible clarity.

"Husk," she said. "I'd never realized it before. Husk killed Spindrift. He tried to kill Juniper. The one she trusted. He was Juniper's father."

"No, he couldn't be," stammered Juniper.

"Oh, he was," she said. She was calmer now. "I thought about it, after that. I think he already wanted Aspen. Wouldn't do to be linked with a simple squirrel from the rocks and her child. Wouldn't suit his plans. Pushed her down the cliff with the baby in her arms. Put her in a leaky boat and pushed her out to sea, saw the baby was still alive. Tried to drown him. Everyone thought she'd gone with a sailor from another island."

Juniper held her paw as firmly as he could, but he shook. Sepia hugged him tightly.

So this is what it all came to. The thing he'd always wanted to know. The missing pieces of the puzzle. The lifelong question of who he really was. He wished he had never found out.

If only, if only, he had never let her think he was Brother Fir. If only he could go back to that moment of decision and tell her that Brother Fir was not there. He could have sent for one of the captains, she might have told a captain, and he could have gone away, and he would never have known. It would have been better that way. If only he'd never, never, never . . .

. . . if only I'd never been born, he thought bitterly. *I am Husk's son.*

Sepia held him, wishing she could bear the pain for him. A sudden cry from Damson pierced them both with shock and sent a shudder through Juniper.

"You won't tell him, Brother Fir? You won't tell Juniper? You see why he must never know!"

"Yes," said Juniper. He managed the words slowly, forcing out one at a time. "He mustn't know."

"And can you forgive me? I know I should have told, but . . ."

"Forgive?" he said. Forgive her for saving him, caring for him, sacrificing her freedom, and keeping the terrible truth from him? He wanted to take her in his arms and hug her, thank her, bury his face in her fur as he had done when he was tiny—but he was supposed to be Brother Fir.

"Peace, daughter," he said gently. "There is nothing to forgive. You have done well."

"But I should have told!" she cried.

"You are completely forgiven," he said. He laid a paw on her head. "The Heart loves you, forgives you, and rejoices in you. Heart bless you. Sleep, daughter."

He stared ahead of him, seeing nothing, aware of Damson's rough dry paw in his. Sepia's arms were still around his shoulders, but in his loneliness she might have been on the other side of the mists.

Husk's son. Husk's son. He hadn't pretended to be Brother Fir for his own sake. He hadn't meant to pry, to hear a confession that wasn't meant for him. But he had been curious about it, and he *had* heard it, and it was too late to change that. He knew who his father was, and he would have to live with that knowledge for the rest of his life.

Damson's breathing seemed to be slower. There was a pause between the breaths, as if she might not take the next one. Before dawn she opened her eyes again, and he gave her a drink.

"Is that my Juniper?" she asked.

"Yes, I'm here," he said, and as she struggled to sit up, he raised her and cradled her. He had been ready for her death. It was inevitable now; she had brought him up until he could take his place on the island, but he yearned for her to stay. She had always been there.

"You've been"—she wheezed painfully—"you've been a good son to me, Juniper. Good lad. Proud of you."

Juniper rocked her and leaned down to press his cheek against hers.

"You're my mum," he told her. "I'll always love you, Mum."

He raised a paw and said the blessing over her—*May the Heart claim you with joy and receive you with love. May your heart fly freely to the Heart that gave you life.* He did what he had longed to do, and for a few precious seconds he pressed his face into her fur. Then he could only wait, softly singing the lullaby to her and holding her in his arms until sunrise, when she died.

CHAPTER TWELVE

H E LAID HER DOWN IN THE NEST. There were other sick animals to be visited. He had to do that now. It was vital, and it would take his mind from that terrible truth. But he was too numb now to think clearly. His instinct drew him to stay with Damson as if he could slip back to a safe, happy time when she was alive and well, and there was no disease on the island, and he had no idea of who he was.

"I'll fetch Apple," said Sepia, and scampered away. When she returned with Apple dabbing her eyes on a leaf, Juniper packed his satchel, rubbed vinegar lotion on his paws, and wrenched himself away from Damson's nest.

He walked away uphill, not caring where he was going. No matter how far he walked, he couldn't get away from who he was.

He had recognized the greatest enemy of Mistmantle, but here was another enemy. It was his past, which he could never change or escape.

Urchin, Needle, and their friends were all, in one way or another, heroes. But he was Husk's son, born under a dark shadow to a cruel tyrant and murderer. *I am not fit for Urchin's company*, he thought. *I don't belong with decent animals*. It was as if everyone would hear his new name following him on the air. *Husk's son*.

Cedar held the naming shawl in both paws and faced her old enemy, Smokewreath the Sorcerer, across the empty cradle. Bones, claws, and feathers swung from the cords on his robe, he smelled of death, and his eyes stared with malice. He stretched a scrawny, stained claw to the naming shawl. If he took that, he could keep Catkin forever, trapped with his malice and bound in curses. He must not have it. But she couldn't stop him, she couldn't move, couldn't even cry out for help, couldn't call on the Heart, she was frozen. . . . She woke, her eyes wide with terror, struggling for breath, telling herself it was a nightmare. She must look at the cradle in case Smokewreath really was there. Forcing herself to breathe, she sat up. She had staggered back to the tower so exhausted that she had fallen onto the bed with dust, dirt, and blood still in her fur, and slept instantly, but not for long.

Was there someone outside the door? She twitched her ears and told herself that the guards were there. She felt at her side for a sword and remembered that she had not worn a sword since she came to Mistmantle. She had not needed one. But did she face enemies whose evil was too great to fight with a weapon? What was the enemy? And where? The tap at the door was light and gentle, but she bit her lip.

"Queen Cedar?" said the soft voice of a female hedgehog.

"Thripple!" called Cedar thankfully. "Come in!"

Thripple walked lopsidedly into the chamber, carrying a candle. "They only just told me you were back," she said. "I thought I'd better come down in case you couldn't sleep."

"I did," said Cedar, shivering. Thripple wrapped a coverlet around her. "I wish I hadn't."

"Did you have your nightmare again?" asked Thripple.

Cedar nodded, and pressed her paws to her eyes as if she could obliterate Smokewreath's face forever. "I have to look at the cradle," she said.

They stood looking down by candlelight into the empty cradle. Cedar picked up the naming shawl and stroked it.

"I can't help wondering if Smokewreath the Sorcerer really is still alive," she whispered. "Or if he's . . . well, if he's . . . if he's dead, but still . . . you know. Was he . . ." With a great effort, she said the word. "Was he *cursing* me as he died? Did he curse every child I'd ever have?"

Thripple sighed. "I can't say whether he did or not, madam," she said. "But as to whether his curses had any power against you, that's another thing. No curse can stand against the Heart. Perhaps you'd sleep better for a wash and a hot drink, now?"

Cedar didn't argue, but voices in the corridor sent her dashing to the door in case there was news of Catkin. An agitated squirrel

144

seemed to be arguing with the guard moles at the door as she flung it open.

"Mistress Hammily!" she said.

"Beg pardon, we didn't want you disturbed, Your Majesty," said one of the moles with a glare at Hammily.

"Oh, please, Your Majesty," gabbled Hammily in a high, tense voice, "I wouldn't dream of it, but you said to tell you if he got worse, and if he wanted you . . ."

"I'll fetch my things," said Cedar. "Thripple, vinegar mixture, please!"

Fingal turned the boat and felt her swing into the wind as smoothly as a bird in flight. He raised his head to the sunrise, the salt breeze, and fine rain, almost laughing with exhilaration, tasting the moment. All his life he had been in and out of boats, but nothing compared with this—*his* boat, with her perfect lines, responding so lightly to his touch and his heart, that she was somehow part of himself.

What name would be good enough for her? *Queen Cedar? Catkin? Joy? Joy* was the nearest word he knew to the way he felt now.

As soon as the little ones were allowed out of the Mole Palace, he'd give them rides in his boat. He'd already taken Tide and Swanfeather out in it but now, with simply himself and his boat in the great sea and the wide air, he felt wonderfully happy.

Thinking of the little ones, he remembered that he'd promised to

145

look in on the Mole Palace. The children grew restless in there and needed someone to organize games, and anxious parents were eager for news of them. With regret he turned for the shore, sensing a waft of turbulence on the air. Sailing in that would be fun, and already he was looking forward to taking to the sea again tomorrow. Tomorrow would soon come, but it felt too long.

The queen had said Hobb had been fortunate. He had caught a very mild case of fouldrought and recovered within hours, so he'd be immune to it after this. But he didn't feel at all happy now: in the middle of a large burrow with a lot of animals expecting him to tell them what to do about fouldrought, and Husk, and not being able to let the little ones out of our sight except, of course, we had to take them to the Mole Palace, and it's not fair, and is there a curse on the Heir of Mistmantle? and somebody ought to talk to the king about it, and it's no good expecting the queen to understand anything because she's a foreigner. Some were even angrier than he was. They all seemed to think he should be the one to speak to King Crispin. The big hedgehog was most insistent about it.

And, of course, he should. He'd wanted for a long time to give the king a piece of his mind, and His Majesty had somehow heard about their grievances and had arranged to meet them here this evening. He had a feeling that somebody might come out of this looking ridiculous, and it wouldn't be King Crispin.

The Mole Palace was becoming pleasantly noisy, apart from the corner where Jig and Fig, the mole sisters, were telling old stories of mole princes and princesses to the small animals, who sat sucking their paws and gazing up at them. One little mole, perched on a tree root, put up his paw and asked if they could have a story about Gripthroat, but Jig firmly said no, not today. Gripthroat was a terrifying mole from ancient legends, and stories about him were sure to give the little ones nightmares.

A hedgehog and an otter were giving lessons to some of the older ones. Whenever a question was asked, paws would shoot into the air.

"What can any of you tell me about the Heartstone? Yes, Flynn?"

"Please, miss, it rolls about and you can't hold on to it unless you're the true ruler or the true priest. . . ."

". . . please, miss, if you're not you drop it . . ."

". . . please, miss, I saw it at the coronation . . ."

". . . miss, so did I . . ."

"And why must you never go beyond the mists?"

"Please, miss, because you can't leave by water and come back by water."

"Please, miss, Urchin did . . ."

". . . and so did Brother Juniper, miss!"

"Yes, they did, because the Heart made that possible. What is the most times anyone has ever left the island and come back?"

"Twice, miss."

"Miss, if anybody leaves a third time, they can't come back at all, not any way."

"We're not sure about that," said the hedgehog. "Nobody ever *has* come back. That might not mean that nobody *can*, but it's never happened so far, except for . . ."

"I know, miss!"

"Go on, then."

"Except for a Voyager."

"Except for a Voyager, yes, but that's very rare. The island goes for many, many generations without a Voyager. There are pictures in the Threadings of the last two Voyagers—there was one called Lochan the otter—but they were long before the memory of anyone alive now."

"Please, how can you tell if someone's a Voyager?"

This question was too difficult for the teachers, and there was nobody they could ask. They changed the subject.

Fingal was met by such a rush of infants that Jig hardly had time to say "mind his burns!" before they could hug him. The older children were helping to look after the little ones, and the squirrels who usually sang in Sepia's choir were rehearsing as well as they could without her, but as they never managed to come in on the same note and at the same time, there was a lot more giggling than singing. Hope the hedgehog was telling anyone who'd listen that this was where he grew up, Mother Huggen was holding a baby hedgehog against her shoulder and patting its back, and some little mole girls were playing clapping games in a corner, or playing at weddings and pretending to be Moth's bridesmoles. Tipp appeared to be directing a battle against Gripthroat.

Mother Huggen had insisted on the strictest and highest standards of cleanliness. One of the palace rooms had been made into a laundry, where towels and clothes were pounded furiously to get them clean. The strong smell of vinegar and herbs was now so familiar that the animals who used to hold their noses and pull faces no longer noticed it.

A few squirrels, bored with games of First Five, began to chase each other. They ran shrieking along a corridor where a door stayed shut.

"Out of there, you lot," called Fig. "Urchin's asleep in there."

"Should think he'd sleep through a landslide," said Mother Huggen. The baby on her shoulder burped thunderously. "Beg pardon, you? He's been up all night with the king on the search. I hear they tracked Linty down, but she'd gone, and the king wanted Urchin to stay the night here because he was soaked, and it was a long walk back to the tower. They think they've got a track somewhere not far from here. If that poor Mistress Linty would just leave Princess Catkin with me and run for it, that would suit me. I'll have no peace until that baby's home. Don't know where the queen went."

"Is she looking after that whiny Yarrow?" called Fingal. Mother Huggen sat herself down in the rocking chair and settled the baby in her lap.

"I've never known anyone work so hard as the queen," she said. "I think it gets her through."

Behind the shut door, Urchin was woken by a screech from somewhere in the Mole Palace. He sat upright and reached for his sword, but the screech was followed by a cry he found completely unbelievable.

"Hope hit me!" screamed someone.

The idea of well-mannered little Hope hitting anyone was so astonishing that Urchin sprang up and ran from the chamber. Fingal, laughing, was holding back Hope as he struggled toward a small, red-faced, and very astonished hedgehog.

"Hang on to this warrior for me, Urchin!" he called. "He might strangle Cringle. It's hard holding a hedgehog at the best of times, especially with burned paws."

"Hope, calm down!" ordered Urchin, and the eager little crowd that had gathered parted to make way for him, whispering with excitement. He took Hope's paws firmly and knelt to look into his face. "This won't do, Hope. What's it all about?"

"He hit me!" screamed the hedgehog. He was now clinging to Jig, who was biting her lip with giggles.

"I'll defend you!" cried Tipp.

"No, you won't," said Fingal.

"No, you won't," said Todd. Tipp didn't answer, as he wasn't at all sure who needed defending, and why.

"I know I shouldn't have hit him," said Hope.

"Certainly not," said Fingal, his mouth twitching.

"Absolutely," said Urchin, with a huge effort not to look at Fingal. "This isn't like you. You don't go around hitting animals."

"It was because of what he said," said Hope, glaring past Urchin at the hedgehog.

"I never!" said the hedgehog.

"Ooh, he did!" squeaked an excited little squirrel in the crowd. Urchin recognized Siskin, one of Sepia's choir. "About the queen and King Crispin, we all heard him say it, sir."

"Well, it's true!" said the hedgehog, and ducked behind Jig.

"It's true, but you never said it?" asked Fingal.

"We all heard it!" said Siskin eagerly. "He said the queen's gone mad!"

Tipp tried to draw his toy sword, but it stuck. Hope lunged forward in fury. Urchin dragged him farther back from the cowering hedgehog, who was stammering in an effort to say something.

"But . . ." mumbled the hedgehog, "it's only what they say at home."

"I see," said Fingal, and knelt down beside the frightened hedgehog. "Who's 'they'?" he asked gently. "Who's been saying things about the queen?"

"My mum and dad," whispered Cringle wretchedly. "And my big brother, Quill. And his friends." He sniffed. "Sir."

"We won't be angry," said Fingal, "but we need to know what

islanders are saying. Hope won't hit you again." He looked over his shoulder and raised an eyebrow at Hope. "Will you, Hope?"

"He didn't understand what he was saying, Hope," said Urchin. "You know perfectly well that you don't sort anything out by hitting animals, don't you?"

Hope looked down at his paws and muttered an awkward apology.

"Good lad," said Urchin, and cautiously let him go. Cringle looked uneasily at his paws, then at Fingal.

"Quill and everyone," he said, and shuffled a little closer to Jig, "they say that"—he lowered his voice—"they say that the queen let her baby get stolen so now she's gone mad and she goes round whispering to the ground and singing. Well, she does, doesn't she? We all know that, it isn't a secret. Maybe it's because she's a foreigner."

Urchin, noticing a movement in the shadows, glanced up and caught his breath. Crispin and Padra had slipped into the Mole Palace and were standing half-hidden in a tunnel. Rain soaked their cloaks and made their fur gleam. Urchin was about to tell Fingal, but Crispin put a paw to his lips.

"And we didn't have no diseases like this before the queen came," went on Cringle, gaining confidence as he realized nobody would hit him this time. "My mum says maybe they're all mad where she comes from. And we know Captain Husk's come back and they're not telling us, that's what Quill says Master Hobb says, they say the king doesn't want us to know about it, and there was this bit of muslin or something in the woods, and . . ."

152

"Slow down, young hedgehog," said Fingal. "We don't know Captain Husk's back, because he isn't. How can I explain this? Listen. He isn't coming back, he can't, he's dead. Got it?"

"No, no, my dad says nobody ever saw him dead," gabbled Cringle. "He's back, he poisoned the water, and it's true, because my dad's friend saw him one evening, and he's taken the baby away and killed it, and he's going to . . . ow, ow, ow . . . help!"

The cry was because he was being lifted into the air. Padra had slipped in behind him and picked him up very gently. As Cringle kicked in the air, Padra turned to Crispin, bowed, and carefully placed the trembling hedgehog in front of him.

Everyone had fallen silent. Those who were not too flustered or excited remembered to bow or curtsy to Crispin. A few glanced nervously at each other, and Fig hurried forward with towels for Padra and Crispin, but Crispin had already knelt down to be on the small hedgehog's eye level.

"Cringle," said Crispin gently. "I'm not cross, and nobody's going to hurt you. Do you like it here?"

"Y . . . y . . . y . . . yes, Your Majesty," stuttered Cringle miserably. Crispin put out a paw and gently smoothed his quills. A sense of relief settled on the chamber.

"Dear Cringle," said Crispin. "I don't want you to be afraid of me. I'm not a monster." He looked over Cringle's head and said to the wide-eyed, openmouthed animals, "I don't want any of you to be afraid of me. Cringle, will you do something for me?"

153

Cringle nodded his head. "Yes, Your Majesty, please, sir," he said.

"Good," said Crispin. "When you leave this place and go back to your family, you will have something to tell them. Tell them from me that the queen has nursed both Yarrow and Hobb back to health, and her efforts in the search have brought us very close to finding Catkin. And you may tell them that Husk is dead. If you were an adult, spreading slanderous rumors against your queen, I would deal severely with you. But you are young and need to learn who to listen to, and when to speak."

"Yes, Your Majesty, sorry, Your Majesty," said Cringle.

"Off you go, then," said Crispin. "Good lad. Go and talk to Mother Huggen. Hello, Hope!" He toweled energetically at his wet fur and turned to Urchin. "Cedar believes that the infection is past its peak, but I don't want to let the little ones out yet."

"Are you any nearer to finding Catkin, Your Majesty?" asked Urchin.

"We thought we were getting close," said Crispin. "But the wretched thing is that we had to call off the tunnelers. There's fresh digging, as if she's trying to make new tunnels, and with the weight of last night's rain it could lead to a landslide."

With Catkin underneath it, thought Urchin, but he didn't say so. He glanced at Padra, but when he saw that Padra was looking past him at something, he turned to see what it was. A trickle of water, thin as twine, twisted gleaming down the wall.

"I don't remember that being here before," remarked Padra.

"It's only water," said Fingal. "Can't harm them if they don't drink it."

"It's water in the wrong place," said Padra and looked up into the earth ceiling, inspecting it from different angles. "It's filtering through a tiny gap in the tree roots."

"Is that a problem?" asked Fingal.

"There shouldn't be any gaps at all," said Padra. "This place is supposed to be impenetrable. We need some good moles."

"I'll find some, shall I, sir?" said Urchin.

"I'll send a messenger," said Crispin, coming to Padra's side and craning his neck to look up at the leak. "We may need you here. And I'll send a message to Hobb's lot to put off my meeting with them. This is more urgent." He leaped into a tunnel and called orders, sending squirrels darting away in search of Captain Lugg and his best moles. When he inspected the wall again, he drew Padra, Urchin, and Mother Huggen to one side.

"Dangerous," he said quietly. "It's raining heavily now, and this could turn into a landslide. All the sudden rain is pouring off the hills and soaking into the ground, so it's too heavy over the tunnel networks. Farther uphill, it could dislodge earth. We have to move everyone out of here, but without alarming anyone. Don't look at that leak too conspicuously," he added, as Urchin tilted his head to look. "We've drawn enough attention to it already. We don't want to panic anyone; we'll just quietly get them moving out."

The thought of it made Urchin heavy with exhaustion. He seemed to have hardly slept before being woken up by the quarreling hedge-hogs, and his eyes wanted so much to close. The prospect of escorting dozens of small animals to safety made his limbs feel heavy as stone. He tried not to think about it. It was easier not to.

"Where shall we move them to?" asked Padra.

"Those who have homes near enough can be taken back there," said Crispin. "But only if there's been no disease there over the last few days, and they're not close enough to be in danger of landslide. If possible, they can move in with their friends. We could get some of them to Falls Cliffs, where there's plenty of room and no danger of landslides, but it's a long way, and the paths will be slippery. We can always pack them into the tower. But it's not only the Mole Palace that's in danger."

"Yes," said Padra. "If there's a landslide, we don't know how wide-spread it might be."

"I suspect," said Crispin, "that Linty's efforts at digging a way through might have disturbed the network and weakened it. Squirrels aren't expert tunnelers, she wouldn't know what to listen for, or how to feel for the qualities in the earth."

For a second Padra rested his paw on Crispin's shoulder, and on the otter's grave, calm face Urchin saw the thing they were all think-ing. He was too young to remember the last great landslide on Mistmantle, but he had seen pictures of it in the Threadings, and had heard the older animals talking about the terrible rushing of the pow-erful earth, faster and faster, unstoppable, rumbling and roaring, with the smell of wet soil and the agonized creaking of tree roots as mud and boulders stormed down the hillside. Crispin himself had lost family in that landslide. No wonder he took this seriously. And this time, where would Catkin be if the weight of earth crashed through tunnel roofs?

"When the moles get here," said Crispin, "we need them to feel for the vibrations and tell us where the danger areas are. We need calm, quick messengers to alert everyone in the tunnels and burrows and get them out of the way, and we could do with some Circle animals. Any diseased animals have to keep well away from the rest, wearing masks, if we have enough. Padra, we need otters to watch the watercourses from the hilltops down, so we know if the water is getting faster or the rivers bursting their banks. We need to redouble the watch for Linty in case she gets scared and makes a dash for it. Huggen?"

"Quiet a minute, Cringle," said Mother Huggen to the young hedgehog, who was chattering earnestly to her. "Yes, Your Majesty?"

"Choose a sensible female to go to the queen, please," said Crispin. "She needs to know what's happening."

"She was just out visiting that Yarrow," said Mother Huggen, in a voice which showed exactly what she thought about Yarrow. "I'll send someone to her."

"Urchin," said Crispin, "when did you last eat?"

"Just before I fell asleep, Your Majesty," said Urchin.

"Any idea how long you slept?"

"Um . . ."

"I see," said Crispin. "For the moment, go to the surface, into the tree growing above the leak, and make sure nobody comes within three squirrel's leaps of you. The ground mustn't be disturbed. Can you stay awake?"

"I think so, Your Majesty."

"I'll send someone to take over from you as soon as I can," said Crispin. "I know I'm asking a lot of you."

"It's all right, Your Majesty," said Urchin, already feeling less tired now that he had something to do. Knowing that Crispin trusted him gave him new strength and energy.

"And the whole island must pray," said Crispin. "And Brother Fir and Juniper need to know what's happening."

Trying to look casual, Urchin glanced at the trickle of water. Was it his imagination, or was it getting bigger? Remembering Crispin's orders he darted to the surface, but long before he reached it he heard the hard, furious drumming of torrential rain.

All that day, it seemed to Juniper that he tumbled without thinking into the burrows where he was needed, attended to the sick expertly, hardly noticing what he was doing, and lurched out to begin again somewhere else, not staying anywhere long enough to be asked for his advice, or prayers, or a blessing. At last, through drenching rain and wind, he stumbled to the tower. He didn't want the peace and quiet of Fir's turret. He didn't want the time and space to reflect on what had happened. Anger, pain, and confusion flung him staggering up the stairs of the tower, to the thing he felt driven to do.

"Are you well, Brother Juniper?" asked the mole on guard. "You look . . ."

Juniper rushed past him and limped up the stairs to the turret which would never seem the same now. Nothing would. He had been Fir's novice, Urchin's friend, Damson's foster son, and life had been sweet. He had never realized that until now, when it all seemed to be over. He could never enjoy life again. He was Husk's son. In all his life he had never truly hated, but he hated his father now.

He lurched up the last winding stair, just remembering to pause outside the door and knock softly. There was no answer, and he opened the door in complete silence. The fire burned low, and a single lantern shone steadily on a windowsill. In the little bed Brother Fir lay asleep, one wrinkled paw on the quilt, his face serenely still.

I will never be so peaceful as that, thought Juniper. Never again. I don't belong in the same world. He knelt shivering at Fir's bedside and yearned for his blessing, not sure if he could ever receive it again.

Brother Fir would not like what he was about to do. He should ask for permission first, and it would almost certainly be refused. But he had to do it.

"I'm sorry," he whispered, not wanting to wake the priest. "I have to do this."

He knelt at the hearth and with both paws, lifted out a loose stone,

159

taking care not to let it scrape against the others. With a reverence that made his paws shake, he reached into the space and lifted out the oval box made of dusky pink stone that glowed softly in the lantern light, the box that held the Heartstone. Flecks of gold and silver glinted in it.

He hated himself. But he had to find out something about himself, and only the Heartstone of Mistmantle could tell him.

He lifted the lid and looked down at the pale stone where it nestled like a bird's egg in a nest of straw and muslin. Only a true priest or ruler of Mistmantle could hold on to the Heartstone. He had seen it lie in Crispin's paw at the coronation, as peacefully as if it had come home.

Fearful and trembling, on his knees, he laid a shaking paw on the Heartstone. Then he gasped, turned hot and cold, and could not move. The door was opening.

CHAPTER THIRTEEN

TYPICAL!" PROCLAIMED HOBB to his audience. "The king keeps us all waiting, then he says he's not coming! Couldn't look us in the face! I managed to get here, and I haven't been well!"

It had been a great relief to Hobb when the king's messenger arrived, soaked and breathless, to tell them that due to an emergency the king must put off his meeting with them. Hobb had waited until the messenger was out of the way before telling his friends what he thought of the king. The sense of relief made him confident.

"May as well go home," shrugged a hedgehog.

"It's pouring," said a squirrel.

"Want to call on Yarrow, Master Hobb?" suggested a mole, and Hobb said that he might as well. It was nearer than going home, where his wife would tell him to stop strutting about and putting the island right, and mend the toasting fork.

161

Urchin perched in the tree with his shoulders huddled against the rain and his gaze on the waterlogged ground, watching for approaching animals and also for any sign of trembling in the earth. Now and again a movement would catch his eye and alarm him, but it was always a mole or a hedgehog popping to the surface to call "All's well," or "The roof looks poor to me." As the darkness grew, lanterns were lit and flickered in the storm, and more lights moved and swayed in procession far off, as little animals from the Mole Palace were led over the hills to safety. He hoped not many of them were making the long journey to the tower and Falls Cliffs, not in this driving rain, not in this wind that rocked the tree where he stood.

A squelch of wet paws behind him made him dart around to warn whoever it was to stay back, but the pawsteps had already stopped. Twirling his tail for balance, squinting against the rain, he saw that Fingal had spread-eagled himself on the ground with his paws outstretched and his head raised.

"I can't come near," called Fingal, "and I have to lie like this to spread my weight. Padra's upstream. There are streams bursting their banks and rain making the mud waterlogged, and mud and rocks and all that stuff, they're all coming down. Padra's leading a team to build a dam to stop the water and a channel to divert it so it'll go over the, you know, that whatsitswhiskers. The rocky bit that won't collapse. The ridge."

"Do they want me up there?" Urchin called back.

"No," yelled Fingal. "There's a danger of rockfalls from below the dam. We have to look out for them." He suddenly gave some sort of a nod, turning his face to the side to keep out of the mud, and Urchin turned to see Crispin behind him with Captain Lugg, Longpaw the messenger, and a young squirrel at his side. Rain streamed from Lugg's blue cloak and sparkled in lantern lights on Crispin's tail and whiskers. Fingal, still sprawled on the boggy ground, took a deep breath and repeated all that he'd just told Urchin.

"Then I'll get you some help, and you can go to the channel and keep it clear of rocks, Fingal," said Crispin. "Longpaw, we need three or four young otters to help him." Longpaw dashed away toward the shore, and Crispin guided the young squirrel forward. "Urchin, Dunnock is here to take over from you."

"Can I have Urchin to help evacuate the animals from the burrows around here, Your Majesty?" asked Lugg. "He's fast and light, and he's been in so many tight places I know he can cope with another one."

"It's too risky, and he's done enough," said Crispin. "He needs a break."

"I'm volunteering for it, Your Majesty," said Urchin hopefully. Cold and wet as he was, the challenge was irresistible, and it would be good to be at the heart of the action by Captain Lugg's side again. "If not me, somebody has to do it."

"He'd only get swept away in a mudslide if he stayed here, Your Majesty," called Fingal, raising his dirty face from a tree root.

"They're brave lads, these," remarked Lugg.

"Please, Your Majesty?" pleaded Urchin, and Fingal said something that sounded as if he had a mouth full of mud.

"Go on, then," said Crispin. "Fingal, get out of there. Backward, very slowly. And Urchin," he went on as Urchin ran down the tree trunk, "the first sign of a shaky tunnel and never mind being a hero, just get yourself out, understood?"

"Yes, sir," said Urchin, stepping as lightly as he could to Lugg's side.

"Keep an eye on him, Lugg," said Crispin. "If anything happens to Urchin, one of us will have to answer to Apple, and sooner you than me."

Juniper could not move. He could only wait, kneeling on the hearth in the dim turret, trapped in his nightmare, as the door opened. What could he say? He didn't know. His mind, like his body, failed him.

The sight of Sepia, sweet-faced, wet, and worried, trailing a soaked cloak behind her, flooded him with relief. He had been caught out, but by one of the few animals who might possibly understand.

Sepia took in the gentle light of the chamber, the sleeping figure of the priest, the warmth from the fire—not as warm as she would have liked, but far better than outside—and Juniper crouching on the hearth with alarm and fear on his face. Or was it guilt?

She had been so worried about him. She had hunted for him through the lashing rain, growing more breathless and anxious as the light faded, guessing that he might go to Urchin, but where would Urchin be? Darting through treetops rocked with storms, calling to every animal she met, she had heard that Urchin was with the king and Captain Padra, and they were moving the little ones away from their hiding place and trying to hold off a landslide, and it all looked very dangerous. But was Juniper with him? Please, *please*, had anyone seen Brother Juniper?

Nobody had seen him at the landslide site, but somebody had seen a squirrel who looked like Juniper—at least it might have been Juniper, hard to tell in this light and in this weather, you can hardly look up—hurrying to the tower. Limped like Juniper, come to think. She had sent a message to tell her family she would not be back tonight and had struggled on to the tower as the wind whipped the branches under her paws. Drenched, tired, and anxious, she had reached the turret at last—and here was Juniper, kneeling on the floor with a box before him.

She slipped nearer to the bed to see if Fir was sleeping and was relieved to find that he was. She huddled on the hearth beside Juniper.

The firelight showed clearly the pale pink box and the stone nestling at its center. Sepia gasped. When she managed to speak, her words were barely a whisper.

"What are you doing? That's the Heartstone!"

"Yes," said Juniper harshly. "Watch this."

"Don't touch it!" whispered Sepia in horror. "Juniper, *please* don't, you mustn't!" She put out a paw to stop him, but he jerked away from her, held his right paw in his left in a failed attempt to stop it from shaking, and scooped up the peach-pink pebble. It rolled softly onto the floor.

"Put it *away!*" urged Sepia with a glance toward the bed.

Juniper swept the Heartstone back into the box. "I had to do it," he said, and the wretchedness in his voice made her hurt for him. "I had to prove it to myself. I'm not a real priest."

"You're a novice!" she said. "It just means that you're not a real priest *yet*, and you knew that!"

"But I told Damson I was, and I heard her confession," said Juniper. "And I wish I hadn't. And I wouldn't have heard it, if I hadn't pretended I was the priest. I should never have done it."

"But you didn't do it just to hear her confession," said Sepia. "You did it so she could die in peace, and she did. Think what it would have been like for her if you hadn't!"

Juniper stared into the deep orange glow and white ashes, wrapped in his own misery. He knew Sepia was right, but he was wrung out with grief and guilt and the weight of his secret. Into the silence came a single sound, soft with weakness, but so familiar.

"Hm!"

"Brother Fir!" gasped Sepia.

"Plagues, lice, and fire," grumbled Captain Lugg, shoving his head and shoulders into a tunnel. "Get out, you lot, quick about it, and be light on your paws."

"I've not been very well," moaned a voice from inside. "I can't hurry."

"That's Hobb, is it?" said Lugg. "Well, you'll be worse if the tunnel comes down. Is Yarrow the squirrel down here anywhere? Yes, I know you've been ill, you're not the only one. Get out. Plague and lice! Urchin, tell 'em not to move anyone out of the burrow below this one yet. Let's get this one clear first. Don't want too much coming and going at once. We need more pit props."

Urchin leaped lightly forward through the tunnel, scampered up the next layer of burrows, and called for pit props. He looked up to the hillside, where storm-tossed lanterns rocked in a wild dance as otters and hedgehogs worked furiously, building dams and channels. Wild clouds whipped across the sky. Crispin, with a few Circle animals, stood up to his knees in water, stopping the dislodged stones that rolled down the hillside. Urchin ducked into a burrow.

"Be ready to leave when Captain Lugg calls for you," he ordered. "Till then, don't move unless you absolutely have to."

Above him, a tree root shook. Rough and ready props for holding up tunnel roofs had been made from whatever timber Twigg and the other carpenters could supply and from branches wrenched away by the storm. Urchin darted out of the burrow to find one. Lightning flashed, followed by a rumble that he hoped was only thunder.

"That's all we need," muttered Lugg, pushing Yarrow into the open. "And you needn't think I can't hear you muttering about Husk, because I can. Can't see how he could make it thunder. Watch out, young Urchin. It's getting worse."

167

"Dearest Juniper," said Fir, when Juniper and Sepia had told their story. "You hate yourself now because you heard Damson's confession. If you had not done it, you would hate yourself for that instead."

Juniper found that his despair was not quite as heavy as it had been. Miserably, with the gales battering the dark windows and the lamp casting a steady light on Fir's calm, wise face, he had poured out his story to Brother Fir, and Damson's story, too—"She meant you to hear it, sir," he said. Sepia had plumped up the pillows for Fir, built up the fire, and heated cordials. The firelight cast a warm light on her face and flickered on the walls. Juniper was aware of peace around him, even if he wasn't at peace himself.

"It had never occurred to me," said Fir, "that Husk might be your father. I remember Spindrift. We thought she had left the island with someone from one of the ships. A quiet, shy little squirrel with a gentle nature. She must have loved you very dearly. So, Juniper, now you know. May the Heart rest her, and dear Damson, too."

"She was the only parent I ever had," said Juniper. "I wish I had her here. I'd rather have Damson alive than know the truth about my father."

"I know, I know," said Brother Fir sadly, "but that's not the way it is. The Heart brings good from all things, all things, however impossible that may seem. Bring your wretchedness, your anger, and your unwelcome knowledge to the Heart."

"I can't, sir," said Juniper.

"You can't yet," said Fir, "but you will. Life consists of doing the impossible. Thank you, Miss Sepia," he added, putting down his empty wooden mug. "I feel much better for that cordial. What else is happening on this wild night?"

"They're moving the little ones out of the Mole Palace," said Sepia, cupping her paws around her drink. "There are streams bursting and water rushing off the hills, it's so heavy that they're building defenses and things to prevent a landslide. The king and Captain Padra and everybody, they're all there, getting people out of burrows."

"That's dangerous!" said Juniper.

Sepia hesitated. He was right, but if she said so he'd want to go straight there. Juniper didn't wait for an answer.

"Is Urchin there?" he demanded.

"Well . . ." said Sepia, already wishing she hadn't said anything.

"You mean he is?"

"The king will not put Urchin in danger," said Fir mildly.

"The king can't be everywhere at once!" cried Juniper, jumping to his paws.

"And neither can you," said Fir. "You have had more than enough for one day, and you are distressed."

"I'll be a lot more distressed if Urchin gets hurt," argued Juniper, "without me lifting a paw to help him. There should be a priest there. You can't go, so I must."

"I will not forbid you to go," said Fir, "but I would advise against it."

169

"I have to!" said Juniper. "I have to prove to myself that I can rise above being Husk's son!"

"You rose above it, long before you knew about it," said Fir. "If you must go, remember that you must not put Urchin or yourself in any greater danger. And however much you want to be a hero, remember that you are inexperienced. Obey orders, whether from the king or from a captain."

"Yes, Brother Fir," said Juniper. "May I have your blessing anyway?" He knelt for the touch of Fir's paw on his head and the murmured words of blessing, took the dry cloak that Sepia held out to him, and pattered down the stairs.

Fir sank back onto the pillows, his eyes closing. Sepia, not sure whether he was praying, falling asleep, or both, settled the blanket gently around him to keep him warm.

She couldn't do much good at the landslide site. There were enough animals there already. After the long day, the leaping flames and surrounding quiet made her realize how tired she was.

It would be nice to go home and be in her old nest with her sisters, but it was too stormy to go home now, and too far. The quiet, sleepy breath of Brother Fir made her intensely lonely. He could sleep and she couldn't, not after all she had seen and heard that day. Once, he stirred in his sleep and said "stars" very clearly as if he were awake, but he slept peacefully after that. She wrapped herself in a cloak and, reluctant to leave the fireside, looked into the kindly fire, holding Damson and Juniper in her heart. She had sunk into a light, restless sleep when someone tapped softly at the door. She jumped up, took the lantern, and slipped to open the door.

"Your Majesty!" she said, and bobbed a curtsy—then when the light fell on the queen's face, Sepia stepped back, holding the door wide, and stretched out her paws.

The queen was thin and haggard, her eyes red-rimmed with sorrow and tiredness, the catkin blanket clutched in her paws. Her flame-red coat had grown dull, and the familiar smell of herbs and vinegar hung about her. She looked wild with grief, and Sepia saw more than the Queen of Mistmantle. She saw a mother facing yet another long, terrible night of not knowing where her baby was.

"I went out to see to Yarrow," she said. She looked tightly huddled, as if she were cold. "He's had fouldrought badly, but he'll live. I've washed, I've done all the right things. I came to see if Brother Fir was all right."

"He's much better. He's asleep now," said Sepia. "Come in, Your Majesty. Come and get warm."

The queen knelt by the fire and sipped the hot cordial Sepia put into her paws. She still looked cold, so Sepia put an arm around her.

"Shouldn't you go to bed?" she said gently.

"Thripple keeps telling me that," said Cedar, but she put down the mug. "I don't want to sleep. I have nightmares. But I'll go."

"No, don't!" said Sepia. "I mean, not if you don't want to. Not if you'd rather be here. Excuse me, I won't be long."

She ran quietly down the stairs and, with the help of a mole maid, fetched the quilt from the royal bedchamber. Back in Fir's turret, she warmed it by the fire and spread it on the floor while Brother Fir talked to the queen.

"You stood up to Smokewreath in Whitewings," he was saying. "Stand up to him in your dreams. And tell him no curse can stand against the Heart. Tell him that!"

At last, the queen drifted into a few hours' sleep. It was as if Brother Fir's quiet breathing had a power to soothe. Sepia slept, too. She dreamed of stars, mists, and Catkin, while Brother Fir dreamed of exactly the same things. Halfway through a dream in which stars danced around Mistmantle Tower, she woke.

What had woken her? She sat up, aware of the empty space beside her where the queen had been, and of the figure of a squirrel looking out of a window.

"Your Majesty?" she said.

"Did I wake you, Sepia?" said the queen softly. "I slept well for the first time since . . . for the first time. Then I woke and realized I hadn't said good night to her. I always do that, wherever she is." She leaned from the window. "Heart bless you, Catkin," she whispered. "Mummy's here."

Sepia rubbed her eyes and remembered her dream. It seemed important.

"Your Majesty," she said. "You know on the night of riding stars before . . ."

The queen shuddered.

"Sorry, but, you know the stars circled the tower?"

"Did they, Sepia?"

"Well, that's supposed to make you think of your hopes and dreams," she went on. "And, I mean, I think it's because, when they go around the tower, they disappear, as if they weren't there anymore. As if your hopes and dreams had just gone away and disappeared. But you see them again, Your Majesty, they always come around."

"I suppose they do, Sepia," sighed the queen, and put a paw to her mouth as she yawned. Sepia slipped downstairs. She'd fetch some pillows and lavender, and perhaps, in the soothing peace of the turret, the queen would sleep without nightmares again.

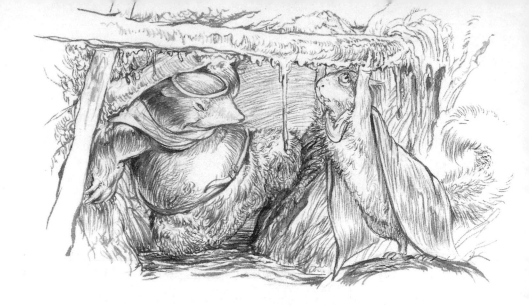

CHAPTER FOURTEEN

PLAGUE, LICE, FIRE, AND VERMIN!" cursed Lugg, ankle-deep in mud. Through the drenching rain and darkness, he passed an armful of wet pit props to Urchin. "Them otters must be dislodging as much as they stop."

"They're not!" yelled Crispin. "They're doing a great job up there. This will soon stop!"

"Not blooming soon enough!" growled Lugg as another wave of mud and stones slithered downhill toward them. "Are them hedgehogs out of that burrow?"

"All out and accounted for," said Urchin, struggling through mud as he passed along the pit props. "But there's another burrow beyond it. What's their best way out?"

"Top way, sharpish," said Lugg. "Give 'em a shout, but don't go up there if you can help it."

Urchin shouted, but he knew his voice would be whipped away in the wind. There was no choice but to scramble to the top of the bank, unbuckling his sword to make himself lighter.

"Come out the top way!" he yelled. "Quickly, one at a time!"

He heard Crispin shouting something, strained to hear the words, and turned with rain driving into in his eyes. Looking uphill he saw Crispin cupping his paws, shouting, and Padra, waving and pointing to a wave of mud and stone lurching furiously downhill.

He sprang backward as mud, grass, and stone cascaded toward the burrows. Animals with lanterns were running in all directions as Crispin, Padra, and Lugg shouted orders—*Stay back!—Over here!—Spread out!* The churning mud gathered power and speed, hurling rocks ahead of it, huge and savage as a monster in a nightmare.

The slope shallowed. The landslide slowed, spreading its weight, thinned to a trickle, slithered over Crispin's paws, and finally stopped.

There was a brief and total silence, then a cheer that was almost a sigh of relief, and a low whistle from Lugg.

"Not bad for a practice run," he remarked.

Crispin climbed onto a mound of earth. He was so daubed with mud that the white patch on his chest was obscured, and his ears were the only clean part of him.

"Anyone harmed?" he called. "Urchin, come farther back. That would have been a lot worse if not for the work the otters are doing at the top there. This lot was way below the dam already. Is anyone in those burrows?"

"Yes, Your Majesty, and I can't see them getting out in a hurry," replied Lugg. "We were going to get them out the top way, but that lot will have blocked it solid. The only other way now is a twisty one that goes well under the hill, in and out and I don't know what. Dead ends all over the place. They'll need an escort to get them out. Permission to do it myself, please, Your Majesty. I don't fancy asking anyone else to."

"You may, Lugg," said Crispin. "And choose who you want to help you. No unnecessary risks." He called a few hedgehogs to his side and squelched back up the hill. Urchin watched Lugg run along the bank, scrabble at an almost invisible entrance, and wriggle into the darkness. There were a few muffled words, and something about needing more props.

The stack of pit props had been thrown in all directions by the mud slide. Urchin, seeing some sticking up through the mud at wild angles as if reaching out to be rescued, crawled to gather a few together.

"Pit props, Lugg!" he called, and lowered them down, wriggling and angling them as they jammed against tree roots. From the calls of "Mind me snout!" he knew they were getting there.

"Move, littl' 'uns!" yelled Lugg. To a chorus of mutters and curses, two terrified young squirrels ran from the entrance, looking over their shoulders with wild, frightened eyes.

"It's caving in!" squealed one.

"Get clear, then!" yelled Urchin, but they huddled beside him. They looked like brothers, and he remembered meeting them before. "It'll cave in even faster if you stand on top of it," he insisted. "Go . . ."

He could see Docken guiding animals to safety. "You see that tall hedgehog? That's Docken of the Circle. Go to him. Crawl, get farther up and onto the driest ground you can find."

The older squirrel retreated backward, leading the younger by the paw, but with a heartbroken wail of "Mummy!" the little one pulled with all his strength toward the entrance.

"Sh, Pepper," said the older one. "Master Urchin and Captain Lugg will get them out. Please, Master Urchin, sir, I'm Grain and he's Pepper, and our mum and dad and Mistress Wheatear are still in there."

"And they'll want you to be safe, so go to Master Docken," insisted Urchin. "Captain Lugg will get them out, if anyone can."

"Do you need this, sir?" said Grain, heaving with his free paw at a log sticking out of the mud.

"Thanks," said Urchin, dragging it into place to give to Lugg. "Now, GO!"

There was another length of timber almost buried in the mud, but when he heaved it out he saw it was too short to hold up a tunnel roof. "More props!" he yelled to anyone who could hear.

."There's no more!" yelled Docken, taking Grain and Pepper by the paws. "None big enough!"

"Pass whatever there is, then!" Urchin shouted back. The timbers someone passed to him were too short to hold up a tunnel, but perhaps an animal could hold them up, or wedge them against a tree root. . . . From underground came a terrifying rumble.

"PLAGUE!" bellowed Lugg. "Where's the plaguing props? LIGHT!"

177

"Someone bring a lantern!" yelled Urchin. Twigg slithered toward him, one arm wrapped around a bundle of timber and holding up a lantern in his other paw.

"The wood might not be long enough, but it's all I could get," panted Twigg. "And here's your lantern."

Urchin lowered the wood, but the lantern was too awkward a shape to ease into the tunnel. Hind paws first, holding the light above him, he clambered down into the tunnel and held it high. In its warm circle, he saw Lugg heaving pit props into place. Mounds of fallen earth, leaves, and mud lay on the ground around him. Three squirrel faces peered out from a dark corner.

"Shall we make a run for it, Captain Lugg?" asked one.

"Not yet!" grunted Lugg. "Urchin, what in plagues and fire are you doing here?"

"Bringing your lantern," said Urchin.

"Good lad," he muttered. "Got any props?"

"Only these, and they won't be long enough," he said. "Will it help if I hold one up?"

"If all else fails, I suppose so," grunted Lugg. He winked at the squirrels and jerked his head at Urchin. "Just because our Urchin's been through the mists and back, he thinks he's indestructible. Find a stone to climb on, Urchin. The best thing to do with that bit of stick you've got is to ram it across the roof, then wedge it in amongst the tree roots to keep it in place."

A scatter of earth fell about Urchin as he stepped onto a stone. He stifled a cough and rubbed his eyes. The earth grumbled. He had heard that sound all night, but now that it was over his head, his fur prickled with fear. He tried not to imagine what it would be like if the tunnel caved in. Without him saying anything, Lugg understood.

"Don't even think about it, son," said Lugg. "Concentrate on what you're doing."

Ashamed of the trembling of his paws, Urchin placed the lantern gently on the ground. There must be no sudden movements. For a moment the squirrel hair bracelet on his wrist caught the glow of light, and it made him feel stronger.

"Heart help us all," he whispered, and climbed up to wedge the branch between the tree roots.

Juniper sprang through treetops, raced across open ground, and heard the shouts of the animals long before the glow of storm-blown lanterns was in sight. His cloak, whipped about by the wind and snagged on branches, now hung limp, torn, soaked, and tangled. Bands of otters still struggled furiously, reinforcing the dam and digging out channels to divert the flooding streams, and below them he could just see animals and lanterns moving among banks of mud and stone. The landscape had changed so completely that he no longer recognized anything. Leaping downhill, he was stopped by Captain Arran and Russet of the Circle, carrying lengths of old, polished timber in their arms.

"Stop!" cried Arran, and Russet leaped forward to put a restraining paw on his shoulder. "You'll have the whole hillside down!"

"I need to find Urchin," gasped Juniper. "Is he safe?"

"None of us is safe, if you come thundering around like that," growled Russet. "Come with me the long way around. Still, you're small and light, you might be useful. Do exactly as you're told, and for everyone's sake, be light on your paws."

"And take these for me," said Arran, unloading the timbers into Juniper's paws. "Then I can get back up the hill."

With his arms full of planks, Juniper followed Russet to where Docken stood. Docken's eyes brightened when he saw the wood. "Captain Lugg's been yelling for those," he said.

"Where's Urchin?" demanded Juniper.

"In that lot." Docken nodded toward the burrows. "You're a priest, just say a prayer that he gets out in one piece."

"I'll take these to him," said Juniper. "Russet, give me your lot and I'll take those too."

"I'll do it," said Russet.

"I'm smaller and lighter," said Juniper. He caught the look that passed between Russet and Docken and knew what it meant. *Yes, it would help if Juniper could take the timber to Lugg, but we can't send another young animal in there.*

He didn't wait for an order. Here was something he could do to set against the harm his father had done. Tucking the longest and strongest lengths of timber under his arms, he crawled facedown through the mud, not looking around when he heard Docken's sharp bark of "Juniper!" There was a low-voiced answer from Russet. "Let him try." Raising his chin from the mud, he crawled on.

Voices guided him to the burrow. He eased the pit props down the entrance first and scrambled down after them.

"Well, look what the Heart sent us!" exclaimed Lugg.

"Juniper!" cried Urchin. He was balanced on a twisted root, pressing the prop hard against the roof as sweat trickled down his neck. There was one second of delight at seeing Juniper's face, then his heart twisted. Juniper was here. One more valuable life would be lost if the burrow collapsed.

"Juniper, what are you doing?" he demanded. "What are you doing *here*?"

"Getting you out," said Juniper. "Here, let me hold that. Urchin, get out."

"Be quiet and give us those props," said Lugg. "That long one, use it to hold up that side, there. That short one, hold it up over here, like Urchin's doing. Here, by me. That's it."

Juniper took his place, far from the burrow entrance. Urchin was much nearer to the way out than he was. Good. That was what he wanted.

"Now," said Lugg. "Ready to go, you lot. One at a time. You first, mistress."

A squirrel darted from the burrow, her ears flattened, her tail streaming behind her as she flew past Urchin. His shoulders burned with the strain of holding up the prop, but he must not move.

"Next!" commanded Lugg. "Give us a paw, then, madam." The next squirrel scurried as quickly as she could from the burrow. As Lugg helped her to get a claw-hold on the tree roots, trickles of earth fell on Urchin's head. He blinked away dust.

Get out, he thought, *out, quickly.* He mustn't move, though his neck was cricked, searing pain flickered down his arms, and sweat trickled through his fur. There was still one more squirrel to get out.

"Urchin and Juniper, when the last one's out, get yourselves out," ordered Lugg. "Sharpish. Captain's orders. I'm not going till you're out, and as I'd like to get out alive, you'd oblige me by looking nifty."

"Captain Lugg . . ." began Juniper.

"Do as you're lousy well told," said Lugg.

"Captain Lugg," said the remaining squirrel. "If you think I'm going to stay here while there's two young lads holding up the roof for me . . ."

"Fair enough," said Lugg. "Juniper, Urchin, scarper. Now. Captain's order."

"I'm nearly a priest," said Juniper, struggling for breath as he held the timber in place. "I should stay. If there's nobody to hold up the roof . . ."

"I'll hold it up," said Lugg. "You're more trouble than all my daughters. And the grandsons too."

"Can't we all go together?" asked the squirrel.

"All those paws pounding along at once?" said Lugg. "You two young 'uns, get out, spread yourselves on the ground, and be ready to give us a paw. Urchin, move over."

The squirrel slipped into place beside Urchin and stretched to hold up the beam just as the pain began to burn into Urchin's elbows. Lugg took over from Juniper, and with last anxious glances over their shoulders, Juniper and Urchin sprang as lightly as they could to the tunnel, clambered one at a time through the entrance, and stretched themselves on the ground. From far below they heard Lugg bark a command, then there was a racing of quick light paws. They reached down into the burrow to haul the other squirrel to safety.

"Run, you two," he said. "I'll wait here for Captain Lugg."

In the rain and darkness Urchin couldn't see Juniper's face clearly, but he didn't have to. He knew he was about to argue.

"Come on, Juniper," he said, crawling backward. "We're only increasing the weight by staying."

"Crawl away in different directions," came Lugg's muffled voice from belowground.

"Over here!" called Docken from behind them. Cautiously, reluctantly, they began to crawl away. For a second or two, Urchin thought he heard mole steps underground, but the pounding rain made the vibrations confusing. Then, from far beneath them, came a rumble and a creak that grew louder.

Urchin, glancing over his shoulder, saw that he was almost within reach of Docken's outstretched paw. Then he looked back toward the burrow, and his skin prickled with horror.

Juniper was flailing in the mud, stretching out his forepaws and struggling to crawl as he slipped farther and farther away. The mud was sliding, dragging Juniper down the bank toward the burrows, and there was still no sign of Lugg.

Urchin sprang across the sliding bank, falling and staggering, dodging sideways and sideways again to avoid shifting, slithering mud, hearing voices shouting but neither knowing nor caring what they said. Something flew through the air past him, and he ducked, then saw what it was. It was a length of timber. Docken had thrown him a prop. He sprawled and stretched to reach it, and held it out to Juniper.

"Grab that!" he yelled, but already Juniper was too far away. Claw by claw he crept forward, heaving across the mud, until at last Juniper's paws had clutched at the wood.

He pulled hard with both paws, gritted his teeth, and heaved again, but the weight of the wood and of Juniper sinking in the mud was too much. Though his muscles strained and burned, and he heaved with all his strength, it was as if Juniper and the wooden beam were both sealed in stone. His paws shook with effort.

"Hold on!" he yelled, and then the thing he had dreaded most was happening. The earth beneath him, slowly, unstoppably, was moving, and he, too, was sliding out of control.

Strong paws grasped his heels. Somebody was dragging him backward. Juniper too was sliding free from the mud. Russet and Heath had appeared and were hauling at the beam, pulling Juniper to safety—he heard Crispin's voice.

"You're all right, Urchin. I've got you."

The ground was firmer now, and he could stand. Then Docken, Crispin, and the newly rescued squirrels and hedgehogs were around them, wrapping blankets around their soaked and muddied shoulders and patting them on the back.

"Where . . . where's Lugg?" stammered Urchin through chattering teeth. Nobody answered.

"Lugg!" he cried. Without thinking he lunged toward the burrow, but Crispin caught him and held him back. Docken held on to Juniper. Below them the ground squelched, sighed, heaved like an enormous wet slug, and sank with a creaking of roots into the place where the burrow had been.

Urchin stared. He wished he didn't have to believe what he was watching.

"Well, that's sorted," said a voice behind them.

"Lugg!" cried Urchin again.

Captain Lugg stood behind them, his claws in his belt. He bowed to Crispin.

"Sorted, Your Majesty," he said.

"But you were . . ." began Juniper.

"Ah, well, I reckon the earth's on my side," said Lugg. "Treat it with respect, and it'll treat you the same way. When it shuts one tunnel, it usually opens another one. Tight squeeze, though. And I'd say we've had the worst of it now."

There was nothing but paw-shaking and hugging and congratulating each other for several minutes after that, with Lugg commenting that tunnels were getting tighter these days, Your Majesty. Then Crispin put his arms around Urchin and Juniper.

"You've done well," said Crispin. "Very well. Go and get yourselves washed, warm, and dry."

"Where do we go, sir?" asked Urchin. The thought of the long walk back to the tower was exhausting.

"Mistress Apple won't have 'em in the burrow in that state," remarked Docken.

"There's a row of empty burrows halfway up the hill, above where the otters are working," said Crispin. "We've had them prepared for casualties. Arran's up there."

They trudged uphill, their paws sinking into the mud that made every step a struggle. Urchin was too tired to say much and supposed that Juniper's silence was just because he, too, was tired. As they scrambled over a ridge they saw lanterns glowing at the entrance to the burrow, making Urchin feel warmer already.

"Looks welcoming," he said, and when Juniper didn't answer, he added, "Are you all right?"

"Damson died," said Juniper. He'd have to tell Urchin that much sooner or later, and it gave him a good reason to be quiet.

"I'm sorry," said Urchin, and put a paw on Juniper's shoulder, but Juniper didn't seem to notice. In the darkness, Urchin glanced toward him, but Juniper was staring straight ahead of him, and it was hard to see his face. Urchin thought about how he'd feel if it were Apple who had died, and he hurt for his friend, but it was as if Juniper had retreated somewhere many miles away, beyond the mists, and Urchin could not reach him. At the entrance to the burrow he stood back to let Juniper go through first, then asked the guard hedgehog where Captain Lady Arran was.

"I'll send someone for her," said the hedgehog. "Get yourselves inside. Captain Padra gave orders to be ready for you."

The burrow formed a neat row of chambers, each with a wooden door, some connecting to the next one. The hedgehog opened a door for Urchin and Juniper and showed them into a plain, clean, and wonderfully warm chamber, with a dry sandy floor and a fire burning in the grate with a steady, orange glow beneath it, welcoming them like a friend. Wooden tubs of hot water stood before it with steam rising into the firelit air and neatly folded towels beside them.

"Have yourselves a good wash," said the hedgehog. "I've never seen squirrels in such a mess. Might have to change the water a few times. How's it going at the digging?"

"Everyone's out of the burrows, and the worst seems to be over," said Urchin.

"Thank the Heart for that!" said the hedgehog, and trotted away to spread the news and find Arran. Urchin and Juniper were left alone.

Urchin reached to unbuckle his sword, then realized he'd left it at the diggings. He plunged his paws into a tub of hot water and felt the heat seeping through to his bones so wonderfully that the only thing to do was to tip himself headfirst into the tub and scrub hot water into his fur, over his head and ears, between his claws, and into his

187

tail tip until the mud and sand had floated away, and he felt as clean as a freshly washed sponge. Then he scrambled out, perched on the edge of the tub, and leaped onto the towel, rolling himself in it.

"It's wonderful!" he said to Juniper. "Try it!"

Juniper had curled up tightly, hugging his knees. He could never be part of Urchin's world again. It was as if he carried something worse than fouldrought.

Alarmed, Urchin knelt in front of him. "Juniper!" he said. He put a paw on Juniper's head, but Juniper didn't move. He must be in shock, Urchin thought. He's just lost Damson, then nearly died in collapsing burrows.

"You'll be all right now, Juniper," he said. "We'll get you through this. You'll feel much better after a soak in the hot water. You should try it." Then he leaped back, startled, as Juniper sprang up.

"What do *you* know about it?" he cried. "Do you think you know it all? Do you think you understand everything, and it can all be put right with a hot bath and a fire? You have no idea!"

"I'm sorry!" gasped Urchin.

"You don't know anything!" yelled Juniper bitterly. "Don't you understand? I went in to save you, and you ended up saving me, because you always have to be the hero!"

"Juniper, what . . ." began Urchin, but Juniper wasn't listening.

"So what if I'd died saving you!" cried Juniper. "I wanted to! I would have done one noble, worthwhile thing, and then it would have all been over, and I wouldn't have to live with this!" The rage in his eyes turned to terrible pain. "You don't know who I am!"

CHAPTER FIFTEEN

THE DOOR OPENED. Tall and commanding with her no-nonsense air, Arran marched into the chamber.

"Scream louder," she commanded. "They might not have heard you on Whitewings. What's going on here?"

Neither of them spoke. Neither had any idea where to start.

"Have a wash, Juniper," she said briskly. Subdued by her presence, Juniper climbed into a tub, washed, and was drying himself off when Padra and Crispin, smiling and filthy with mud, strode into the chamber. To Urchin, everything immediately looked more hopeful. With Crispin and Padra, he always felt everything would be all right.

"Well done, you two," said Crispin.

"Excellently done, the pair of you," said Padra. They threw their swords and cloaks into a corner, and Urchin's sword, too, and leaped

189

with two splashes into the washtubs. As they wallowed about washing themselves, Urchin hopped to Juniper.

"This isn't just about Damson, is it?" he whispered. "What did you mean about knowing who you are?" As Juniper didn't answer, he went on earnestly, "Whatever it is, tell Crispin. It's important."

Juniper felt the firelight seeping into him, and the presence of Crispin and Padra was reassuring. He should tell Crispin. The king had a right to know, and so did Padra, as senior captain. He probably wouldn't be allowed to be a priest now, and they'd have to know why not. This way he'd only have to tell it once, and get it over—but he couldn't, not when Padra and Crispin were splashing about in the water and looked as if they were having fun for a change. They must have enjoyed the challenge and struggle of the landslide. For a short time, it had taken their minds from Catkin.

"Juniper," whispered Urchin, "you said I don't know who you are. Well I do. I told you on Whitewings, we're brothers."

"I won't hold you to that," said Juniper.

It became quiet. Crispin and Padra had dried themselves and had noticed the urgent whispering between the two young squirrels. Arran placed another log carefully on the fire, and sparks fluttered upward.

"Is something the matter?" she asked.

"Go on!" whispered Urchin.

"Juniper?" inquired Crispin gently.

Juniper shrugged and glared at Urchin. "There isn't time," he muttered.

"Whatever it is, you'd find it a lot harder later on," said Crispin kindly. "Padra, would you make sure nobody interrupts us?"

While Padra was out, Crispin ushered Juniper and Urchin to a place by the fire and asked them whether they'd been hurt in the rescue at the burrows. They had a few scratches that they hadn't noticed at first and Urchin's shoulders ached, but none of it seemed important. Then Padra swished into the burrow with jugs of cordial and warm spiced wine, and a pawful of mugs, which he set beside the fire.

"I've given orders that we mustn't be disturbed except for the most urgent of needs," he said, pouring out dark and spicy drinks that steamed in the firelight. "Get that inside you, Juniper. Whatever you have to tell us, it's probably not so bad as it seems."

The cordial was rich and sizzling hot, and Juniper felt better for tasting it. Then he set his mug on the hearth. Sometimes looking at the fire, sometimes at his paws, and sometimes into their faces, he told them everything. He told them of his decision to hear Damson's confession. Finally, keeping his voice as steady as he could, struggling to look Crispin in the face, with every word growing heavy and reluctant, he told them about his mother's murder.

"And because she stayed out of the way, it was years before Damson saw him again, and heard him, and realized who he was," he said. "It was . . . Your Majesty, it's the worst person it could be."

He took a deep breath. One short syllable, and it was out forever.

"Husk," he said.

He was aware of Padra and Arran both shutting their eyes tightly as if they'd been hurt, but Crispin continued to look at him without flinching. Juniper felt he should repeat it, in case Crispin hadn't understood.

"Do you understand, Your Majesty? I'm Husk's son, and he murdered my mother."

"It was brave of you to tell us," said Crispin softly, and took Juniper by the shoulders. "Well done. You can't help who your father was."

"I'll never be happy again, sir," said Juniper, his head down, not looking Crispin in the eyes. "When I heard about what Urchin was doing at the landslide I went because I wanted to take over from him, do something worthwhile, and get killed."

"Oh, Juniper!" cried Arran.

"I'm very glad you didn't succeed," said Crispin. "It would have been a great loss to all of us. The whole island would be a poorer place without you."

"But I'm something to do with him," said Juniper. "I could turn out like him."

He hunched up with his head on his knees. Urchin offered him a beaker, and for Urchin's sake he drank.

"Why should you turn out like him?" asked Crispin. "You haven't up to now. I knew Husk, and you're nothing like him."

"I'm not that good, either," said Juniper.

"Good enough for us," said Crispin. "Brother Fir thinks so, and so do I. If there's anything very bad about you, you must be hiding it well."

"Husk made people think he was good, sir," he said, and wished

Urchin hadn't been there. He could only hope their friendship would pass the test.

"Brother Fir says that Husk was jealous of you, Your Majesty, when you were young tower squirrels, and that was one of the things that brought out the worst in him," he said. "And I get jealous. I don't mean to, but I can't help it."

"Jealous of anybody in particular, Juniper?" asked Crispin.

It was the question that had to come. Looking at his paws again, he said, "Urchin." He glanced sideways. "Sorry, Urchin. I can't help it."

"But we've always been friends," said Urchin, who was finding this difficult to understand.

"Oh, yes," said Juniper. "But I'm jealous of you, all the same."

"I should think lots of animals are," remarked Crispin.

"But you risked your life to save mine!" said Urchin. "Twice!"

"Because it was worth saving," explained Juniper. "and because you're my friend and my brother, but I'm still jealous of you. I can't help it. You helped to save the island. You get to do the exciting things, you even rode on a swan. And when you learned the truth about your parents, you found out that they were heroes."

"Juniper, you're a hero yourself!" said Padra. He left Arran's side, knelt before Juniper, and took his paws. "Look at me, Juniper. After Spindrift died, the only parent you had was Damson, and she was rightly proud of you. Husk *chose* evil. He wanted power and glory for himself, and he'd do anything to get it. You haven't chosen that way, you've chosen love and loyalty. Look what you did, going to

Whitewings! You're loyal to Urchin, even though you're jealous of him. You have excellent qualities. Fir chose you. Your father's blood isn't what makes you who you are. You chose the Heart that loves you, and the Heart keeps you. You are free from your past."

"More than that," said Crispin. "You're something good that came from Husk's life, in spite of all he did."

"And you're my brother," said Urchin.

"Please, Your Majesty," Juniper asked, "do other people have to know?"

"I don't see why," said Crispin, "and certainly not yet. Don't try to make decisions yet, when you've only just learned this. Sleep on it. That's something we all need to do. None of us got much sleep last night. Padra, Arran, wouldn't you rather go home to Tide and Swanfeather?"

"Oh, yes, please," said Arran. "We've had to leave them with Mother Huggen and Apple so much lately, I'm afraid they'll forget who I am, and I . . ." She stopped suddenly, and finished, "I do want to be with them." Urchin guessed that she had nearly said something about worrying that they'd go missing and stopped herself just in time.

"Tell Cedar everyone's safe," said Crispin. "And tell the night watch guards I'll sleep here tonight, so they can wake me if anything happens. But I don't think it will."

Urchin twitched his ears and gave himself a shake to try and stay awake. Suddenly, his eyes wanted to close. He tried to look wide awake and alert, but it was hard to do that while putting both paws to his mouth to stifle an enormous yawn. It was no good hoping that Crispin hadn't noticed.

"Urchin, you're exhausted," he said. "I'll send someone for blankets."

Padra and Arran left to return to the tower, and bedding was brought for Urchin and Juniper, who rolled themselves in blankets before the fire. The excitement of the day and night meant that Urchin lay awake for a long time, looking into the fire. He slept at last, lightly and uneasily, dreaming of tunnels caving in, and floods, and dark tunnels opening to show the face of Captain Husk. He woke scared and sweating, staring into the dark.

I'm safe. I'm in a refuge burrow, with a fire burning and Juniper beside me. He sat up, hugging the blanket around himself, looking into the deep orange embers. There were voices outside, but it was Crispin and Lugg, speaking in low voices. They must be trying not to wake anyone.

"Floods and landslides, Your Majesty," Lugg was saying softly, "I can deal with those. You can see what you're doing with those—see it, hear it, feel it. I'm more worried about things that are being said on this island, Your Majesty, if you'll pardon me raising the subject. There's another bright spark hedgehog swears he saw Husk last night. Drunk enough and dense enough to say anything, if you ask me. No normal, sensible squirrel can go home in the dark without some busy-body wailing that they've seen Husk."

195

"And until they get it firmly into their heads that he can't harm them, they'll be afraid," said Crispin. "One day, Lugg, this will be over. Disease will have died away, the island will be calm and safe, and Cedar and I will put Catkin to bed in her own cradle. We have to keep believing that. Now, where are the injured animals from the landslide?"

"Chambers at the end of this row, Your Majesty, and Heart be thanked, there's nobody killed. But, Your Majesty, it's not just Husk they're talking about."

"What now?" asked Crispin, and Urchin heard the weariness in his voice.

There was a moment's pause then, so quietly that Urchin could barely hear it, Lugg said, "The queen," and what followed was whispered so softly that he couldn't hear anything at all.

"Get a few hours' rest, Lugg," said Crispin at last. "That's an order. I'll look in on the injured."

Urchin heard the soft padding of paws as they moved away. He was falling asleep again when another voice made him jolt with surprise.

"Urchin!"

"Juniper? Are you all right?"

"I couldn't sleep," said Juniper, propping himself up on his elbow. "I just heard Lugg and the king talking."

"So did I," said Urchin. "I suppose we shouldn't have listened."

"I'm glad I did," said Juniper. "When the animals aren't muttering about—you know, him—they're saying the queen's mad. Brother Fir says the most dangerous enemies are the ones you can't see. You could see Husk, we could see King Silverbirch and Granite, and Smokewreath, and they were bad enough, but you can't see rumors. We have to do something about them."

"Such as what?" said Urchin.

"That's what I'm trying to work out," said Juniper.

He stared into the darkness, silently repeating his prophecy in his head. The impossible prophecy. But now the fatherless had found a father—or, at least, he knew who his father was and what had happened to him. The hills had fallen to earth. Perhaps there was hope, then, emerging from his own despair. Somewhere in the future lay an outstretched claw, a glimpse of blue—where had he seen that shade of blue?—and the flash of a knife.

"Urchin," he said at last. "Are you still awake?"

"Not much," muttered Urchin.

"I can't sleep," said Juniper. "I'm going back to the tower to be with Fir."

"Now?" said Urchin.

"I can't just lie here waiting for morning," said Juniper.

With reluctance and a great effort, Urchin sat up. He hadn't slept much, but at least he had been warm and resting. "I'll come with you," he said.

"No, don't," said Juniper. "The king might need you in the morning. If anyone asks, tell them where I've gone."

Crispin sat alone by a dying fire. He could have called a guard, or woken someone, but it would be no good. He had to face the loneliness of being the king.

Landslides and disease, they were struggles, but struggles he could cope with. He had fought worse things. Lying awake night after night, he had asked himself if Husk might really be back, and whether he could have tricked Linty into bringing Catkin to him. He had wondered if he would ever see her again and even, when the nights were longest and darkest, whether there really was a curse on the Heir of Mistmantle. And after all that, he had to face what Lugg had told him. Cedar had been such joy, such warmth and strength for the island and for himself, and what was the latest silly gossip? The foreign queen comes from a land of sorcerers where they don't know how to do things. Can't even look after her own baby. It's all her fault. Fouldrought, everything.

He could not remember feeling so coldly, bitterly angry since the day his first wife died. He could feel sorry for easily led animals who believed rumors about Husk. He could understand the frightened animals who hardly dared let their young out of their sight. He could understand them criticizing him—he was the king, the island was his responsibility. But they had turned their gossip against Cedar, picking and clawing at what was dearer to him than his own heart. There was ignorance to fight on this island and a battle within himself. Before he could speak to the islanders, he must face his hurt and anger.

Brother Fir would have been able to help him, but Brother Fir was far away in the tower. From long years of experience, he must ask himself the questions Brother Fir would ask. He imagined the priest, sitting on the hearth with a beaker of cordial in his paws, saying, "Think, Crispin, think! Haven't I taught you to think? I must be a poor sort of priest. Ask yourself questions. So some animals—only *some* animals—are being unpleasant about Her Majesty. Hm. Ask yourself the right questions."

Crispin asked himself the questions Fir would have asked. *Why? Why are they behaving like this? What have you just said to yourself? Question, question. What are the enemies we face? Ignorance, yes, weakness, yes, and ? Come on, think!*

Then he knew what the island's greatest enemy was and realized that he had always known it. It was obvious. He lit a candle, and smiled at last.

There was no point in sitting here, doing nothing, waiting for morning. He went again to visit the injured animals, then climbed out to the fresh air, ran up to the best viewpoint, and, as the darkness lifted just a little, looked down over Mistmantle. He felt his heart grow with love for this island and its animals.

Why did anyone think that kingship was about ruling, ordering, and holding power? To him, it was simply looking after the island for his lifetime, nurturing it, being like a father to the island as he was to Catkin. *Little Catkin. Heart protect you. We're looking for you. I can't bear this, I can't bear not holding you.*

Somebody was calling him. He turned to see Urchin climbing the hill toward him, carrying a spare cloak in one arm and Crispin's sword and sword belt over his shoulder.

"Can't you sleep either, Your Majesty?" he said. "Cloak?"

"Thanks, Urchin," said Crispin, who didn't feel the need for a cloak but let Urchin put it around him. "We may as well go down. It'll soon be dawn."

They walked along the ridge as it sloped gently toward the woods. Somehow they were both looking in the same direction at the same time when they saw him.

In a cluster of trees far away below them, not far from an entrance to the Mole Palace, one dead tree, an old lightning-struck tree, stood out from the rest. At its top was a dark shape that could almost have been a nest, but who would build a nest there? But it moved, and they recognized the arch of a squirrel's tail. Then, dimly in the gray dawn, they saw a silhouette that made Urchin's blood chill, his ears stiffen, and his mouth dry. He had never thought to see that profile again.

He looked up at Crispin and saw him gazing at the same spot, calmly, and almost smiling. When Urchin looked back at the tree, the squirrel had vanished.

"Your Majesty," whispered Urchin. "*Husk!*"

Crispin watched for a moment, as if waiting for the squirrel to appear again.

"It may be," he said simply. "I'll set a watch on that spinney. Courage, Urchin. This time, we'll be ready for him. Back to the tower, I think, before we gather the island together."

CHAPTER SIXTEEN

WHEN THE SUN WAS FULLY UP, Padra's eyes were still too heavy to open, but the constant nudging and nuzzling of Tide and Swanfeather was too much to resist. With an effort he heaved himself up, tucked a twin under each arm, and trudged out to the spring where he slipped the small otters into the stream and splashed cold water on his face. Squealing with delight, Swanfeather twisted and somersaulted her way toward the sea, while Tide followed in a smooth line and overtook her.

"Stop when you get to the waves," called Padra. The tide was half in, half out, and it would take them a while to reach the water's edge. He rubbed his face, shook his wet whiskers, and looked out at the morning after the storm.

He had seen worse. But it was bad enough.

The pale golden sand was streaked with gray-brown mud.

201

Everywhere he looked, fallen branches lay among a litter of leaves, drifting on the sea, on the shore, sprawled over the rocks, tangled with seaweed. Of the scattered driftwood and debris, some was recognizable as bits of people's lives, swept away from wrecked burrows during the storm—misshapen wheels of wheelbarrows, splintered tools, a low stool, a battered hat, a kettle. Padra ached for the animals who had lost homes and treasures. Much of the splintered wood and muddied fabrics were no longer recognizable as anything, though some of the timbers had enough shape left to show that they had been part of a boat.

The otters' boats were small, but they were sturdy. It had been a terrible fury of a storm to sweep up those boats and smash them on the rocks. The crafts that had survived—probably those tied up in the most sheltered of the coves—were on the water now, as otters rowed and stopped and rowed again, scooping up anything that could be salvaged. More otters glided through the water, bobbing to the surface, looking about them, and appearing again, sometimes carrying a beaker or a broken hoe, dragging it to the nearest boat. Padra felt someone at his side and knew without looking that it was Arran.

"At least the harvest's all in, and safely stored," she said. "It could have been a lot worse."

Neither of them said that Linty and Catkin could have been under the landslide. Both of them thought it.

Swanfeather scampered up the beach dragging a muddy cloth in her mouth. As Padra knelt to take it from her, Apple's voice rang out from behind him.

"Ooh, my goodness, what's she got there, bit of old curtain or cloak or something, what a morning, Captain Padra, morning, Captain Padra, morning, Captain Lady Arran, what a morning, what a night, what have you found, little Swanfeather?"

"It's one of the pennants from the tower," said Padra, examining the soaked and torn cloth. "Swanfeather, stay where it's shallow."

He looked up at the turrets. Not a pennant remained in place, and even the flagpoles were splintered. It was the least of their problems, but the sight was disheartening.

Swanfeather squeaked and splashed. An otter had bobbed up and waved a paw at her before disappearing underwater again.

"It's Fingal," said Arran, trying not to yawn. "He must have been out early." Fingal surfaced again and pounced on the kettle as it drifted past. He turned onto his back and sculled to the shore, holding the kettle against his chest.

"Your kettle, Mistress Apple?" he asked with an elegant bow.

"Not mine," said Apple. "Could be Mistress Duntern's, I'll take it to her, what I come looking for is . . . oh, my goodness, there it is, look, my hat, floating out to sea and off on its way to the mists!"

The otters turned to look. The wide brimmed hat bobbed far away on the waves as if it were teasing them.

"I had it out 'cause I reckoned I should wear it for poor Mistress Damson's funeral," she complained. "And the wind snatched it away like it were out of pure spite, and there it is. . . ."

Fingal was already skimming to the rescue, gliding underwater and surfacing now and again to check exactly where the hat had got to before trying to pursue it any farther. Apple was worrying loudly that it might lead him beyond the mists, and Arran was reassuring her that it would be all right so long as Fingal could move faster than a hat, when two otters loped from the water dragging a piece of driftwood between them.

"Bit of a boat, Captain Padra, sir," said one, before shaking his whiskers and returning to the sea. "Nice piece of wood, and it's still got most of its paint."

"Yes, I see," said Padra. He looked more carefully at the timber, frowned, and looked out to sea where a ripple indicated Fingal's presence underwater.

"Aren't you two supposed to be on shore watch?" he inquired.

"We were," said one. "But the king told us to come out this morning and try to rescue the things like pots and furniture and bits and pieces, sir, that people have lost. I suppose we shouldn't have bothered about that driftwood, but it's a nice bit of timber, sir."

"I'm glad you found it," said Padra. A swift movement caught the corner of his eye, and he turned to see Longpaw, the messenger, dashing toward them.

"Gathering at Seathrift Meadow at noon, sir and madam," he said, and raced away. In the distance other squirrels were rushing through treetops, presumably with the same message.

"Why not the Gathering Chamber?" said Arran.

"Seathrift Meadow is a little bit nearer for animals who've had a rough night," said Padra. "For those who are still getting over illness and injuries, it means they don't have to get up the tower stairs, and if anyone's still infectious, it's better not to crowd them all indoors. It's the sort of thing Crispin . . ."

He was interrupted by squeals of excitement from Tide and Swanfeather, who were pointing out to sea. The hat was still bobbing cheerfully on the waves when a ripple and a splash rocked it alarmingly.

"Ooh!" cried Apple. "Me hat!" Then the hat rose from the water with Fingal's grinning, whiskered face beneath it, and he wore it in triumph as he swam to the shore. Scrambling up, he took it off with a flourish, shook the water from the brim, and presented it with a bow to Apple.

"Madam—oh, hang on a minute," he said. He removed a few fronds of seaweed and a live crab from the dripping rosebuds. "Madam, your crown."

"Ooh, what a love you are!" said Apple, and squashed him into a hug that left him gasping for breath. "Ooh, look at me now, soaked through, that comes of hugging wet otters, bless you, Heart bless you, young Fingal, you're as good an otter as your brother and that's saying something." She held the hat at arm's length. "I'll have that as good as new, no time, it'll need doing up new, but it did anyway, I've had those rosebuds since before I found our Urchin and he's nearly a member of the Circle now, can't believe it, can you? I think I'd better get this dried off." She waddled happily away toward Anemone Wood.

"I wish I could be like that," said Padra. "Made perfectly at ease and happy by the finding of a hat. Arran, there are injured otters who can't work and able-bodied otters clearing up after the storm. Crispin must have reduced the shore watch for Catkin and Linty."

"He's got fewer otters and more squirrels keeping a sharp lookout for anything that looks suspicious," said Fingal.

"And weren't you supposed to be off duty?" inquired Arran.

Fingal shrugged and scuffed at a pebble in the sand. "I just came out to see . . . you know . . . well, nobody could sleep through that lot, and after a storm . . . I just thought I'd come and see . . . just about things, you know."

"Fingal," said Padra sadly. He put an arm round Fingal's shoulders. "There's a bit of driftwood over there, I don't know if you noticed it."

"Yes, I know," said Fingal. He glanced over his shoulder at the drift-wood, then looked away again quickly. "I went out early. A few of the boats were missing, and I thought mine might just have been washed out to sea or something, so I swam around a bit for a look. I found a few bits. Must have been thrown onto the rocks." He shrugged again, with a brave attempt at a smile. "It was only a boat, it's not as if any-one was in it."

"Oh, Fingal, your boat!" said Arran. "Are you sure . . ."

"Oh, yes, I know the bits of my own boat," said Fingal. "I'll just have to start again. Sorry, I'd promised to take the twins out in it. They can go on having rides on my back instead."

"I'll help you build another one," said Padra. "We'll get Twigg onto it. There's still lots of timber in the yards."

"There can't be, not after last night," said Fingal. "And there's burrows and things to be repaired. They still don't know where Catkin is, animals have died in the epidemic, and whole families lost their homes in the landslide. It was just a boat."

"It was *your* boat," said Padra, and tightened his hold around Fingal's shoulders. "We know how you feel about it."

Fingal wriggled free of Padra's arm. "Any chance of breakfast," he asked, "or do I have to go and catch it?"

Later that morning, animals began to scurry, trundle, clamber, and leap to Seathrift Meadow. In the burrows high on the hillside, badly injured animals remained with those who looked after them, but the rest made their way to the meadows. After a quick bite of breakfast and a wash and fur brush, Urchin, Juniper, Lugg, and King Crispin came down from the tower.

"Put the best face you can on this," said Crispin. "We've all had a long, hard night and not enough sleep, we're all bruised and aching. You've done magnificently up to now. What we have to do this time is to walk down to the meadows with our fur clean and our steps firm— or as firm as can be, with a quagmire to walk on. We have to look strong and confident for the sake of the others."

"Yes, Your Majesty," said Urchin, knowing that trying to look strong and confident to convince other people is as good a way as any of convincing yourself. "Is the queen coming with us?"

"I advised her to rest and stay with Brother Fir," said Crispin.

Urchin felt that Crispin wasn't telling him everything. Perhaps he had things to say that would be best said when Cedar wasn't there. He wouldn't want to embarrass her. Urchin squared his sore shoulders and raised his chin, stopping now and again as Juniper seemed to be falling behind.

"It's all right," called Juniper, "I'm waiting for Lugg. I'll catch you up."

"Glad it's down them stairs, not up them," muttered Lugg, who seemed slower than usual this morning.

"You know all that shoring up we did last night," said Juniper, "will it last?"

"Wait and see," said Lugg, trying to get his breath. "Land needs time to settle, and it's still soft down there. Maybe we'll need to shore up the roofs a bit more. Last night we were holding 'em up with whatever we could get."

Juniper remembered the previous night, with pit props crammed into place against walls and ceilings. There hadn't been much time to think about things then, but something had puzzled him.

"Those pit props," he said. "Some of them were just whatever branches we could find, but there was some proper wood—sawn up, with marks on it as if it had been used before, even polished wood. It wasn't new, so I don't suppose it came from Twigg's yard—and besides, it would have taken too long to get it from there. So where did it come from?"

"Good question," said Lugg. "Well, you see, in the business of what's been happening, what with little Catkin and that, I've been awful busy about tunnels. All sorts of tunnels, all over this island. Old ones, mostly, that had been blocked up long, long ago and were meant to stay that way, but the king wanted 'em looked into, just in case anybody, by any chance, had found a way in but couldn't get out again. The longer the baby's hidden, you have to admit, the more it looks like something like that could have happened. So I've got doors unblocked that should have been blocked, and soon will be again. I've had tunnels and chambers opened out just enough to take a peek into them, in case anyone's hiding in there. Opening 'em's one thing, closing 'em up again is another, when you've got more than enough to do and half the island coming down on your head. I've got doors half-unblocked that I hadn't finished before the landslide started. So, when we needed wood for pit props, I knew fine well where to find it."

"Wood from closed-off tunnels!" exclaimed Juniper.

Lugg chuckled. "There's no law against it," he said. "If there was, Mistress Tay would have found it before now. Mind you, I don't think she knows about this, so . . ."

"Don't worry," said Juniper quickly. "I won't tell her."

"There's tunnels all under the tower was meant to be searched for the princess," said Lugg. "Would have done it by now, if not for that plaguing rain and its plaguing landslide."

"When Catkin first went missing," said Juniper, "Urchin and I had to search the Chamber of Candles, and Hope came with us. He said there was another layer underneath."

Lugg chuckled. "You can tell that one was trained by moles," he said. "Oh, yes, that's how prisoners got away from the pit, all that long time ago. There's all sorts of ways down there, but I don't know what they're like. Dunno what's fallen in and what hasn't." He stopped, wheezing, and waved Juniper ahead. "I need to catch my breath again. You go ahead."

"No," said Juniper, "I'll wait with you."

"Do as a captain tells you, cheeky little twitcher," said Lugg. "Do they teach you no manners?" He waved a paw. "Get along, the king might need you."

The rocks gleamed, and beyond them the turf was spongy with rain. Here and there, wet autumn leaves had drifted into heaps. Rose hips glowed on a thornbush. With an air of busyness and excitement the Mistmantle animals were gathering together. Those who lived nearest advised the others as to which bits would be boggy, and young hedgehogs and squirrels jumped into them anyway, just to see if they really did sink to their knees in mud. An occasional breath of wind ruffled the fur. Anxious parents hovered near their young. A few children began to play Find the Heir of Mistmantle and were instantly silenced.

Russet, Heath, Docken, and the rest of the Circle were quietly going from one group of animals to another, keeping order, listening to accounts of the damage done by the storm, and making sure everyone could see the rock where Crispin would presently stand. As so many animals had made long journeys to get here, Arran had arranged for refreshments to be served before as well as after the gathering, and aproned hedgehogs and squirrels wove their way through the crowd with mugs on trays and baskets laden with berries and nuts. Needle and Crackle were doing their best to keep the excited little ones occupied, which was difficult as the squirrels only wanted to run off and find trees to climb; and a very small hedgehog fell down a burrow, and Needle had to heave him out with Scufflen clinging to her other paw because he had been told to stay with Needle and refused to let go of her. Hope had offered to help, but in fact was staggering under the weight of a very contented sleeping baby hedgehog sucking its paw, and was telling everyone that this was his baby sister, Mopple, "and I look after her because she likes me."

Needle, brushing down the rescued hedgehog, was wondering where Urchin was and wishing he'd turn up and help. Sepia and Scatter would have been useful, too, but they were on duty in the tower where Brother Fir or the queen might need them. It was a great relief when Urchin finally did turn up, with Jig and Fig, the mole maids.

"The king told me to find you," he told her. "He asked me to find someone to do—well, the sort of thing you're doing already. I found

Jig and Fig." A plump little mole caught sight of Fig and hurled itself into her arms. "I wonder where Juniper is? I can see Lugg on his way, but not Juniper. I hope he's all right."

"I haven't seen him for days," said Needle, trying hard not to be irritated. She sometimes felt a touch of resentment about Juniper. Urchin and Juniper got on so well. They were both squirrels, both boys, they'd shared adventures and dangers together. She was a girl, a neat-pawed workroom animal who'd been the one left to save Mistmantle while they found themselves in prison on Whitewings without ever meaning to go there. She could understand that Urchin liked having a brother. But she'd always been his best friend.

Never mind that, she told herself, and gave her spines a shake. Just to show that she did care about Juniper, she waved at the kind-faced otter-wife who was looking after Padra and Arran's twins. "Mistress Inish, have you seen Brother Juniper?"

"Funny you should ask," said Inish, balancing a wriggly Tide under one arm and an even more wriggly Swanfeather under the other. "I wondered if he was going to see Brother Fir. One minute he was cramming leaves into his satchel, and the next he was running off to the tower." She heaved at Swanfeather, who had turned upside down. "I couldn't see what leaves they were, but . . . sort yourself out Tide, that's your own tail you've got hold of . . . I don't think they were anything for healing. But he was off at such a rate!"

"Thanks," said Urchin, and wove his way in and out of the crowds to the rocks where Crispin and Padra were speaking with the Circle animals. Tay stood with her arms folded and a look of stern disapproval on her face, oblivious to a small spider dangling from her whiskers. Needle had scrambled onto the rock, and Padra was coming to speak to them both when Urchin said, "Look! There he is! Juniper!"

Padra and Needle turned to look. Juniper, with a bulging satchel over his shoulder, was hurrying lamely toward the tower.

"He should be here," said Padra. "Go and round him up, Urchin."

"Yes, sir, if that's an order," said Urchin, anxiously watching Juniper. "But I'm worried about him. With Damson dying, and"—he remembered just in time that Needle didn't know about Juniper's father—"and everything, I don't think he's himself."

Padra nodded. "Go after him, Urchin," he said. "You're nearly a Circle animal. Use your own judgment and do whatever you think best. I'll explain your absence to the king if necessary."

"Thank you, sir," said Urchin.

"And if you haven't come back by the time Crispin dismisses us all, I'll send someone to find you," said Padra.

"Please, Captain Padra," began Needle, "I'm nearly a Circle animal too, and it might be . . ."

"Get along with you, then!" smiled Padra, but he stopped smiling as the two young animals hurried away, and watched until they were out of sight.

"Heart keep them," he said quietly, and raised a paw toward the tower. "Heart keep them safe."

Urchin and Needle pattered away after Juniper, Urchin making an effort to slow down for Needle, and Needle making a bigger effort to keep up with Urchin. On the rocks around the tower, Juniper veered off to the left.

"He's not going into the Tangletwigs, is he?" said Urchin. "We'd never find him in there."

Needle crouched down, her bright eyes alert and her nose twitching. "There he goes!" she said. "Into the hill!"

Juniper had turned sharply right and ducked into the rocks beneath the tower. Needle and Urchin hurried after him.

"It's where Twigg's carpentry yard used to be, before he moved," said Needle. "What's Juniper doing in there? Shouldn't we call him?"

"Not just yet," said Urchin. He wasn't sure at first why he said this, but he knew there was a reason and had to ask himself what it was. "He's in a terrible state. He means to do something. If we ask him about it too soon, he'll avoid saying anything. We have to ask him at the right point, and I don't think this is it."

"If you say so," said Needle, and followed him to the cave, where sawdust still lay soaked into the ground outside. Inside it was clean, swept, and completely empty.

"Where's he gone?" whispered Needle.

CHAPTER SEVENTEEN

CRISPIN LEAPED TO A HIGH POINT on the rock and rang his
sword against it for silence. Chatter stopped, apart from one
crying baby otter, and a shrill-voiced squirrel saying, "Ooh, look,
there's a spider on Mistr . . . ooh, sorry." But when Crispin stepped
forward, the silence became complete.

Crispin's keen gaze traveled slowly across the crowd, engaging the
animals at the back, moving forward, scanning row by row until every
animal felt that the king knew about him or her, and cared, and
understood. Then he began.

"Animals of Mistmantle," he called, "we have come through so much
together this autumn. I know how you have sweated in the sun for the
harvest and hunted by night and day across the island for Catkin. We
have struggled together against disease, storm, and landslide, and you
have shared it all with courage, love, effort, and perseverance that I can

215

only wonder at. I count myself glad and privileged to be one of you. To be an islander of Mistmantle! There is no greater honor than this!"

"Isn't he a love!" muttered Apple to the otter next to her and received a quick dig in the ribs.

"The worst of the fouldrought is over," said Crispin. "And we have three of our young animals to thank. Fingal, Scatter, Crackle, come here!"

Crackle, who hadn't really been listening, jerked at the sound of her name. Was there anybody else here called Crackle? Scatter pulled on her paw.

"That's us!" she whispered, dragging her forward. "Where's Fingal?"

Paw in paw, they wove their way through the parting, murmuring crowd to the rock. Fingal scrambled up, too, looking a bit embarrassed, which wasn't like him. Crackle was thinking that they were very high up, and then realized that it really wasn't a high rock at all, it was just that everybody else was down below them looking up, when someone passed bouquets of autumn flowers to Crispin.

"Well done, Crackle," he said.

This is really me, really here, and the king is putting flowers into my paws!

She turned to face the crowd. Applause! There was applause! Warmed and happy, she held the flowers against her face. Mistmantle loved her! Beside her, Scatter received a bouquet from the king's paws, beamed with joy, and wondered if it were possible to burst with happiness.

Crispin turned to Fingal. "Please don't give me flowers," said Fingal.

"The queen thought you would prefer this," said Crispin, and fastened a bracelet of plain silver on Fingal's wrist, taking care to do it gently. "How are the burns?"

"Almost gone, sir," said Fingal. Crispin turned him to face the crowds. Fingal grinned, gave a brief wave, and jumped down, and Crispin went on with his speech.

"And I know you want to thank the teams of healers," he said, "who have traveled day and night to care for the sick, going without sleep and putting their own health at risk. All of you, from the oldest and wisest to the newest apprentices, gatherers of herbs and makers of medicines, we thank you from our hearts. The queen has told me of all your hard work, and she marvels at it."

He paused while a few murmurs of thanks and approval ran through the crowd, listening hard for any resentful mutterings and the pockets of silence.

"I know it's been hard," he went on. "If you have complaints, if you are discontented, if you feel our problems could be dealt with better than they are now, animals of Mistmantle, tell me! Tell me now! I am your king, and I am here to care for you. Tell me your needs! Tell me your doubts! Help me to help you!"

There was silence. A few animals shuffled their paws.

"Then everything's perfect?" he said. There was a little uneasy laughter.

"Last night," he went on, "I was forced to cancel a meeting with a delegation of animals who had problems to discuss with me. Good creatures, will you talk to me now?"

Hobb and Yarrow stood very still, looking hard at the ground. Quill stood behind Gleaner and hoped nobody could see him. Somebody nudged Hobb in the back.

"Leave us alone," he muttered.

"Then is all well?" demanded Crispin. "Disease has carried off our dear ones, my daughter is still missing, burrows are flooded. Is all well?"

Animals looked at each other. A bright-eyed young squirrel, one of the choir, piped up, "No, sir, but it's not your fault!" and there was more nervous laughter.

"Thank you, Siskin," said Crispin. Siskin, astonished that the king knew her name, went a bit shaky and had to sit down. In the middle of the crowd, somebody prodded Yarrow in the arm.

"Ow!" said Yarrow. "Get off!" Heads turned toward him.

"You had enough to say before," said Hammily loudly. "You can say it now."

"You're the one who can do the talking," muttered Yarrow to Hobb.

"But I never . . ." began Hobb, but it was too late. Animals were steering them toward the rock where Crispin stood. Quill's father shoved him forward, and he was carried along unwillingly to the front of the crowd. A few of the other hangers-on, looking resentfully over their shoulders, were pushed along with them and almost bundled into the king's presence.

"Gently!" called the king. He reached down a paw to help Quill onto the rock. "Good animals, don't heave them about as if they were timber!"

Embarrassed and wretched, the animals dusted down their fur as they stood before him.

"I'm not here to blame you, judge you, or trick you," said Crispin. "And I'm certainly not here to show you up. Whatever you have to say, say it to me, and not to your neighbors in the burrows. I'm here so that we can know the truth and treat it as the truth. There's no point in anything else. Now—" He raised his voice. "What did you want to ask me about? What are your complaints?"

Yarrow and Hobb still looked at their paws. Quill decided it was up to him.

In a voice so nervous he could hardly shape the name, he whispered, "Husk, sir."

"Husk!" called out Crispin. A shudder of fear ran through the crowd. "Well done, Quill! Don't be afraid, it's only his name! What about Husk?"

"They say he's back, sir," whispered Quill.

Crispin knelt in front of him. "Can you tell me who says it, Quill?" he said. "Well, never mind, you've made an effort. Good lad." He stood up. "Can anyone say *who* says Husk is back?"

"Lots of animals, sir," said a voice in the crowd.

"But he is, sir!" said a hedgehog. "I saw him!"

Various animals, gaining courage, told their stories. They had seen Husk against the skyline. Well, it looked like Husk. Yes, it was dark. No, it wasn't for long, but they thought it was Husk. And, Gleaner said, what about the muslin that had been stolen from Aspen's grave?

"So, you think he's back," said Crispin. "I'll talk to you presently about Husk. Is there anything else that worries you? Anything else that needs holding up to the light?"

There were more shuffles and murmurs. A squabble appeared to be breaking out between Gleaner and the hedgehog next to her.

"You said it was," hissed the hedgehog.

"No, I didn't, I only said that Yarrow said it."

"You didn't, you said that she . . ."

"Yes, you did!" said another hedgehog.

"It wasn't me, it was Quill!"

Gleaner suddenly realized that everyone around them was silent. Everyone, including the senior animals on the rock, was watching them.

Well, let them, she thought. I'll say what I think. Crackle and Scatter have had their moment of glory. I'm going to have mine. She stuck out her elbows, pushed through the crowd, and marched to the foot of the rock where she stood, paws on hips, looking up at Crispin.

"It's the queen," she announced. "She's all wrong."

There was a gasp and a stunned silence. Everyone watched Crispin as he took a deep breath and exhaled slowly.

"Thank you for your courage, Gleaner," he said. He unbuckled his sword and sat down at the edge of the rock, close to the crowd, scanning their faces. A few looked embarrassed, or defiant, or just guilty. Most were shocked. There was a little murmuring in a corner of the crowd as Tipp insisted that if anyone said anything about the queen he'd fight them, and his mother shushed him.

"The queen," said Crispin. "Cedar, who overthrew Silverbirch and Smokewreath on Whitewings and put their rightful queen on the throne? Cedar who brought Urchin, Juniper, and Lugg safely back to us? Cedar who healed you? Cedar who helps me to be a king? You don't really believe that she brought fouldrought, do you? You don't really believe that she didn't know how to look after Catkin, so why blame her?"

"We don't, Your Majesty!" cried a voice in the crowd. Paw after paw was raised as animals competed with each other to tell about the queen's kindness and wisdom and how she had healed and helped them.

"In that case," said Crispin pleasantly, "why does anyone complain about her? Tell me!"

Yarrow leaned toward Gleaner. "Tell him!" he whispered.

"Tell me what, Yarrow?" asked Crispin, without turning his head.

"Nothing, Your Ma . . . I mean . . ." stammered Yarrow, "I mean, it's not her fault that she's not in her right mind."

There was a hiss of shock from the animals. Crispin was about to speak when Thripple raised her paw.

"May I speak, Your Majesty?" she asked. Crispin extended a paw to help her onto the rock, and she turned unevenly to speak to the crowd of animals gazing upward. She looked as she always did, lopsided, standing to one side to adjust to the weight of her hunched back.

"I don't usually do things like this," she said. "But I can't hold my peace now. When my little boy was born he was taken away for the cull, and it was Captain Crispin, as he was then, who hid him and saved him. I know what it's like to be separated from my child, and I've sat by the queen day after day and night after night, and I can assure you that she's as sane and strong as any animal on the island. And saner and stronger than some!" she added with a glare around the crowd. "She's behaving exactly like a mother needing to find her baby, and why shouldn't she! I know what it is you really think! You're thinking she doesn't come from Mistmantle! If you want to blame anyone, you'll blame the queen, because you think she's not one of us! Well, she is now! And quite right, too!"

A stunned silence followed. Subdued, Thripple turned to the king.

"Beg pardon, Your Majesty," she said. "I didn't mean to go on like that."

"I couldn't have done it better myself," said Crispin, and stood up. It was time now for the next stage.

Linty woke up with a jerk. There was chaos on the island now, storms, landslides, floods—it wasn't safe to fall asleep. Everywhere, they were out looking for Daisy to kill her. Daisy? Catkin? The baby. She mustn't fall asleep in case they came for the baby, so she forced herself to stay awake.

Fresh air would help. It was a risk, but it was one she could take. Leaving the baby asleep in her solidly walled hiding place, she wriggled through the twists and byways of tunnels, covering her tracks, blocking the way behind her, scrabbling through sandy soil until she sniffed the salt air of a cave.

She squeezed into a cleft in the rock where she could stay hidden but still have a good view of the bay. Patrolling otters strolled past, picking up driftwood and debris. They were dragging something, something that shushed through the wet sand. It was coming toward her! Louder! Nearer!

Linty turned cold with terror. She pressed further into the rock, sweat chilling on her skin, her heart hammering. They were coming for her! They were coming for her baby! Let them try. She breathed deeply, flexed her claws, and bared her teeth. She would fight if she had to.

"Whose boat is this, anyway?" asked one of the otters. "Young Fingal's is missing, but it doesn't look like his."

"No, his was smashed to bits," said the other. "Don't know that this one belongs to anyone in particular. She's well maintained, though, and she survived the storm. Needs bailing out, but she'll do. Leave her in here, it's a high tide tonight and we don't want her floating away. I reckon the tide'll bring the mist with it. Are you yawning?"

"We're all yawning. Don't think anyone got any sleep last night."

Linty stayed absolutely still until they had gone, then wriggled back into the rock. A boat. A high tide. And the otters on patrol were tired. She would never have another chance like this. She would take the baby far beyond the mists, and nobody from Mistmantle could ever come near them.

CHAPTER EIGHTEEN

URCHIN AND NEEDLE STOOD SIDE BY SIDE in the entrance to the cave that had once been Twigg's workshop. Apart from a few planks resting against the walls and some rusty and battered old tools, it was empty.

"There must be a way through the back," said Urchin. "One of those very tight places that you get in caves." He put his paw against the wall and walked slowly forward, feeling for gaps, working his way steadily into the darkness at the back of the cave.

"Look out!" gasped Needle. As she spoke, he felt a draft of cold air at his paws. With a hop backward he looked down into the gaping space where a trapdoor had been left open, its lid thrown flat against the ground. He flung himself down on the edge of the empty, black square and peered down.

"I can't see much," he said. "Just a big, black space that looks as if it wants to swallow us. I wish I'd brought a candle or something. I expect Juniper did."

"Your eyes will get used to it," said Needle, trundling up beside him.

"I think those are steps," he said. "Yes, there are steps cut in here. It's some sort of cellar, Twigg must have used it for storage. I'll go first, I can see better in the dark than you can."

He pressed both paws against the walls, felt for the first step, then ran down on all fours. He was about to warn Needle that the steps were uneven when the sound of something rolling down toward him made him jump back against the wall and stay there. A ball of prickles bounced past him and landed with a bump at the bottom.

"I didn't mean to do that, sorry," she whispered, poking her head out.

"Are you all right?" he asked and then raised his voice. "Juniper! Where are you?"

There was no answer. They waited. A circle of faint light appeared ahead of them to the right, growing wider and stronger. It was a candle, casting a ghostly light on Juniper's face as he emerged from a corner.

"How did you know I was here?" he asked.

"We followed you," said Urchin. "We were worried about you."

He tried to think a step ahead, working out what to say if Juniper told them to go away and leave him alone. But Juniper only said, "I'm glad it's you. The stairs are all different, by the way, it's safest to jump or roll."

Urchin sprang down, Needle rolled, and the three of them

gathered in the light of Juniper's candle. "So what are you trying to do?" he asked.

"Everything's falling into place," said Juniper, and though his voice was quick with excitement, his face in the candle glow was perfectly calm. "The only way to prove that Husk is dead is to find his body, and let anyone see it who wants to."

There was a gasp from Needle, who put a paw to her mouth. Urchin closed his eyes and wished with all his heart that this wasn't happening. It wasn't the time, or the place, to tell Juniper what he and Crispin had seen at dawn, but Juniper had to be told. He couldn't continue weaving his way underground looking for a body that wasn't there.

"It's so simple," Juniper went on, and lowered his voice. "It's the prophecy." He didn't even glance at Needle, but Urchin understood. She didn't know Juniper's secret, and it wasn't the time and place to tell her.

"Needle," he said, "could you just check for any shaky ground or anything?"

Boys! thought Needle in disgust. What do they want to talk about behind my back? But she was too proud to argue, and scurried away to investigate.

"'The fatherless will find a father . . .'" said Juniper in an excited whisper. "I'm the fatherless."

"'and the hills will fall into earth,'" said Urchin. "They did! But the dead paw . . ."

"It's not enough to know who my father is," said Juniper. "I have to find him. I think that's it. I don't understand this thing about pathways on the sea, but I've worked out the other thing, too. Mistmantle's greatest enemy."

"Yes, but, Juniper, wait," said Urchin. He glanced to see where Needle was, drew Juniper as far away as possible, and whispered, "You think you can find his body, and I might have thought so, too, but this morning"—he barely spoke the words—"*I saw him!*"

"You *think* you saw him," said Juniper, and looked as if he would have said more, but Needle had run out of corners to pretend to inspect and was coming to join them. "Just take my word for it, Urchin," he whispered quickly. "You didn't see him. I can't explain now, but . . . found anything, Needle?"

"Of course not," said Needle. "Now, if you think we have to go looking for a body, I suppose we should get on with it."

"We all have to recognize the island's greatest enemy for ourselves," said Juniper. "You know it, Urchin. You met it on Whitewings, when you stood before King Silverbirch."

"I met it long before that," said Urchin, thinking of the night when he had followed Captain Husk through dark tunnels.

"Oh, I know what you mean," said Needle, remembering a trap she had fallen into.

"And we have to face it and not let it win," said Urchin. "I think you're right. We have to find Husk, if he really is still there."

"I was talking to Lugg on the way down," said Juniper. "Between unblocking doors in the search for Catkin and removing wooden barriers for pit props, none of these places are as thoroughly sealed as they were. He'll have to seal them again soon, so if we're going to find Husk's body, this might be the only chance. And this is when it has to be done, because some of those animals really do believe that he's back."

"But you've no idea where to look!" protested Needle.

"I think I've worked it out," said Juniper. "We need to be directly underneath the Chamber of Candles, and we know it's very deep. Twigg used this as a storeroom, and he said there was a blocked door down here and probably another one behind it. And we need to go more or less southeast. Some doors have been partly dismantled and some might be decaying, but I expect we'll still have to do some digging and scrabbling to get through."

"You'd never have done it by yourself!" said Urchin. "Why didn't you ask us in the first place?"

"Couldn't, could I?" said Juniper, and Urchin decided it had been a silly question. Juniper couldn't have asked anyone to join him in something like this.

"We'd better get on with it, then," said Needle briskly, "before the king sends anyone looking for us."

"This way," said Juniper.

They followed the candlelight to the right. There, in a recess, was a wooden door that looked completely solid. Juniper tried the handle, found it firmly locked, and gave it a determined shove with his shoulder. It creaked, but didn't open.

"This is the door Twigg told me about," he said. "It's not blocked, we just don't have a key."

"A sword might help," said Urchin. He stepped back and looked the door up and down. He'd learned to use his sword for fencing and useful things like cutting down ivy and fishing lost cloaks from the sea, but he wasn't sure if it would be any use for this. He tried wedging it between the planks, but they were too firmly in place to be prized apart.

"Couldn't we find something to batter it with?" he suggested.

"In a carpenter's store?" said Needle. "There must be some tools or—oh, there was an ax upstairs. It was an old rusty one, but . . ."

Urchin scrambled back up the rough steps into the old workshop and returned to the top of the steps carrying the ax in one paw and dragging something like a flagpole in the other. It looked as if it might come in use.

"Look out!" he called, and threw the pole down the stairs. He leaped down after it with the ax in his paw. "If the ax is no good, we can take a run at it and batter it down."

They took turns swinging the ax against the door and found that Juniper, who, having grown up among otters, was a strong swimmer and an excellent stone-skimmer, had a powerful swing. When he had splintered the wood enough to weaken it, they lined up along the flagpole, with Urchin at the front and Needle at the back, and charged.

The impact jarred Urchin's sore shoulders horribly and threw

Needle backward. "Just as well I *was* at the back," she muttered, picking herself up. Urchin gritted his teeth and rubbed his shoulder.

"That door's giving way," he said. "One more."

Under another blow, the wood wrenched and tore. A few more ax blows from Juniper made a hole big enough for them to throw the tools through first and scramble in after them. Needle's spines and Juniper's satchel caught on the splintered edges, but with a lot of tugging and a paw from Urchin, they had broken through into complete darkness. Apart from the draft from the broken door, they could feel no air currents at all. It was a shut-in place.

"We've made a terrible mess of that door," remarked Needle.

"I don't suppose anyone will mind," said Urchin. "That wasn't too difficult."

As soon as he had said it, he realized that it was going to get a lot harder. Things always did. Juniper was holding the candle high, turning slowly, and Needle was licking a deep scratch on the back of her paw.

"We're in another chamber," said Juniper. "Earth walls. I'd hoped it would be a tunnel or a stair."

"Let's have a good look," said Urchin. "It was too much to hope we'd only have to get through one door. But that last one was only locked, not sealed, so it could have been used not long ago. And as it leads to this chamber, somebody could have been here recently, too. The moles might already have started work on a way through."

They shone the light around the chamber. Urchin drew his sword, ran the point around the walls, and nearly overbalanced when it suddenly slipped into a soft patch of earth.

"That's it!" he said.

"There are scuff marks on the ground," said Needle, peering at the earth. "Mole prints. Lugg and his teams might have been here. This must be one of those doors that's been partly unblocked already."

"Stand back," said Urchin. "Juniper, you're best with the ax." After some chopping, barging, and scrabbling they had made a hole big enough to squeeze through with Juniper going first, carrying the candle, Urchin following with one paw on his sword hilt, and Needle close behind, peering over Urchin's shoulder. Juniper stopped suddenly.

"What have you found?" whispered Needle.

"Nothing," he said, reaching with his free paw into his satchel. "I'm putting down a leaf. Try not to get it stuck to your paws, it has to stay where it is."

"Laying a trail," said Urchin, "so we can find our way back." Needle was about to say that she thought Juniper was supposed to know where he was going, but decided that it wouldn't help. Still, it was just as well she was here to take care of Urchin if he had to go running after Juniper on some silly dangerous quest that would probably get them nowhere. And when the king might need them, too. How were they to answer to Crispin?

The path twisted and turned so much that Needle soon lost all sense of where they were. Juniper paused now and again to put down a leaf, once stopping so suddenly that Needle, who was trying to work out where they were, walked into Urchin's back.

"Sorry!" she said. "I wish you wouldn't do that." She sniffed the air. "There's a branch of this tunnel going off to the right."

"I know," said Juniper. "There are lots of them. But this is the right way."

"How do you know?" she asked.

"I can tell," said Juniper. He was paying absolute attention to every signal in the walls, the drafts, and the changes from cool to cold. He listened, too, to the drawing of his own heart that compelled him to the place and, at the same time, made him afraid of what he would find.

"Don't worry," said Urchin. "He understands things that the rest of us don't."

Squirrels! thought Needle. Sometimes, they were more trouble than they were worth. But now Juniper was holding the candle high and saying something about steps.

"A spiral stair," he said, shuffling to one side. "Stay close."

Even by staying as close to him as possible, it was hard for Urchin and Needle to see the candle as Juniper turned and turned with the curling of the stair which seemed to go on forever. How far had they been doing this, and how far down were they? The cold and damp of the air was enough to tell that they were far, far underground.

It must stop somewhere, thought Needle, plodding on down the stairs. Adventures can get really boring sometimes. Then she realized that Urchin had stopped, the light had stopped, and they stood together on a landing with a dead end before them. Juniper held the candle high.

"It's another blocked entrance," he said. Needle's heart sank. "If you look carefully, you can see the outline of the doorway. There may still be a wooden door behind it when we break through."

"Let me through," said Needle. If they had to break through yet another sealed entrance, she may as well find out how difficult this one would be. She raised her nose to the earth wall. "I can smell wood somewhere," she said, and pulled a face. "And decay. Definitely a smell of decay."

Urchin sniffed at it, and that smell of decay carried such terrible memories that he found he was shuddering. It was as if this was the door to the greatest fear of his past, and he could feel again the raw terror of running through corridors of darkness with unseen things scurrying about him, cobwebs catching on his face, nameless things under his paws, Husk, the smell of evil, death, and decay. . . .

"Urchin, are you all right?" asked Juniper.

He nodded. Brother Fir had cleansed that terrible dungeon and had made it a place of blessing. But the place they were looking for now, the bottom of the pit where Husk's body lay, was deeper and darker than anywhere he had ever been.

"I know what you think," said Juniper. "But I don't sense evil on the other side of this. Only sorrow."

"Are you sure this is the way?" asked Needle.

"Oh yes," said Juniper. "We have to get through that door."

Knowing that they were getting good at this, they threw all their energies into hacking, stabbing, and scrabbling the earth away. This wall seemed far thicker than the others, and they worked on with loose earth falling into their fur and ears, irritating their eyes, and blackening their paws. Urchin longed to give himself a good shake, but as he couldn't do that without spraying more soil over the others, it was better not to think about it, just as it was better not to think of what lay on the other side of this. Perhaps Juniper was wrong, and after all this they'd find themselves in the wrong place.

It took a lot of hard work and grazed paws. The earth wall was so deep that when at last they had made a hole big enough for all three of them to crawl into, they were still not through to the other side.

"But it's thinner," said Needle. "Take care, we don't want this lot to fall on top of us."

"We should dig out the next bit one at a time," said Urchin. "Two of us can watch the one who's digging and get them out if it looks as if anything might cave in."

There was no point in asking who would go first. Juniper scrabbled furiously until he had to stop to rub the thick layer of soil from his paw, and Needle said, "Here, let me have a go."

"Yes, get your breath back, Juniper," said Urchin.

Needle clambered into the hole. Juniper had reached a long way.

"We're nearly through to the wood," she called back, her voice so muffled by the surrounding earth that they strained to hear her. "There might be a soft bit somewhere. I think—yes—I think I've—oh! Ow!"

There was a scuffle, a sound of falling stones, and a scream. Urchin and Juniper crammed themselves into the space, but the scream had already died away.

"Needle!" they yelled. By the light of the outstretched candle they could see something that looked like broken steps and a rocky slope that disappeared into blackness.

"Needle!" they yelled again.

A faint whimper of pain came from somewhere far below. Juniper lunged forward, but Urchin held him back.

"Steady," he said, putting his sword back into its sheath. "Whatever's happened to Needle, we don't want it happening to you too." He called out again. "Needle! Can you hear me?"

A faint voice reached them. It seemed to come from impossibly far below them, and he had to twitch his ears and strain his hearing.

"It's rocky . . . and very steep . . . a cliff . . . don't fall . . . ouch!" gasped Needle.

"I'm coming, Needle," he said. "Juniper, shall I take the light?"

With Urchin holding the candle, they crept forward. There were a few broken steps, then Urchin jerked backward. His paws tingled. The drop beneath was a sheer cliff. At its foot was a ledge, then two more steps, and a rough slope cluttered with broken stone, too long for him to see where it ended.

Urchin was used to running down walls. At the tower, he did it all the time. But he wasn't used to coming upon them as suddenly as this, threatening to catch him by surprise and break his neck. He put out a paw to warn Juniper.

"It's a vicious drop," he said. "We could jump it, but I think it's safer to run. Shall I go first?"

He handed the light to Juniper and leaned over the edge. "We're on our way, Needle!" he called, and twisted to look over his shoulder at Juniper. "I'll get as far as the ledge and wait there for you. It should be easy after that." Then he tipped himself over the cliff and ran, slipping and scrabbling.

Juniper tried to breathe deeply, remembering at last to open his heart to the Heart and receive the strength he needed. Some time, far in the past, before all his other memories, there had been darkness, Husk, a scream, and a cliff. Now, in this terrible place with darkness behind and before him, he was coming to the end of this particular journey. There was still this plunge into the unknown before he could complete it. He had to do this, before he could start on the next stage of his life.

Urchin was waiting for him, Needle was injured, and there was no time to think. He tipped himself over the edge.

The smoothness of the rock took his breath away. There was nothing to grip, nothing to balance on. He was slithering, faster, falling on the ledge, rolling onto the slope—and Urchin had caught him. Side by side they dashed over the slope, dislodging pebbles, stumbling and scrabbling on loose scree, twisting and somersaulting to get their balance.

"Look out, Needle!" yelled Urchin as pebbles slipped from under his paws and left him sprawling on his back. The candle fell from his paw and went out. "Curl up!"

"I *am* curled up!" came a cross, muffled voice. She sounded like herself now.

Urchin reached the bottom of the slope and dusted himself down while he became accustomed to the cold and darkness. "Where are you?" he called.

"Here," said a voice to his left, and if he strained his eyes he could see a ball of prickles. He knelt beside her.

"Are you badly hurt, Needle?" he asked.

Juniper was scrabbling in his satchel for flints and more candles. He struck a spark and placed a light beside Urchin and Needle, holding another in his paw.

Urchin began to take in where he was. The air felt empty, as if nobody who left this place would ever return. The far-remembered smell of decay and fustiness hung about, and he was glad he couldn't see much. It had the coldness of a place that had never been lived in and never known sunlight.

"Can you stand up?" he asked Needle.

Taking his paw in her left forepaw, she pulled herself up. When he tried to take her right forepaw, she flinched away.

"I've done something to that paw," she said, and held it to the circle of light from the candle. "I heard something crack."

The paw had already swollen from elbow to wrist. "Can you wiggle your claws?" asked Urchin.

"Not much," she said.

"Juniper's got his satchel," he said. "He should be able to bind it for you." He turned to see where Juniper had gone and saw him walking away from them into the deeper darkness, with one small candle in his paws.

Juniper walked on into unknown shadows, cold and sorrow, and the end of his journey. It was not fear that filled this place, or a sense of danger, but a sadness heavier than anything he had ever known. Old white bones littered the ground. This was a place of grief and desolation.

Aware of something above him, he looked up, and to his great relief saw a faint glow of warm yellow light far above him. He was right, then. They were directly under the Chamber of Candles. He held the candle as close to the ground as he could, to see what lay there. When his hind paw touched something hard and cold, he flinched as if it burned.

It was nothing. Only a bit of old metal. He held the candle to it.

In the pale light, he could recognize the tip of a sword blade. He knelt, holding the candle to follow the line of the sword from the tip of the tarnished blade, the elegant and dented hilt, and the empty socket where a jewel had fallen out. Beyond the sword hilt lay the fine skeleton of a paw that had finally lost its hold. The claws curled as if they beckoned.

He raised the candle higher. Delicate white bones gleamed. There was a paw, the long bones of an arm where shreds of fabric still clung, and a few gold threads. He stood up and walked around it, stepping carefully around the dull and twisted circlet that had rolled from the shattered and splintered skull. The teeth remained bared, as if crying out. He walked on around the other outflung arm, the fragmented ribs and collarbone, the legs and spine, all broken in the fall. Something that looked like grit seemed to gleam gently and might have been precious stones, as if the hem of the dusty, tattered robe had been jeweled. There was little of it left now. Tiny creatures must have nibbled it away.

He looked up to meet Urchin's eyes. The two squirrels stood on either side of Husk's skeleton, each holding up a light.

"I've found him," said Juniper.

Urchin came to stand beside him, looking down on the circlet, the sword, and the robe that he had last seen when he had seemed to have been much younger, when the gleam of that circlet and the magnificence of that robe had drawn the whole island to Husk's power, when murder had always been in the air. So here was the end of Husk's story. Shreds of nibbled cloth, dulled jewels fallen from a battered circlet, a tarnished old sword blade, and shattered bones.

"I wish none of it had happened," whispered Juniper. "All the things he did and what he became. But it did, and we can't change the past. We can only make a difference now." From the scene of old death, he looked up to the reassuring glow from the Chamber of Candles above them. "Now," he added quietly, because he didn't want Needle to hear this, "nobody can ever see me in a dim light, from far away, and think they've seen my father."

Urchin stared at him. He was about to say that Juniper didn't look a bit like Husk, but, now that he came to think of it, there was something, just now and again, in the turn of his head—seen from a distance, in a poor light, he would look a bit like Husk.

"I climbed to the top of the dead tree this morning," said Juniper.

"I know," said Urchin. "In the trees. Crispin and I were just coming out of the burrow."

There was a little gasp from Needle, and they turned sharply to run back to her. She lay on the ground, her mouth tight with pain.

"I tried to walk," she said, "I think I've done something to the hind paw on that side, too. I'm a bit bruised down one side. I'll be all right in a minute."

"Try taking deep breaths," advised Juniper.

"I did," she said, "but it hurts."

"We need to get her out quickly," said Urchin to Juniper. "We can't get her up there without help."

"Excuse me, I'm still here," said Needle with all the indignation she could manage.

"Sorry," said Urchin, "we need to get *you* out, and we need help. We need a team with a rope or a sling, or a basket or something, to fetch you. None of us had the sense to bring a rope. Needle, it's best if Juniper stays with you because he's the one who knows about injuries. I'll tell Crispin what we've found and get a rescue team down here."

"Fast as you can, Urchin," said Juniper. Suddenly hungry for warmth, he realized that Needle would be cold, too. He took off his cloak and wrapped it around her as she flattened her spines.

Urchin stood back to take a long look at the way they had come, weighing up the angle of the slope, the steps, the ledge, and the sheer cliff. Making a good, fast run up the loose stones and gravel would be difficult, but without that he hadn't a hope of getting up the cliff. Even with a good launch, it would be hard. He couldn't remember running up anything so smooth and so high. He ran up the scree, took a deep breath, and gathered all his powers for the spring.

It was a strong, stretching leap that took him far up the cliff, but the height still above him was daunting, and he felt himself slipping as he scrabbled for a claw hold and slithered helplessly back to the ground. Angry at himself, both for failing and for failing in front of his friends when Needle needed help, he took a few deep breaths and with all his strength and skill launched himself at the cliff, scrabbled, and fell again.

He had done all he could, he had used all he had to give, and it had not been enough. The strength he needed was beyond anything he knew. Deep in his heart he prayed, and felt that Juniper was praying, too.

Heart who brought me through stars and sea and over the clouds, give me your strength. Heart who brought me through the earthquake, help me. Be the strength of my strength. Be the Heart in my heart.

He thought of woods in spring, with young squirrels racing and chasing from tree to tree, faster and higher. He thought of flying, with a flicker of joy. He sprang.

Think higher, think higher, he told himself, stretching out his claws into the air. *Fly!*

He landed not far from the cliff top, but still not close enough, and felt himself slipping. This time, he didn't scrabble to stay up. *Fly!* he thought, and pushing his paws against the cliff, he sprang once more, stretching out his claws for the cliff top and heaving himself over the edge.

"Well done, Urchin," yelled Juniper. "Heart speed you!" Then Urchin was running back the way they had come, sniffing the air, feeling in the dark for Juniper's marker leaves as he ran for Crispin.

CHAPTER NINETEEN

INTY, WITH CATKIN IN HER ARMS, pressed herself against the back of the cave and gave thanks. It had been hard, dragging the supplies here through tunnels and cave ways, and, of course, with every trip she had to carry Catkin, who seemed heavier every time. But she was ready now. She had only to load the boat, and conditions at sea were perfect. The tide had brought in the fog, and soon it would be twilight. No such chance would come again.

"We're going in a boat, my little Dais—Catkin—my little one, my baby," she whispered softly, rocking Catkin. "The tide will carry us away from here, and evil Husk will never get you, and we'll never come back here, we'll find a lovely place to live, and your mother and father . . ." She hesitated, twitching uneasily. "I'm your mother now. I'm your real mother. It's me that's looked after you. You're my little baby."

"How's the forepaw?" Juniper asked Needle. He held her tightly in the cloak, both for her warmth and his own.

"It's better since you bandaged it up," she said.

"And the hind paw?"

"So's that. And the bruising isn't so bad as long as I keep still. Aren't you cold?"

"Not me," said Juniper. "I don't feel it." He reached into his satchel as carefully as he could, not wishing to move her. "Have another drink."

She drank from the bottle of cordial. "Was it worth it?" she said drowsily. "Coming all that way to see *him*?"

"It was for me," said Juniper. "But I'm sorry this has happened to you."

"Oh, I'll be all right," she whispered. It had been worth it for her, too. She'd learned to like Juniper. If she had to be lying injured at the bottom of a dark pit, Juniper was a good animal to have with her. It was almost as good as having Urchin there—better, really, because Juniper knew more about injuries than Urchin did. They were part of each other's lives now, all three of them.

In Seathrift Meadow, King Crispin sat on a rock and looked down at the young animals. He didn't look like a king rallying the island, more like an uncle telling stories.

"When I was a very small squirrel," he said, "my parents would sometimes take me to tea at the cave of an elderly otter, on winter nights. It was meant to be a treat—and it was, she made a wonderful tea. But I feared those outings. I feared them because of a stone that stood by the cave entrance. It was almost black, and strangely veined. In daylight, it was a stone. But as the shadows grew, I felt that stone behind me. If I turned to look at it, I knew that those veins would look like a hideous face that would follow me home. Not looking at it was worse, because I knew it was watching me. It became a horror."

He looked down at the young animals gazing upward. "Do you have things like that? Things that frighten you?" Wide-eyed, they nodded. Each one could think of a twisted tree root or strange shadows in the firelight.

"I'll tell you what I did about it," he said. "I told myself it was only a stone, and there was no point in spoiling a good tea by being afraid of it. I asked the otter-wife what it was for, and she said she had rolled it over a place that had let the draft in. So I went up to it in broad daylight, had a good look at it, and kicked it. It hurt my toes, and I limped all the way home, but it was worth it."

The little ones laughed shyly. Crispin went on, "I'm sure you all have something like that, something you're afraid of," he said. "When your parents and grandparents were little, they were scared, too. Scared of a twisted tree, a pattern in the cliffs, or an animal they were shy of. We all have fears like that, and we all have to learn that it's nothing to be ashamed of." He raised his head, looking out at the crowd. "Isn't that true? Weren't you all afraid of something when you were young?" Then he sprang to his paws, and his voice rang from the rocks. "So you're afraid of Husk! You're worried that he could be alive and among us. Maybe he is! Heart help us, he's only a squirrel! Paws, ears, and a tail, like the rest of us! He only took over the island before because we let him! He has no power over us unless we give it to him!"

"And we're not going to!" piped up Hope, then curled up as everyone laughed.

"Well said, Hope," said Crispin. "We won't! For myself, I have enough to do with fouldrought, landslides, floods, and Catkin missing, without one troublesome squirrel who doesn't know how to stay dead!"

Thripple gasped. Lugg grinned.

"Good at this, isn't he?" he said.

"What are your fears?" demanded Crispin. "Be honest with yourselves! What do you fear? Do you fear a ghost? Do you fear the unknown? Because the queen comes from a place strange to you, are you afraid of what she might do? Are you afraid of what you see in nightmares or hear in rumors? Are you afraid that I won't govern you well, that Cedar and I and the captains will let you down?"

He stepped forward. All eyes gazed at him.

"Good creatures," he said more slowly, "I know what the island's greatest enemy is, and it moves among us. It has been among us all this time, setting paw against paw, mind against mind, heart against the Heart, as Brother Fir warned. It is the child of ignorance. Its name . . ."

He paused. The silence was tight with waiting.

"Its name is fear," he said. "Fear! I don't mean the healthy fear that makes you careful, but the overwhelming fear that cripples you! Dearest animals, don't plot and whisper about each other. Fill your lives with the enemies of fear! Take love, take hope, take friendship, take music, take laughter, support one another. The Heart has no room for fear!"

There was a brief pause, then the younger animals decided they should applaud, and did, and everyone did, more and more, in a wave of cheering, clapping, and stamping. A breath of wind drifted across the rock, and it was as if that light wind lifted the gloom, the discontent, and the spoken name of fear, and swept it away to sea. The air felt clean.

Crispin held up his paw for silence.

"Now," he said. "If you have questions to ask, come and ask me, or one of the captains. Presently, food will be brought from the tower kitchens so nobody goes home hungry." He turned, scanning the small group of animals behind him. "Where's Juniper?"

"He asked permission to be absent, Your Majesty," said Padra.

"Then I'll give the blessing myself," said Crispin, and raised a paw. "The Heart bless and keep each one of you as you go, as you lie down tonight, and as you rise in the morning."

Some of the animals who lived nearby were wrapping themselves in their cloaks and going home, but most stayed for the warm drinks and food being carried down in carts from the tower. They drifted into little knots and sat down together, chatting and eating and reassuring each other that of course the king was right, or at least, they hoped he was, and how could anybody be unkind about the queen, poor dear? Padra, watching for anyone who wanted to approach the king but might be too shy or uncertain, decided it was time to have a word with Crispin about Juniper, Urchin, and Needle, when a loud, urgent cry of, "Your Majesty!" made all the animals on the high rock turn and be silent. The crowd, too, picked up the silence, put down their bread and beakers and turned to look.

Running from the tower, breathless and dirty, came Urchin. Dust and soil clung to his fur, cobwebs hung from his ears, and blood was on his paws, but in his eyes there was a strength and depth that Crispin had not seen there before. Paws reached out to haul him onto the rock.

"Your Majesty," he gasped, "Needle needs help, and Juniper is with her. And, Your Majesty, nobody need ever question again whether Husk is alive. Juniper has found him. He lies where he fell, broken, with his sword and circlet. I have seen him, Your Majesty. I have been there."

It took very little time for Urchin to explain the situation to Crispin and the captains and for them to assemble a rescue party and send for ropes, slings, and lanterns. While they were doing that, Arran raised the question as to whether other animals should be allowed to go down.

"Oh, I don't know," said Lugg. "There's plenty would be glad of the chance to make sure he's good and proper dead. If they've got the guts to go down there, that is."

"Yes," said Crispin, "but we don't want animals going down just out of curiosity, to have a good look. He's not something to gawp at for entertainment."

"I think the prospect of going down to the bottom of the pit will be enough to put most of them off," said Padra. "But some of them should go. It's not enough for the captains to go down there and say, yes, we've seen him dead. The doubters and worriers should see for themselves."

"Then I'll get the species to choose a representative each," said Crispin. "They can go down in the morning, but they have to be chosen tonight and set to guard the entrances to the place. That way, nobody can claim that the evidence has been tampered with. Two of each would be best. Docken, Russet, Heath, sort them out, please. Now, are we ready? Has anyone found Needle's parents? Urchin, lead the way."

"Well done, Crispin!" said Padra. "That was the work of a real king."

"If you say so," murmured Crispin. "It's marvelous what we can do together—stop landslides, fight off plague, quell rebellion—those three have even found Husk. But between us we can't even find one wild-witted squirrel and my daughter." He lifted his head and raised his voice. "Ready, everyone? Forward!"

When the rescue party had gone, Sepia and Scatter sat on their paws on a landing in the tower. There was nothing they could do to help with the rescue of Needle and Juniper, nothing but wait until they were brought out, and they had decided to do that here, in the quietness of the tower as twilight grew. It was good to be away at last from the bustle of animals scurrying about outside, and Sepia felt she needed time to be quiet and think about Damson. So she sat on the stairs watching the sky behind the window turn dim with twilight, holding Urchin, Juniper, and Needle before the Heart, because sometimes her friends seemed too heavy for her own heart to carry. They had been away for such a long time, or perhaps it just seemed like that. Then Scatter, who was getting bored but didn't like to say so, said, "Shall we go and see if Brother Fir is all right?"

"Oh, yes," said Sepia. "We ought to see if he needs anything." They pattered up the stairs to the turret, tapped at the door, and waited to be called in—but when they stepped into the chamber they both curtsied, because the queen, thinner than ever, sat at Brother Fir's side.

"Your Majesty!" they said.

"Well, what excellent company," said Fir, and though his voice was frail he seemed to Sepia to be more like his old self. His deep eyes twinkled. "Three of the finest young animals on the island, all at once. I must be a dangerous old scoundrel, you know, if it takes three of you to keep me out of mischief."

"We came to see if you needed anything, Brother Fir," said Scatter.

"That was most kind of you," said Brother Fir. "As you see, I am finally out of bed, and the queen herself made up cordials for me. But I shall go back to bed soon. Sepia, Scatter, my dears, would you be most kind and close my window?"

Glad to have something to do, Sepia scurried across the floor to fasten the window. In spite of the gray fingers of fog coming in with the tide, it was turning into a beautiful evening. The sky was gray-violet now, with a few stars and a track of moonlight reflected across the rippling sea.

Something was moving on the water. It must be a boat from the other side of the island or one of the otter patrol. But, as she narrowed her eyes, she could see it wasn't an otter rowing it . . . it could be . . .

"Please, Your Majesty," she said, "come and look at this."

Then Cedar, Scatter, and Sepia were leaping down the stairs, calling for the guards, the messengers, and Crispin.

At the top of the underground cliff, Crispin, Padra, Lugg, and the other chosen animals stood surrounded by lanterns and candles. It seemed so much safer to Urchin, now that all the others were there, and there was more light. With a long rope tied to Docken's waist, and the strongest of the animals lined up in front of him all holding firmly on to it, a sling was lowered over the edge of the cliff. There were a few muffled squeaks and a clanking of buckles, then Juniper's voice came echoing from far beneath them.

"Haul her up gently," he said. "She's hurt."

"Ready!" called Docken. Presently, Needle's taut, brave face appeared over the edge of the cliff, and in a few seconds Crispin had lifted her clear of the sling.

"Lower it for Juniper," he ordered. "Needle, how are you feeling?"

"It hurts," said Needle. Her voice wasn't very strong, but she tried to smile. "I'll be all right. Hello, Urchin."

"Take her back up to the top, Urchin," Crispin ordered, "to your own chamber at the Spring Gate. Lugg, they'll need help. Can you carry her between you?"

"How heavy do you think I am?" demanded Needle weakly. Crispin left Urchin and Needle exchanging stories as she was carried away, while he looked over the cliff edge as Juniper was hauled up. He was dirty, bloodstained, and trying not to shiver, but on his face was a calmness that nobody who saw it ever forgot. He looked, they thought afterward, like Brother Fir. Crispin looked gravely into Juniper's face.

"Well done, Juniper," he said. "Well done. Are you all right?"

"Yes, Your Majesty," said Juniper, and knew that he should explain to Crispin why he'd done what he'd done, and he supposed he should apologize because it was his fault that Needle was hurt—but somehow he couldn't find the words. And Crispin said nothing to question or to blame him, but just held him by the shoulders and said, "Is it all over now?"

"I didn't just do it for me," said Juniper. "It was for the island. And for you. There was a prophecy."

"I understand," said Crispin, and took off his cloak. "Put that on, you're frozen. Now, I want to go down there and see for myself. Don't bother with the sling. If those two can manage a jump like that, so can I."

He took a step or two back to prepare for the leap. But before he could move farther, there was a racing of paws toward them, and Longpaw flew through the doorway.

"Your Majesty!" he cried. "Catkin! Linty, in a boat, heading for the mists!"

The wind was rising as Sepia ran around the shore and scampered onto a high rock to give herself the best possible overall view. Animals were clustered on the shore around Arran who was giving instructions, holding back those who were determined to swim out or already hauling their boats down to the water.

"If she's desperate enough to row for the mists, she's desperate enough for anything," called Arran. "She's rowing a heavy boat against the tide, which should slow her down. The queen has given orders, all the way through this, that we mustn't make Linty panic. Still, I'll see if she'll listen to me." She took off her circlet and passed it to a small otter called Skye. "Hang on to that for me, please. I'll go alone, or she may take fright. Have two or three boats ready, but don't do anything until you have orders from the king or Padra." And she launched herself into the water.

Sepia stayed where she was, hugging her cloak about her against the chill, watching for every squirrel and every mole who ran across the shore. She had to think of Urchin and Lugg now, who had gone beyond the mists twice and somehow returned safely. Nobody had ever done it a third time. Catkin might not be the only one who needed saving.

She could see them, Urchin and Lugg, carrying Needle between them, with two adult hedgehogs who must be Needle's parents. It looked as if Lugg and Urchin were going to end up in the same place, which made her task a lot easier.

Following them was easy, too. They were slowed down by carrying Needle, and by stopping now and again to ask some passing animal what was happening. The Spring Gate, it looked as if they were on their way to the Spring Gate. Good.

She wasn't sure if she could ask the Heart to help her in what she meant to do, but perhaps she could ask to be forgiven for it. *Heart, please understand why I'm doing this and I'm sorry, but I have to.*

She caught up with them as they headed to the Spring Gate, chatting, asking after Needle, running ahead of them to open the chamber door, strike a spark for the fire, and shake a blanket over Urchin's nest. She filled a jug of water from the spring. Then, leaving them all fussing over Needle, she slipped quietly out and closed the door behind her.

There was no lock on that door. Pity. She looked about and found a heap of driftwood which was probably meant for fires. She took a plank that looked about the right size, jammed it under the door, whispered "Sorry!" and ran.

She flew up the nearest stair, racing along empty corridors, up flight after flight of stairs, past Threadings, and empty workrooms, past windows that opened to the twilight, until she stood breathlessly at the door of Fir's turret, feeling the fierce, fast pounding of her own heart.

She had done one bad thing for a good reason. Now, she would have to do another. She *had* to. Trying not to think of what she was doing, she slipped in. There was enough light to show the loose stone in the hearth.

"Heart forgive me," she whispered.

When Juniper had taken the Heartstone from its box, she had been deeply shocked. But once before it had helped to bring Urchin home, so perhaps it would protect her, too. She wouldn't even open the gleaming box, just pick it up and put it in a satchel.

No, she wouldn't.

She couldn't. Every instinct told her not to. She turned to leave.

"Dearest daughter," said Fir.

"Door's jammed," said Lugg. "Give us a paw, Urchin."

Urchin hopped to his side and tugged at the solid, heavy, old door.

There was no movement at all. He curled his claws against the edge and tugged, but nothing happened.

"We're trapped!" said Needle.

"We're not," said Lugg, who was lying down inspecting the floor. "There's a great plank under here. Dunno how it got there, but we'll get it out. Perhaps you two hedgehogs could give us a paw?"

The plank was wedged so tightly that not all their heaving could move it. Lugg stood back, gulping for breath.

"We'll have to scrabble the earth away to loosen it," he said. "Everyone get scrabbling."

Sepia gazed toward the window as she told Brother Fir why she was there.

"I'm sorry for what I meant to do," she said. She couldn't believe she'd intended to do anything so terrible. "It's just that I think Linty might listen to me because she won't be afraid of me. She's trying to get beyond the mists, and on a night like this, it's hard to tell what's real Mistmantle mist, and what's just the weather, I mean, the fog sort of mist. I'm afraid of following her and not being able to get back, so I wanted the Heartstone to help me. But when I got here, I knew I couldn't take it."

"Of course," said Brother Fir.

"So I'd better go now," she said. "I've wasted too much time already."

Brother Fir smiled with such kindness that she wished she could stay there, drinking in the wisdom and love in those eyes. "Then go, child. Put your trust in the Heart, not the Heartstone. And go quickly, with my blessing."

Sepia dashed back down the stairs. Brother Fir hobbled to the window, where he raised a paw and turned his face to the shore. Between mists, fog, and gathering dark, it was hard to see anything much. Brother Fir prayed steadily into cloud and darkness.

CHAPTER TWENTY

THE BREEZE WAS STIRRING THE WAVES, thinning and mixing the fog that had rolled in so that it was hard to tell where fog ended and the mists began. Sepia, running to the shore with one paw clasping her cloak, saw boats bobbing on the water and the two figures of Cedar and Crispin, ankle deep in the sea, as they called out. Padra stood a little behind them. Soon she was close enough to see the stretched, strained hope and fear on their faces, and the way Queen Cedar still clutched the naming blanket in her paws, as if she couldn't wait to wrap Catkin in it and hold her. Then Arran glided through the water and shook herself dry.

"She won't have anything to do with me," said Arran. "If I try to get nearer, she just rows farther away. She won't trust any of us. Juniper's in a boat close to her and she hasn't sent him away, but she won't let him any nearer either."

"She'll listen to me," said Cedar.

"I don't think she will, Your Majesty," said Arran. "She's got it into her head that Catkin is her own baby and you want to take her away. If you go near her, she really will go through the mists. You have to stand back, and we'll find someone she'll listen to. Mother Huggen, perhaps? Or one of the young ones?"

Sepia looked about for an empty boat. There wasn't one. Something warm brushed past her leg, and she looked down to see Fingal rolling in the sand, looking up at her.

"Otters are better than boats," he said. "Want a ride?"

"I'll be too heavy," she said.

"You?" he said. "Just let me get into the water first."

As Fingal loped into the shallows, Sepia ran to the queen. "Please, Your Majesty," she said, "Catkin's blanket? May I take it out to her?"

The queen, straining to see the boat as it moved farther away, didn't even seem to have heard her.

"Please, Your Majesty?" she said again, and held out her paws.

The queen seemed to wake from a trance. She pushed the blanket into Sepia's paws.

"Go, then, Sepia," she said. "Heart bless you. Take care, don't . . ."

Sepia ran away before she could hear the queen say, "Don't go beyond the mists," because that might be the very thing she had to do. She heard Crispin shout out her name, as if he might be calling her back, but she was already throwing her cloak on the shore and gasping at the coldness of the water.

"I'll stay at a distance," said Padra, and slipped into the water after them.

As lightly as she could, Sepia hopped onto Fingal's back and twisted her tail for balance. She knelt, holding on with her forepaws, the blanket clenched in her paw to keep it dry.

"Freezing!" she gasped through her teeth as Fingal plunged forward.

"No it isn't!" cried Fingal.

Sepia tried to keep her balance on the smooth, wet body of the otter as he surged through the lifting waves. When she dared to look up, she saw the moon through breaks in the blowing clouds and fog in the wild sky. When she looked down, she saw lapping waves with, here and there, a glint of moonlight or starlight. And as Fingal rushed on, she could see more clearly the outline of Linty's boat, getting nearer and nearer to the mists.

She didn't dare look behind her in case she fell, so she didn't see Urchin flying down to the beach with Lugg lumbering after him. But Padra, twisting in the water, had seen them and swam to meet them.

"If Sepia and Fingal are going, they could do with an escort boat," said Urchin, when Padra had explained everything to him. "And I'm young, so she might not be afraid of me. Let me go, sir."

"Stay this side of the mists," ordered Padra. He waved at Docken, who was in the nearest boat, and summoned him in. "Docken, I could do with you on shore. Urchin and Lugg, row as near to Linty as you can without scaring her. Lugg, take off your circlet. Any sign of a captain, and we've lost her."

"But, sir," said Docken, "if she did try to scarper into the mists, it would be easy enough to catch up with her, and we'd all be more than a match for her, even if she did put up a fight."

"Yes," said Padra, "but in the course of that, the baby could end up in the water, and we don't want a drowned princess. We won't storm the boat unless we absolutely have to."

Sepia could see more clearly now and was balanced more confidently. She held on with one forepaw while taking the blanket from her teeth and holding it round her neck, not to keep herself warm but to keep the blanket dry. Shivering on Fingal's back, she tried to work out what she'd say to Linty. Linty sat forward in the boat, rowing with steady determination. Juniper, seeing Sepia and Fingal, rowed toward them.

"She won't listen to me," he said. "You might have more of a chance, being a girl. Can you get near her? We'll all stay close and come if you call."

"Not too close," said Sepia. "Perhaps if she sees a boat, she thinks someone's going to put Catkin into it. I haven't got a boat, just Fingal."

"*Just* Fingal?" said Fingal. "Shall I see if I can get alongside her?"

"Yes, please," said Sepia, "but stop if I tell you."

He swam on, and all the time Sepia could see more clearly. She saw the intensity in Linty's wild eyes and heard a gentle whimpering from the bottom of the boat.

"Slow down, Fingal," she said softly.

Fingal slowed down just in time. Linty jerked upright in the boat so that it rocked dangerously, and Sepia gasped with fear for the baby. It rocked again as Linty stopped to pick up something from the bottom of the boat, and just in time Sepia ducked low over Fingal's head. A stone flew past her.

"I won't harm you, Linty," she called, "I've come to help. I've brought you the baby's blanket, I heard her crying for it."

"Keep away!" shouted Linty. She scooped up another stone and stood holding it in her upraised paw. The baby's crying sounded louder, so that Sepia longed to hold her.

"She needs her blanket," she urged gently. "Let me bring it for her. It's her own special one, she has to have it. She—she'll get ill without it."

Two small paws appeared over the side of the boat, followed by the tufts of two squirrel ears. With a leap of her heart, Sepia saw the small, bright face of Catkin, gazing in fascination over the side of the boat.

"Get down, my darling," said Linty. "Dangerous." Awkwardly, with a suspicious glance at Sepia, she shipped the oars and reached out for the baby.

"I'm watching you, girl!" she called. With one paw she pressed Catkin back into the boat, waving wildly with the other. "Keep back, you!"

"It's all right, Linty," said Sepia. "I came to help you. Shall I row for you while you look after the baby?"

"You'll try something," muttered Linty, struggling to control the wriggling baby and the boat at the same time, as they drifted toward the mist. "I don't trust you."

"I think you should trust someone," said Sepia. "You can't keep rowing and keep the baby still at the same time, and you don't want her to fall in. What would you like me to do for you?"

Linty held tightly to the baby as the boat rocked. *The girl's right. Pity. Let her row. I can push her out if she's any trouble.*

"Go on, then," she grumbled. "You can take the oars for a bit, just until she settles. Keep that otter back."

"I'll send him back when I'm in the boat, I promise," said Sepia. "But I can't swim and keep the blanket dry at the same time."

"He'll get the oar across his skull if he gets too close," warned Linty, watching Fingal ferociously.

"When I'm in the boat, Fingal, swim away, fast as you can," said Sepia quickly, and struggled to keep her balance as she stood up on his wet back and scrambled into Linty's little boat. She took Linty's place on the wet rowing bench and reached for the oars, the cold air on her wet limbs sending shivers all the way through her so that her teeth chattered. As the moonlight shone through a gap in the clouds, she saw Linty's face clearly.

Linty had grown haggard since taking the baby. Her eyes were wild, suspicious, and, to Sepia, quite insane.

Catkin looked well enough, though, as Linty wrapped her in the blanket and cradled her. The baby looked brightly at Sepia—it was a long time since she had seen any face but Linty's, and this one intrigued her. Sepia smiled, and Catkin smiled delightedly back at her.

"Stop that!" ordered Linty. "Just you row to the mists, girl."

Sepia rowed as slowly as she could. It was so hard to tell whether it was only fog that drifted past her, or the mists. She hoped it was fog. *Trust the Heart and not the Heartstone.*

"Get right away, you otter!" Linty shouted at Fingal. "And that squirrel who says he's a priest, he has to go. Brother Fir's the priest, not him. That evil captain must have sent him."

"The evil captain's dead, Linty," said Sepia through chattering teeth. "He can't hurt you, and he can't hurt the baby."

"I said, send that squirrel away!" shrieked Linty. "And row faster!"

"You'll have to go, Juniper!" called Sepia, and tried to look as if she was rowing faster, though all the time her heart reached out to Juniper and Fingal as they moved away from her. *The mists are at my back and I'll never see you again . . . should I grab the baby and swim for it . . . but she'd kill me and the baby would drown. . . . Heart help me. . . .*

She forced herself to concentrate. She had to stay one step ahead of Linty. She rowed very lightly, knowing that the tide was against them.

"Captain Husk is dead, Mistress Linty," she said. "Nobody's allowed to kill babies anymore."

"Is that right?" asked Linty, but the wary look was still on her face. "You're lying. I heard them talking about him. He's back."

"No," said Sepia. "They were wrong about that. He really is dead." *Admire the baby. She'll like that.* "She's a very beautiful baby. You've taken great care of her."

"'Course I have," said Linty, looking proudly into Catkin's face.

"What's her name?" asked Sepia.

"Ca . . . Daisy," said Linty. "I called her Daisy."

"And whose baby is she?"

"Why, she's mine, of course," snapped Linty. "Whose should she be?" She hugged Catkin tightly. "The king and queen think she's theirs, but they're wrong. This is my baby. They didn't know how to look after their little baby, so they lost her." She yawned, then said again, "She's mine. This is my Daisy."

"I see," said Sepia, thinking hard, though freezing wet fur made it hard to think at all. "Would you like to take Daisy home to her nest? Her own warm little nest that you've made for her?"

"Keep rowing!" said Linty, but she yawned again.

The yawns gave Sepia hope. Nobody could stay awake forever, and Linty must have spent long hours awake, guarding Catkin. As she rowed, she began softly to sing the old Mistmantle lullaby as the boat rocked them. . . .

> *"Waves of the seas*
> *Wind in the trees*
> *Spring scented breeze . . .*

Linty must be tired. Sepia finished the lullaby and without a break began again, Linty singing it with her. But Linty's singing gradually became slurred and broken, and Sepia dared to steal a glimpse at her. Her eyes were closing and opening again.

Sepia still sang. Linty drooped, fighting sleep, then jerked up and pulled Catkin more firmly onto her lap, but every time her eyes closed they stayed closed for a little longer. Gradually, still singing, Sepia lifted one oar and rowed with the other, turning the boat round, all the time watching Linty and Catkin.

Catkin was slipping from Linty's grasp. Should she catch her and risk waking Linty? With a sleepy snarl, Linty scrambled to gather Catkin onto her lap again and settled down to sleep. Sepia still sang, still rowed away from the mists, as Linty opened her eyes a little.

"You've got to get through those mists," she slurred sleepily.

"We are going through them," said Sepia.

She was watching Linty's face so intently that she didn't see the large, rough plank of driftwood bobbing toward them. It didn't hit the boat hard, but hard enough to shake Linty. Startled and fully awake, she looked about her.

"Where are we going? Why are we . . ." she stood up in the boat, clutching Catkin as she gazed about. "That's not the mists, that's a bit of lifting fog! You're going the wrong way!"

"No!" said Sepia. "It's quicker this way, we're . . ."

"Don't you lie to me!" snarled Linty. "Give me those oars! Out of my boat!"

"All right!" said Sepia. "I'll turn the boat around!"

"Out of my boat!" screamed Linty, and in a swift movement she had put Catkin down and lunged with outstretched claws at Sepia. Sepia seized Catkin. The boat was flung from side to side; Catkin was crying and clinging to Sepia who huddled over her. . . .

"Daisy!" screamed Linty—and she hurled herself again at Sepia with a force that sent all three of them tumbling from the boat as it overturned.

The power of shock and cold took Sepia's breath away, salt water filled her mouth, as, desperate and suffocating, she kicked her way to the surface. Still clutching the baby, she shook water from her eyes and gasped.

For a strange, wild moment it seemed that the stars were riding or that she was in the sky among them, but as her sight cleared, she realized that she was looking up at them as the wind blew clouds apart. She looked for the boat, but it was upside down and floating away from her.

Then I am dying, thought Sepia, I must be dying, because I can see silver on the sea, a silver path leading all the way to the shore, and there can be no such thing. Then she blinked again and saw that the track of silver was real. It was moonlight, the trail of reflected silver-white moonlight on water, showing her that same plank of driftwood as it floated just in front of her. She struck out for it with her one free paw, clawed her way onto it, and, soaked, shivering uncontrollably, with chattering teeth, yelled for help, though she was still so shocked and frozen that her voice was a feeble thread.

"Juniper! Fingal! Help!" she cried. "Padra, Urchin, Arran, somebody help!"

Above her voice rose the baby's high wail of distress. She knelt on the driftwood, balancing with one forepaw, clutching Catkin with the other, so chilled that she had to look down to make sure she still held the baby firmly, for her paws could no longer feel anything but the sting of cold. *Oh, Heart help me! When things like this happen to Urchin, the Heart sends riding stars, or the Heartstone . . .* then she heard an otter's voice, and the splash of oars.

The Heart heard me. The Heart sent me the otters. . . . for the sheer joy of hope she was laughing as she rode the track of moonlight, hugging Catkin and crying out.

"Juniper! Fingal! Over here!" She hugged Catkin tightly. "Don't cry, sweetheart. We're nearly home to Mummy."

"Well done, Sepia." It was Padra's voice, calm and reassuring as he and Fingal glided alongside her. With a cry of relief she fell onto his back, sinking one paw into wet fur. Looking over her shoulder, she saw Linty grasping at the driftwood.

"It's all right now, Mistress Linty," said Fingal gently. "I'll take you home."

Sepia crouched over Padra's back as they swished forward, fast and sure along the moon track. She didn't dare look back again for fear of falling, but she heard Fingal shouting, "I'll need some help here," and Padra calling for Lugg and Urchin. Then there was the steady ripple of oars and the splash of swimmers. A boat was riding toward them so that the sea rocked more wildly and she bit her lip in fear, but Padra held his course, and she sang the lullaby for the baby and for herself until strong paws were taking Catkin from her; warm, dry paws were lifting her into the boat; and a dry blanket was wrapped around her.

"Well done, you!" It was her brother, Longpaw the messenger, in the light of moon and lanterns. Then Crispin stepped across the boat and hugged her, and suddenly everyone seemed to be hugging her, so that she had to peer past Longpaw and over Crispin's shoulder to see the one thing she really wanted to see—the sight of Catkin and Cedar hugging tightly and tearfully together on the floor of the rocking boat, as Longpaw took the oars and turned for the shore.

"L . . . L . . . Linty," stammered Sepia. She was still too numb to speak clearly.

"They've gone after her," said Cedar calmly. "Linty will be all right."

CHAPTER TWENTY-ONE

PLAGUE AND LICE, I HATE BOATS," said Lugg. "Might as well be in the water as on it. But I wouldn't have missed seeing Miss Sepia with that baby."

Urchin shipped the oars and leaned forward. "There she is," he said.

Tense and shivering, Linty crouched on the driftwood. She stared wide-eyed into the dark.

"Mistress Linty!" called Urchin.

Her head jerked around. "Who's that?"

"I'm Urchin," he called back. "Urchin of the Riding Stars. Are you looking for your baby?"

A shudder seemed to convulse Linty from head to tail tip. "You got her?"

"She's safe," said Urchin. "We'll take you to her."

"I sent that otter away," warned Linty. She cowered wearily, but she allowed them to row alongside her.

"Give us a paw, then, Mistress," said Lugg. He heaved the soaked and shivering squirrel into the boat, took off his old blue cloak, and wrapped it tightly round her. "There, now, we'll get you dry and warmed up. Your baby's all right now."

"Where's the baby?" she demanded, looking all about her.

"We're taking you to her," said Urchin. He saw the way she gazed at the top of Lugg's head where the imprint of a circlet still showed in his smooth black fur.

"You're a captain," she said. Her voice was low and accusing.

"Me, Mistress?" said Lugg. "Just a plain old mole, that's me."

She continued to stare, and Urchin rowed a little faster. That ring where the circlet had pressed plainly troubled her. Linty did not trust captains. She was deranged enough to have any sort of twisted ideas in her head and to act on them. He rowed harder still. The shore was a long way off. It was a relief to hear Fingal call from somewhere not far away. Help was there if needed. Linty still crouched, her eyes flickering from Urchin to Lugg and back.

The more Urchin thought of that moment afterward, the more he knew that there was no warning, no sound, no movement, nothing to make Linty do what she did. Nobody alarmed her, nothing changed. With a scream of fury and the silver flash of a blade, she sprang at him.

Urchin ducked to one side, pulling in the oars, but she was already upon him, biting and clawing, and he saw the gleam of the knife raised to kill. He tried to stretch out a paw to catch her wrist, but her teeth held his arm. As he thrashed, kicked, fought, and struggled, he heard her howl again, with rage and frustration.

"Get off me, you evil mole!"

Lugg had seized her and was dragging her away. In the furiously rocking boat, Urchin struggled to his paws, pried the knife from her claws, and sprang to help Lugg; but before he could land, Linty had lurched so furiously that she and Lugg hurtled into the sea. Yelling for help, Urchin wrenched the oar from its place and held it out, keeping the blade under the churning waves.

"Lugg!" he shouted. "Grab the oar! Fingal!"

Otters were already swimming toward them. There must be a rope in the boat—he found it and threw it, but there was no answering pull. Fingal and Arran seared through the water, disappearing under the surface where Linty and Lugg had fallen. More otters were swimming to them, more boats were coming, the water thrashed and heaved as Urchin gazed helplessly into the baffling darkness of the sea.

"Get them out!" he yelled as an otter swirled beneath them. "Please, please, get them out!"

A squirrel's paw appeared on the side of the boat. Juniper emerged from the sea, shaking his ears, and Urchin heaved him into the boat.

"The otters have got them," he said. "But it's not good. Urchin!" There was a quick, convulsive shudder. "That knife!"

"Linty's," said Urchin. "We didn't know she had it."

"Oh," said Juniper. "Linty's!" *A knife. A blue cloak.*

With a smooth surge through the water, Fingal and another otter appeared. Between them they held Linty, feebly coughing and spluttering as they towed her to the boat. After them, slowly, as if dragging a heavy weight, came Padra and Arran with Captain Lugg.

Urchin and Juniper reached down to drag him into the boat. There was a cough, and a sort of moan as if he were trying to speak.

"He's alive," said Juniper. "Where's his cloak?"

Urchin pounced on the blue cloak. It lay in the boat where Linty had dropped it, but her wet fur had soaked it.

"We need cloaks and blankets, here, now!" yelled Padra to whichever boat was nearest. He and Arran held Lugg in their arms as he coughed and spluttered seawater from his lungs. "Get him to dry land. I'll swim, the boat will be faster without me. Arran, stay with him. You two, row as you've never rowed."

Someone threw a blanket from another boat, and Arran wrapped it tightly around Lugg as Urchin and Juniper threw all their strength into rowing, powerful stroke after powerful stroke, as if they could hurl the boat to shore. They were within sight of lanterns now, with other boats escorting them, and as the mists cleared they could see the highest lights of the tower. Urchin's shoulders burned as he strained at the oars, but the swirling fog was clearing, and beneath the light of lanterns he could see Crispin and Cedar standing on the shore, looking out to sea, with Catkin cradled in blankets in the queen's arms. Padra and Fingal were swimming around to either side of them, and soon they were behind the boat, pushing and urging her home.

"I'll take a turn at an oar now," said Arran. "You two will be tiring. Urchin, move over."

Urchin changed places with her, taking Captain Lugg's head in his lap. "Nearly there now, Lugg," he said.

"'Bout time, young 'un," said Lugg, with a shaky grin, and Urchin thought he was about to say something else, but the words never came. He seemed to be struggling to speak, or even to breathe. One paw clutched at his forearm as if it hurt, and in an effort to speak, he gasped and wheezed. Juniper stopped rowing and leaned forward, reaching for Lugg's paw.

"Don't try to talk, Lugg," said Arran, but Lugg didn't seem to hear her.

"Well, Heart bless us!" he said suddenly, as if pleasantly surprised. There was a soft, smothered gasp of pain and no more. His head fell to one side in Urchin's lap.

"Lugg!" cried Urchin and bent over him, listening for a breath, feeling for a pulse. In disbelief, he looked up at Arran and Juniper. They had to tell him that Lugg was alive, that he'd be all right, because losing Lugg was unthinkable. They were both feeling for a pulse. Arran listened at Lugg's chest and placed a paw over his heart.

"Do something!" begged Urchin. He rubbed Lugg's cold paws, wrapped the blanket around him, and tried to warm him. "We have to do something! Juniper, do something!"

Arran straightened up.

"It's too late," she said. "There's nothing we can do."

"But it's Lugg!" cried Urchin. "You have to save him!"

"It's too late," she repeated. "I'm sorry, Urchin. He's dead."

It didn't make sense. Lugg had always been there, as if there couldn't be a Mistmantle without him. But there was nothing they could do.

Juniper raised a paw and said the words of blessing.

"May the Heart claim you with joy and forgive you with love," he said. "May your heart fly freely to the Heart that gave you life."

Urchin took the wet blue cloak and covered the old soldier's body. Juniper took the oars as Arran and Padra swam on either side. Crispin waded out to pull the boat in, and together, in silence and with honor, they brought a hero of Mistmantle home.

CHAPTER TWENTY-TWO

ATKIN SLEPT SWEETLY AND SOUNDLY in her own cradle that night. Perhaps she and the little otters were the only animals in the tower who could sleep.

As a fiery dawn crossed the sky, Cedar and Crispin lay in each other's arms, watching Catkin's steady breathing as she slept with her paw in her mouth and her naming shawl spread over her. Sepia, after a hot bath, had been escorted to bed by one of the queen's attendants, but she couldn't sleep and slipped down to the kitchens where she joined Scatter and Crackle to huddle by the grate and sip cordials for comfort.

By the Spring Gate, Padra, Arran, Fingal, and Urchin sat up by the fire, looking into the flames, saying little. Needle had been carried to her home burrow where her mother had made her a nest. It was only after reaching the shore that Urchin had felt the stinging of Linty's bites and scratches, and he had submitted quietly as Padra washed the wounds. Whittle came to knock timidly at the door.

"Master Urchin to the Gathering Chamber, please," he said softly.

"Thanks, Whittle, I'll be up in a minute," said Urchin. He stood up, the scratches hurting as he moved.

"Juniper's been up there with Mistress Cott and the rest of Lugg's family," he explained. "But when they said they wanted animals to stand on watch beside him, I said I'd like to take first watch. I should, because . . ."

"We know," said Padra, but Urchin still felt he had to say it.

"He was saving me," said Urchin. "He was pulling Linty off me when he fell. And I keep going over it again and wishing so much that it could have been different. I can't believe this has happened." He fastened on his sword as he left the chamber, and Padra slipped out after him.

"Urchin," he said, with a paw on Urchin's shoulder, "Lugg's heart was old and tired already. It would have happened, sooner or later. Probably sooner. It might have happened last night anyway, even if he'd been at home in his own bed."

"I wish he had been, all the same," said Urchin, and followed Whittle silently through corridors that felt subdued with grief.

In the Gathering Chamber, a table had been spread with a purple cloth to receive the body of Captain Lugg. He lay in his best blue cloak, his paws folded, like a well-fed and contented mole settling down for sleep. But he wore his sword and circlet, polished until they shone in the candlelight.

Lugg's wife, Mistress Cott, stood at his side, her paw over his, looking down at his face with patient resignation. The three daughters were there, Wing, Wren, and Moth, with their husbands and Twigg the carpenter. Tipp and Todd leaned against their mother. Moth looked pink-eyed and tearful and sat apart from the others talking to Brother Fir, who had been given a chair a little way from the table. A step at the door made Urchin turn, and he bowed, for it was King Crispin, who embraced Mistress Cott in a warm hug and greeted each of the family in turn.

"I suppose, Your Majesty," said Moth, "if his heart was going to just stop like that, he'd be glad to die the way he did. But I still wish he could have died by his own fireside, telling his old stories with all of us around. I wish he'd had that chance."

"So do I," said Crispin. "We'll all tell his stories, and his own story, too. He will be in the Threadings. I, too, wish he could have grown old. Who is on first watch?"

"I am, Your Majesty," said Urchin.

"Good," said Crispin. "I'll share it with you. Mistress Cott, all of you, stay as long as you wish." He knelt to speak to Tipp and Todd. "You'll always remember your grandfather, and you'll always be proud of him, I know."

"I'm going to be like him when I grow up, Your Majesty," said Tipp, with a determined tilt of the chin.

"Everyone says I'm like him already, Your Majesty," said Todd.

"You are," said Crispin. "Both of you." He stood up. "Ready, Urchin?"

After Crispin and Urchin's watch came Padra and Docken, Arran and Cedar, Russet and Heath, Needle and Longpaw, Moth and Spade, as all that day and into the next, animals stunned with grief tiptoed into the Gathering Chamber to pay their respects to Captain Lugg. Apple came by, dabbing at her eyes with a bunch of petals, stopping to squeeze Urchin's paw. Thripple walked past, pink-eyed, holding Mopple in her arms with Hope walking alongside. Hope had brought a posy of autumn leaves and seed heads and stretched up to place them at Lugg's side. Quill, Yarrow, and Hobb came with their families. Crackle and Scatter crept shyly in, and Gleaner, too, who had never even liked Lugg. There was Fingal, leading Tide and Swanfeather by the paws. Tower animals, shore animals, animals from Anemone Wood, the Tangletwigs, the Western Woods, and Falls Cliffs, from trees and tunnels; they filed past, some leaving dried leaves or flower heads beside him until Captain Lugg lay garlanded in the gifts and the love of Mistmantle.

"I've had a long time with the best mole that ever dug the earth," said Mistress Cott. "I'd wish him alive to grow old, but I don't know that it would suit him. And I'd wish him alive to see Moth and Twigg married, and the young ones grown up. But there's always much to wish for and much to thank for, and just now, I'd rather be thankful."

Sepia had returned from the kitchen to the room that had been set aside for her to find a large and smiling hedgehog with an autumn garland in his paws.

"For Miss Sepia, with the thanks of the king and queen," he said. "Breakfast has been laid in your chamber for you."

The breakfast consisted of so many of Sepia's favorite things that she wondered how they knew what she liked. There was hazelnut bread, honey—she was very glad of the honey, as her throat was hurting after a night of damp air and salt water—cobnuts, berries with a dish of cream, and a silver pot of spiced cordial. She ate a little, to be polite, but she wasn't hungry. Presently, Scatter was sent to keep her company and together they slipped to the Gathering Chamber to say their farewell to Captain Lugg, then returned to the chamber so that they could cry without being disturbed. After that, Sepia was just wondering what she was meant to do next and whether she'd be allowed to go home when there was a knock at the door, and a wide-eyed mole maid came in, staring at Sepia as if she were seeing a vision.

"The queen wishes Miss Sepia to go to her chambers, please," she whispered. Sepia brushed down her fur, glanced in the nearest mirror, smoothed her ear tufts, and presently appeared, curtsying, at the royal chambers.

Queen Cedar was holding Catkin against her shoulder, rocking her and patting her back, pressing her cheek against the soft baby fur so that Sepia smiled with delight. It was almost as if they had never been separated.

"Is she asleep, Your Majesty?" asked Sepia.

Cedar turned to show the baby's face. Catkin, clutching her blanket, was not remotely asleep. She gazed with huge eyes at Sepia and squeaked.

"Are you well this morning, Sepia?" asked the queen. "I didn't send for you earlier in case you needed to sleep—or couldn't you sleep?"

"No, Your Majesty, I couldn't," said Sepia. "But that's all right, I mean—I mean I think I was just too excited to sleep."

"As we all were," said Cedar. "Dear Sepia, what you did for the island and for us is beyond measure. The whole island is talking of you, and quite rightly, too."

"Oh!" said Sepia in surprise. For a moment she was lost for words, then she said quickly, "Well, never mind, Madam, they'll soon stop it."

"Sepia of the Singing Voice and the Quiet Spirit," said the queen, smiling, "is there any service the island can give you, after what you have done?"

Sepia, at a loss to know how to answer, wondered if it would be all right to say no. She couldn't think of anything at all that she wanted.

"Perhaps you need time to think," said Cedar. Catkin held out her paws, and the queen placed her gently in Sepia's arms.

"Your Majesty," she said, "what will happen to Linty?"

"She is in the care of the healers," said the queen gravely. "She will stay there as long as she needs to, which may be all her life."

"I'm very sorry for her," said Sepia. "I know she meant well, but . . ."

"Yes," said the queen. "But there's always a reason for animals to behave the way they do. It may not be a good reason. It may be a very bad one, or an insane one, but there is always a reason."

Catkin wriggled to get down and Sepia held her paws as she tried to walk. She had managed a step or two with Sepia behind her, holding her upraised paws, when the door was thrown open, and Crispin came in with Urchin following. Catkin gave a giggle of recognition as Crispin swept her into his arms.

"Hello, Sepia!" he said, and kissed her. "I was afraid Catkin would forget who I was. Urchin and I have just come off duty. We haven't had much chance to talk to either of you two about last night. I assume you've both heard each other's stories."

"I heard what you did, Sepia," said Urchin. "It was wonderful. I would have been there to go with you, but . . ." He looked up at Crispin. "Your Majesty, I haven't told you this yet. Lugg and I both would have got there sooner, but we couldn't get out of my chamber at the Spring Gate."

"Strange," said Crispin. Sepia bent her head over the cup and sipped her cordial.

"Yes, Your Majesty," said Urchin. "The door jammed because there was a wooden plank wedged underneath it. It wasn't there when we went in, or we would have noticed it. We got out by scrabbling away the loose earth around it and wriggling it out. I don't know how it got there."

"Do you think it was done on purpose?" asked Crispin, and Sepia heard the edge of concern in his voice. She stared out the window, seeing nothing, feeling the heat in her face and wondering if it showed.

"I don't understand who could have done it or why," said Urchin. "I don't even know who was around, but it didn't put itself there."

"Thank you for telling me, Urchin," said Crispin. "If anything else suspicious happens, tell me. There may be something going on that we need to be aware of."

Sepia gulped down the rest of her drink so quickly that she spluttered and her eyes watered. The queen sprang to her paws and offered her the water jug.

"I'm all right, really," she croaked. "I . . . um . . ." She gathered her courage and looked up to face King Crispin. "May I speak to you alone for a moment, Your Majesty?"

"Of course you may," said Crispin, and Cedar said something about going to take Catkin to Mother Huggen.

"And may I go and find Fingal?" asked Urchin, and was dismissed.

Sepia stood before the king, feeling very small, trying to control the trembling of her paws. Crispin was always kind and understanding, but she felt sure that even his patience could wear out. She took a deep breath.

"Please, Your Majesty, I'm afraid you'll be angry, but I was the one who shut Captain Lugg and Urchin in the chamber, but I did it because I had to. I pushed that wood under the door so they couldn't get out." There. It was over.

The king's eyes were smiling. Perhaps he hadn't fully understood.

"Remember to breathe, Sepia," he said. "And then tell me why it was so important to shut them in."

"Because they mustn't go beyond the mists," she said. "And they might have done if they'd gone after Linty, especially with all that fog, so they might not even have been clear about where the mists were. Nobody's ever come back a third time, so I didn't want to risk them going."

"There's no certainty that anyone will ever get back," said Crispin.

"I know," she said, "but especially those two. And just now, when Urchin was telling you, you were worried about what had happened, so I had to tell you that it was only me. And"—she looked unhappily down at her paws—"they got out, and Lugg died anyway."

"Yes, you're not a very good jailer, are you?" said Crispin. "I'm glad you told me. You should have left them to make their own decisions and take their own risks, but in the end, they did."

"I meant well," she said. "I really did mean it for the best. It isn't always easy to know what to do."

"I wasn't at all happy about you going off in the boat last night," said Crispin, "but you had to take your own risks, and I made sure you had animals as near as possible to protect you. After this, the queen and I will probably never want to leave Catkin alone in her cradle without being strapped in and guarded, but that's no good, is it? Off you go, now, Sepia, and I'll let Urchin know that there was nothing sinister going on last night. I won't tell him it was you, but you could tell him yourself. He might laugh, but he won't be angry."

Leaving the chamber, Sepia felt she had been in the tower with its sorrow too long. She needed fresh air and ran from the tower to the clean, breathy shore to find Needle, Scatter, and Hope already there. Hope was picking up shells to take to Brother Fir, and an otter was swimming toward the shore, pushing something in front of it.

"Fingal!" she called, waving. As he came nearer she saw that he was steering a plank of driftwood to the shore. Normally all driftwood looked alike to Sepia, but there was definitely something familiar about this piece. He scrambled to the shore, dragged it onto the dry sand, and ran beaming to meet her.

"Look at this!" he yelled, long before he reached her. "Just look at this!"

"It's a plank," said Sepia.

"It smells squirrelly," said Hope, sniffing at it.

"Of course it does!" laughed Fingal. "Oh, come on, Sepia, you know what it is! Tell her again, Hope. Piece of driftwood. Squirrels."

"Is it . . . ?" said Sepia, "I don't know, it was dark, and I was concentrating on what I was doing, but is it the one I rode on last night?"

"The very same one!" said Fingal proudly. "Padra left it propped up against a rock, he said I should go back for it, and I couldn't think why, but look—just look at this!"

With bright triumph on his face he turned the plank over. Traces of deep red and orange paint still clung to it and a decoration of green leaves.

"It's from my boat!" he cried, and flung an arm around her. "It's a bit of my boat! If it hadn't been smashed to bits in the storm, you couldn't have climbed onto it!"

Sepia hugged him and wondered what they'd ever do if they didn't have Fingal. She hadn't the heart to tell him that it was the same bit of driftwood that had hit the boat and woken Linty in the first place. "We'll all help you build your new boat."

"I've talked to Twigg about it," he said. "There's lots of other work to do, so it'll be a long wait—spring, I should think. But that's all right."

When two more days had passed, Brother Fir led the funeral prayers, and the coffin of Lugg of Mistmantle was carried away on the shoulders of four moles through a guard of honor. It seemed impossible to Urchin that they had been without Lugg all this time, but they had survived. The sun still rose in the mornings. Animals, quiet with respect, slipped back to their homes, and Needle, who felt it was time life returned to normal, climbed the stairs to the empty workrooms.

She rubbed her eyes, let herself in, and found a scrap of canvas. She couldn't sew, as her left paw was in a sling, but she needed only one paw to draw, and she wanted to sketch a design for a Threading. It showed a mole in a blue cloak, his claws in his sword belt, as she had so often seen him. But it looked so like him, so familiar, that she had to stop and push the canvas away, so she wouldn't spoil her work by crying on it.

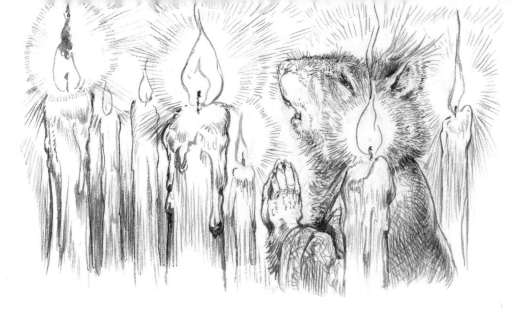

CHAPTER TWENTY-THREE

THE CHAMBER OF CANDLES GLOWED more beautifully than ever, filled with rank upon rank of candles, set in brackets on the walls, arranged in rows and clusters on the ground, tall creamy white candles and tiny white lights. Brother Fir and Juniper sang words of blessing so that the flames nearest them trembled in their breath and flickered on the walls as Crispin, Padra, and Arran, bareheaded, stood at the opposite side of the pit.

Urchin was there, Needle, Docken, and Russet, and two of each kind of animal. Grouped together, standing nervously a little way apart, were Yarrow, Hobb, Quill, and Quill's father, a thickset hedgehog with short spines and—Urchin tried not to notice—a bulging stomach.

"Thank you, Brother Fir, Brother Juniper," said Crispin. "Now, let us finish this business, as it would have been finished long before if not for the discovery of Catkin and the death of Captain Lugg. Juniper had just discovered the remains of Captain Husk. I do not intend those remains to become a curiosity for animals to stare at for the sake of staring, but today, those who wish to see the skeleton and assure themselves that Husk is dead may do so. This is the place from which he fell. I will personally lead you from this chamber to the old workshop and along the route that Brother Juniper discovered to the bottom of this pit."

Yarrow and Hobb looked at each other for help, and Yarrow coughed noisily. They were still lost for words when Quill nervously raised a paw.

"Please, Your Majesty," he said, "I've had time to think about it. And"—he glanced up at his father—"Dad said I should always listen to my elders, and so I am. Your Majesty, I'm listening to what you and Captain Padra and Brother Fir said, and you all say you saw Captain Husk fall and he's dead. So if that's what you say, Your Majesty, it's good enough for me. If you want me to go down there, I'll do it, because I don't want anyone thinking I'm afraid." (Urchin suspected that he *was* afraid, but he was prepared to go anyway and was being extremely brave.) "But I don't need to. Your Majesty's word and everyone else's here is good enough, sir."

"Good lad, Quill," said Crispin.

"And all that goes for me too, Your Majesty," said Yarrow quickly.

"And me, Your Majesty," said Hobb.

"But in the case of you two, it doesn't matter," said Padra briskly, "because you're going down anyway. Don't worry, we'll be with you. And we'll be far better equipped than Juniper was when he first went down."

Yarrow suddenly had a fit of coughing, turning his head away and pressing a paw to his chest. "I'll do my best, sir," he croaked.

"And when we get back, we'll have hot cordials to warm us all up," said Padra. "Urchin, send a message to Apple and ask if she could kindly spare some of her apple and mint cordial. No cough can survive that."

Following the upheaval of sickness, quarantine, landslide, and rescue, the workrooms were pleasantly back to normal. Hedgehogs and squirrels sang softly to themselves as they stitched, wove, and painted. Moles fetched and carried and wound wool on shuttles. In the late afternoon there was a pleasant hum of warmth, work, and good humor. Thripple had been patiently teaching a new apprentice hedgehog to hem velvet while, in the passageway outside, Hope and Scufflen played skittles with empty bobbins and a pebble, but now she had called the little ones in, and they all seemed to be very busy with a large sheet of canvas.

At the window, Needle was making the most of the light before it faded and finishing her design for the Threading of Captain Lugg. She marked in the cloak, the sword, and the round head. Whittle, who had learned all he had to learn about fouldrought, had gone back to learning the Threadings code and was surveying various half-finished Threadings while muttering, "brown for moles, heather for strength, rue for sorrow, oak for a captain . . ." and holding out his paws if anyone needed to wind wool.

"That'll do," said Needle at last, and surveyed her work. There didn't seem to be anything in the Threadings code that really said what everyone felt about Lugg, and as she was now a leading Threading hedgehog, she felt a lot of responsibility. There was a soft knock at the door, and Sepia hopped in with a homespun garment in her paws, the color of oatmeal.

"Mistress Thripple, Needle," she said, "what should we do with this?"

Thripple came to join them as she shook it out and spread it on a table by the light of the window. It was a priest's tunic, very neatly stitched and almost finished, with the freshly woven smell and feel of new fabric about it. But a pattern of juniper berries at one shoulder was not complete, and a dark blue thread hung loosely across them.

"Where did this come from?" asked Thripple.

"It was in Damson's burrow," said Sepia. "She must have meant it for Juniper's ordination, but she never finished it. I thought I might do it myself," she added, plucking at the loose thread, "but I'd only make a mess of it, so I brought it to you."

"Hold it up to the light, please," said Needle. Sepia held the tunic up to the window, and Thripple came to look over Needle's shoulder.

"We can't tell how she meant it to look," said Needle. "But it wouldn't be difficult to finish it, with a berry here and a bit of twig there. Should I work it out on a piece of scrap fabric first? The hard thing would be to do it so that nobody could tell the difference in the stitching, but . . ." She stopped, with a feeling that somehow she was saying all the wrong things. Thripple put an arm around her.

"Do you think," she suggested, "that we should leave it exactly as it is?"

Sepia laid the tunic down, and Needle smoothed it lovingly. Nobody else could complete it quite as Damson would have done. It was her gift, the best she could do for Juniper, as she had always tried to do her best for the injured and abandoned squirrel who had come to her care. Husk had tried to kill every baby born weak or even slightly deformed or shortsighted, and Padra, among others, had risked everything to save them. And now they were just right, those children. What did a curled paw or short sight matter? If some in the community were weaker than others, or slow, or not very bright, there was no harm in that. They were part of Mistmantle, just the way they were. Nothing was ever finished, nothing was ever completely correct. For all the animals of Mistmantle, for the weak and the badly formed, for Thripple with her lopsidedness, and for the unfinished pattern of juniper berries, their imperfections made them perfect.

"We should leave it like this," she said. "It's a different kind of finished."

The autumn day was mild enough for Brother Fir to make the long journey down the tower stairs and onto the shore. Juniper took the stairs very slowly.

"Getting back up won't be a problem, Brother Fir," said Juniper. "Any two of us could carry you, or one strong one."

"I'm glad to hear it," said Fir. "I was afraid you might plan to sling me over your shoulder and take the stairs two at a time." He stopped by a window. A lot of small animals, including Hope the hedgehog and members of Sepia's choir, were scurrying busily about on the rocks below the tower, and more were struggling down the hill carrying something clearly much too heavy for them.

"Are they organizing a game?" suggested Juniper.

"Maybe," said Fir. "But they look purposeful." He raised a frail, thin paw toward them. "Bless them. Hm."

Slowly, they made their way to the Spring Gate. Fir raised his head and sniffed, breathed deeply, and smiled with deep contentment.

"Fresh sea air," he said. "Wonderful. And here's Urchin!"

Urchin was on the way from his chambers with little Swanfeather the otter holding his paw. He usually carried her on his shoulder, but she was getting heavier now and didn't know how to stay still. He walked with Fir and Juniper to the water's edge, which was about as far as Fir could manage in one go, and where there was a convenient rock to sit on. Fir settled down there with his cloak wrapped about him, sometimes with his eyes closed, sometimes looking out to sea with intent enjoyment, swaying a little. Swanfeather pulled at Urchin's paw.

"Come on, then," he said, and turned to Juniper. "I'll take her down to the jetty. She might find some of her friends there."

"We'll join you later," said Juniper, "if Fir feels up to it."

"Hm!" said Fir. "You two, if you have things to do, run along. I'm sure one of these good animals can heave me back to the tower. Are those little ones still busy at whatever it was they were doing?"

As Urchin and Juniper looked around, something that appeared to be a coarse sheet wafted around the corner of the tower. As it came nearer they saw that it was a piece of canvas or coarse linen with small feet propelling it along the shore.

"It walks," said Juniper.

"And it giggles," said Fir, as smothered laughter came from beneath it. As the canvas and its bearers came nearer, they could see Hope, little Siskin from Sepia's choir, Scufflen, and maybe a dozen small animals carrying it along the shore. It sagged now and again and dragged in the sand.

"Shall we give them a paw?" said Urchin, but when he and Juniper ran down to join them, Siskin waved them away.

"We can manage!" she piped up breathlessly.

"Yes, thank you, Urchin, thank you, Brother Juniper, we can manage, thank you!" panted Hope. "We're doing this by ourselves!"

"Here's Apple, too," said Juniper. "Hello, Mistress Apple!"

Apple was waddling toward them, a good-natured smile on her face. She hugged Urchin, then Juniper.

"Morning, Brother Fir," she said, "good to see you up, or should I say down, I mean outside, I been offering to help them young 'uns, but they won't have it, they want to do it all theirselves, bless them, hello little Swanfeather, are you coming to Apple then, ooh, what a lovely hug, I'm all wet now, hello young Fingal and everyone, don't go away, Fingal, I think they might need you."

The procession of small animals stopped, laying the canvas carefully down and spreading it out on the shore. There was a ripple underneath it which suddenly stopped and changed direction, then Todd, the mole, scurried out.

"Fingal?" said Hope uncertainly.

"I'm here," said Fingal, and knelt down in front of him.

"We brought you a sail," said Hope, "because of what happened to your boat, so I asked my mum and she helped us to make it."

"That's wonderful!" exclaimed Fingal. "What a beautiful sail! Thank you all very much!" And he hugged Hope so hard that he had difficulty removing a prickle from his paw. "And thank your mum for me, Hope—no, I'll go and thank her myself—this is so kind!"

Too touched and delighted to find enough words, he hugged the nearest animal, Todd, who quickly wriggled free.

"Don't go thanking her yet," he muttered. "We got something else for you."

They all turned to look up again at the tower. More young animals

294

were processing from the tower, carrying a huge fallen tree trunk like a battering ram. Padra's little son, Tide, was doing his best to help, and the procession was led by Tipp the mole, brandishing a stick as a sword.

"Timber patrol!" he yelled. "CHARGE!"

It wasn't so much a charge as a stagger, with all the other animals running to meet them halfway. Panting for breath, Tipp ordered, "Present tree trunk!" and they laid it down before Fingal. Tipp bowed deeply.

"A tree trunk rescued from the storm," he announced. "To build your boat, Fingal."

"How wonderfully kind of you all!" exclaimed Fingal. "Thank you!"

Juniper and Urchin glanced at each other. They understood that new wood was no good for boat building. Boats must be made from seasoned timber that would withstand hard weather. Fingal would know that, of course, but he was on his knees hugging the young animals as they crowded round him. Fir hobbled forward and bent stiffly to take a good look at the log.

"What do you think, Fingal?" he asked. "I'm no expert on boats, but I'm sure this is just the sort of wood we used to build rafts with. Did you ever have a raft, Fingal?"

"Oh, yes!" said Fingal. "Somebody made me one when I was small, my parents, or Padra, or all of them. Rafts are great fun. You can't take them into deep water, but they're wonderful for the shallows. You need a long pole to push yourself around with."

"Did you ever fall in?" asked Urchin.

"That's the best bit!" said Fingal cheerfully. He pushed at the log. "A bit more wood, some rope, moss, a few empty barrels from the cellar . . ."

The little animals were scattering in all directions, all saying they knew where they could get some rope, or moss, and one saying his grandpa was the cellar otter's best friend, and he'd give them barrels if he asked them. Before long three of them came back, giggling and squeaking and rolling a barrel which seemed to be getting away from them at a dangerous speed, and gabbling out to Urchin that they'd just seen Whittle the squirrel, who said the king wanted to see him.

It was a pity to leave when the raft-building looked like such fun. Urchin left Swanfeather in Fingal's care and ran back to the tower with sand in his fur.

CHAPTER TWENTY-FOUR

THE NEXT DAY NEEDLE AND URCHIN again were to go to the Throne Room, but Urchin made sure he was early. From a squeak and a laugh as he knocked on the door, he knew that Cedar and Catkin were there with Crispin.

"Urchin," said Crispin. "It's time we talked about you two joining the Circle."

"I know, sir," said Urchin, who wasn't enjoying this. He took his paw from his sword hilt to stop himself from fidgeting and said something that was even harder than he had expected. "Please, Your Majesty— Majesties—I don't want to make trouble or seem ungrateful, but could I not join the Circle just yet? Would you mind, Your Majesty?"

He hadn't often seen Crispin lost for words, but he seemed to be struggling now. Finally, the king said, "I have never known anyone not want to join the Circle."

"Oh, I do want it, Your Majesty!" cried Urchin. "I think I've always wanted it. Everyone dreams of joining the Circle. But, sir, it's because of Juniper. He's my friend, we're sort of brothers, I have to look out for him. I know he feels he's in my shadow, sir, and for me to be part of the Circle and not him . . ." Suddenly realizing that Crispin might misunderstand him, he went on quickly, "I'm not asking you to admit Juniper to the Circle at the same time. I know Needle and I are very young to be admitted, and he's younger than we are. It's just that it would be better for Juniper if I waited until he's either admitted to the Circle or ordained as a priest, and so he has an honor of his own."

"You realize," said Crispin, "that if you refuse to be admitted, Needle will refuse too? You won't be admitted without Juniper, and you can be certain she won't be admitted without you."

"Yes, I know," said Urchin, who had already thought of this. "I don't know what to do about that. I don't want to hold her back. They're both my friends."

"And very good friends," said Crispin. "Priests aren't usually admitted to the Circle because they become members of it by right as soon as they're ordained, and it's good for them to be different from the other members. Priests need to be able to put the rest of us right from time to time. As you point out, he's very young. And I can't make him a Companion to the King because he's needed at Fir's right paw, not mine." He glanced past Urchin at Cedar. "Give us time to think about this, Urchin."

A guard rapped at the door with a call of "Miss Needle!"

and Needle trotted in. Catkin squeaked happily at her.

"Hello, Needle, we're just talking about the Circle," said the king. "And there should be an honor for Sepia, too. She's very busy, but I wonder if she'd like to be a Companion to the King?"

"Well . . ." said Needle cautiously, and couldn't help glancing toward Cedar and Catkin.

"I see," said Crispin. "You think she'd rather be a Companion to the Queen? And will you take me to see the Threading of Captain Lugg?"

On the shore, Fir smiled as he raised his face to the sky. He supposed he should never be surprised any more at the way the Heart made good things come from the most terrible circumstances. But he couldn't help feeling surprised, pleasantly so. Catkin was found, disease was over, the islanders were working together to repair each other's houses after the landslide, prayers were being said every day in the place where Husk fell. The little ones were having a wonderful time building a raft. No doubt, after this, they would expect Fingal to spend morning after morning punting them about the shore, and they would shuffle together to see how many animals they could get on before it began to sink. In a quiet cove near Twigg's new workshop, a team of carpenters worked on a boat about which Fingal knew nothing at all. Young animals hopped about the rocks playing Find the Heir of Mistmantle while Siskin told everyone who'd listen that the king knew her name.

All would be well. Whatever happened.

CHAPTER TWENTY-FIVE

T HEY'RE ALL RIVERING UP THE STAIRS!" exclaimed Whittle.
It was impossible even to see the tower stairs as the animals,
in their best hats and cloaks, swarmed up to the door.

"They're doing what?" inquired Crispin.

"I mean, pouring up the stairs like a river," said Whittle, "except
rivers don't go up. It'll be even more like a river when they go down
again."

"Aren't you supposed to be looking after Brother Fir?" said Crispin.

"I think this is a time just for him and Juniper," said Whittle, "so I said
perhaps I should offer to help Mistress Tay today, and Brother Fir said
yes. And I reported to Mistress Tay, and she said thank you very much,
but she couldn't bear any more distractions and responsibilities today,
and I should report for duty to another senior animal. But everyone's so
busy, I can't get near anyone to report to except you, Your Majesty."

"Can he report to me, Your Majesty?" said a mole guard behind him. "Special guests are to go in by the Spring Gate. Nip down there, son, and look out for any special guests, and show 'em up to the Gathering Chamber."

"How do I know if they're special guests?" asked Whittle.

"They're the ones looking for the Spring Gate, aren't they?" said the mole. "Squirrel yourself off, then!"

Whittle leaped for the nearest window, measured the jump, scrabbled a bit, and ran down the wall. A mole at the foot of the main stairway was trying to make himself heard as he shouted, "King Crispin's special guests to the Spring Gate!" It appeared that the special guests all carried leaves bearing Crispin's clawmark and were showing them to the guard. A female squirrel in a dark blue cloak was hurrying toward it, and Whittle quickly caught up with her.

"Excuse me," he said, "aren't you . . ."

"I'm Apple, that's me, son, I'm Urchin's mum, well his foster-mum, you know how it is, I know you, you're the one who's learning the history and the law, it must be wonderful to have all that up in your head, don't know where you find room for it all." She took Whittle's offered arm and let him escort her to the Spring Gate—past the spring and Padra and Urchin's quarters and the back stairway, through a long corridor and up another stair which would bring them to the Gathering Chamber in the opposite direction from everyone else. He had to slow down to Apple's pace.

"Never thought this would happen, never in the old days when I was small," she said. "Think of me, coming into the tower the special guests' way, used to work in the laundry here when I were young, but I always left my heart in the wood, I went back, stopped in the wood all my life, got good friends, and here I am, and my Urchin . . ." She stopped so suddenly that Whittle was alarmed, but after catching her breath and rubbing her eyes she went on, ". . . and my little Urchin in the Circle! And our Needle, she's a little smasher, she made me this cloak special for today."

She turned toward the door of the Gathering Chamber, but Whittle steered her away.

"Special guests in the gallery," he said, and led her up a stairway to the new gallery which had first been built for Crispin's coronation. If she was a little disappointed that the rest of the islanders might miss out on seeing her beautiful new blue cloak and her freshly decorated hat, she was soon comforted, for, as she leaned over the edge of the gallery, an oak leaf fluttered down from her hat and landed on the head of a small Anemone Wood hedgehog.

"Apple!" he squeaked! Heads turned. "Ooh, look, it's Apple!" called someone, and for a few proud and bewildering seconds, Apple stood at the front of the gallery and waved to her friends. Then Needle and Sepia's families came to join her, and they all bustled about putting the littlest animals to the front so they could see and keep at a safe distance from the more prickly hedgehogs, while Scufflen pointed to every Threading he could see and said loudly that his sister made that one.

Apple sat back and admired the decorated hall, garlanded with autumn leaves, berries, and evergreens. Chairs had been arranged on the dais for Crispin, Cedar, and Fir, with more behind for Padra and Arran. The last chair on the row had been spread with a blue cloak, a sword, and a circlet.

In the anteroom, Urchin and Needle sat perched on a chest. It was the chest in which the robes were kept, where, long ago, Urchin had discovered the leaves which had helped to bring about Husk's downfall. He had been up very early in the morning—not difficult, as he'd found sleep impossible—and Arran had helped him to groom himself so that his fur gleamed softly, his ears and tail tip were neatly brushed, and his claws clean and trimmed. His sword was polished to such brightness that it flashed in the late autumn sunlight. Needle, too, was groomed to perfection, her sharp spines neat and smooth. When Needle said, "It's a bit odd, all this, isn't it?" Urchin felt he knew why Crispin had waited until now to admit them to the Circle. Things would have to change now. There would be responsibilities to take, decisions to share. Animals would come to them with their worries.

Usually the captains and Mistress Tay robed in this room, but today they were using the royal chambers, leaving the anteroom to the new members of the Circle. Urchin wished Padra and Arran would stride into the room, talking and laughing and making everything easy and relaxed.

"Are you all right, Needle?" he asked. Needle didn't snap at him or say that of course she was, she just said quietly, "Are you?" and took his paw.

"I am now," he said. "Now I know Crispin has something in mind for Juniper."

"Do you think we'll ever play games in the wood again, and explore tunnels, and all that?" she wondered aloud.

"Oh, yes, of course we will!" said Urchin. It was impossible that they wouldn't. Then Needle jumped up.

"Listen!" she said.

In the Gathering Chamber, a mole was calling the animals to order. After a moment of tingling silence, a fanfare of trumpets and the high, pure voices of the choir announced the coming of the king. Urchin and Needle hopped to the door where they could see the dais.

The Circle animals arrived first, in embroidered cloaks—Russet and Heath, Docken, Tay, Moth and Spade, and Mother Huggen. Juniper followed, wearing a tunic that Urchin couldn't remember seeing before, then Padra and Arran, and, at last, King Crispin and Queen Cedar, crowned and cloaked, and looking happier than they had been since before Catkin first disappeared. It was as if all the island's heaviness had passed from them. Then came Brother Fir, his eyes deeply joyful as he hobbled to his place.

When all were ready, the Throne Room mole hurried to the ante-room door. He took a deep breath and said the words he had been rehearsing.

"King Crispin and Queen Cedar, Captain Padra and Captain Arran, Brother Fir and Brother Juniper, and all the animals of the Circle await Master Urchin and Miss Needle."

Urchin took a deep breath. Side by side, he and Needle walked to the dais—it felt like miles—and stood before the king. Urchin wondered if his fur was sticking up and whether his tail had got dusty in there, but it was too late to check. Crispin and Fir were already stepping forward.

"We have come to the Gathering Chamber," announced Crispin, "because Urchin of the Riding Stars and Needle of the Threadings have been considered and found worthy to join the Circle. Young as they are, they have served the island bravely and faithfully and will uphold the values of our island. Urchin, Needle, kneel."

They knelt. Urchin looked steadily up at Crispin's face and forgot to be nervous.

"Urchin of the Riding Stars, Needle of the Threadings," said Crispin. "Will you love, worship, and serve the Heart?"

"We will, Your Majesty," they said together.

"Will you love, serve, and care for this island and all its animals?"

"We will, Your Majesty."

"Will you live for justice and mercy?"

"We will, Your Majesty."

"Urchin, Needle, be compassionate, be strong for what is right, fight against evil, protect the weak, care for the young and the old. Know how to give orders and how to take them. Be true, be generous of heart and paw, be kind."

"Remember," said Brother Fir, "that if your heart should break, the Heart that cares for us broke with love for us, but it still beats for us, keeps us, and loves us." He raised a paw. "May the Heart enlighten you, enfold you, keep you."

"Stand," ordered Crispin.

Two otters came forward bearing embroidered cloaks across their paws. Urchin stood very still, Crispin's words still in his ears, waiting for the touch of the cool velvet on his fur, surprised at how heavy the cloak was when it came. Fir's paw, firm in blessing, pressed down on his head. Padra held a garland of rosemary and bay high, then lifted it over Urchin's head and settled it on his shoulders. Then there was the paw-clasp of each member of the Circle in turn, and finally he was hugged and kissed on both cheeks by Crispin, Padra, and Arran, and he knew that the smell of bay, rosemary, and warm washed fur would stay with him forever. As Padra turned him to face the gathered crowds, he could still feel the press of Fir's paw on his head.

He folded his paw over the bracelet on his wrist. Perhaps, somehow, his parents could see him. He hoped so.

When animals talked afterward about that moment, they talked of all the cheering and applause for Urchin and Needle. But Urchin himself didn't remember that. He only recalled searching the crowd for Apple's face before he remembered that she'd be in the gallery, and he met her eyes at last, and smiled as she waved both paws and blew kisses.

As the applause finally died away, Urchin realized he wasn't sure what he was meant to do next. He glanced around at Padra and found him already moving forward to draw Urchin to stand at his side at the edge of the dais. Arran was doing the same for Needle, and it was clear that Crispin had something more to say.

"Good animals of Mistmantle," he called, "we have more young heroes to honor today for their service to us all."

Three moles stepped forward, each bearing an autumn garland on a cushion. One was woven with deep red hawthorn berries, one with yellow jasmine, and the third—Urchin's heart leaped when he saw it—with darkly shining juniper berries. Crispin lifted the wreath of jasmine.

"Fingal," he said—and Urchin saw Fingal, who'd been looking the other way, suddenly whisk his head around to pay attention so that Crispin's mouth twitched with secret laughter, "you have given your all in saving Mismantle animals from the contaminated water and from the landslide, and you took part in the rescue of Princess Catkin. Receive our honors, our thanks, and our love, Fingal of the Floods."

There was a moment when Fingal didn't move, and Urchin saw his lips form the word, "Me?" But at a nudge from Sepia he stood up, came forward, bowed to Crispin, and stood still while the king placed the wreath about his neck. Crispin whispered something to him then turned him around to face the cheering animals, and the otters raised the cry of "Fingal of the Floods!" as they applauded, until Crispin had to hold up a paw for silence.

"Sepia," he said, "you cared for the queen in her sorrow and for Mistress Damson at her death. You were gentle enough for Linty to listen to you and brave enough to cross the water to speak to her, though you knew you could be attacked or carried through the mists. You are the one who brought Catkin safely home. Receive our honors, our thanks, and our love, Sepia of the Songs."

Sepia pattered up to the dais, and Urchin heard her say something quietly to Crispin about how she shouldn't really have a garland because she'd only done what anyone would . . . but Crispin put a clawtip gently to her lips, lifted the hawthorn garland over her head, and turned her to face the animals. Amid the cheers were several loud voices calling her to sing.

"She won't sing for you yet," said Crispin, "but I hope you'll hear her later in the day. Sepia, you may sit down."

"Finally," he said, "we honor a most exceptional young animal who had only just come out of hiding when he made the crossing of the sea for which he is now famous, to accompany Urchin to Whitewings. It was Juniper who found good friends to help them escape from the island, so that he, Urchin, and Lugg came safely home, bringing a queen for Mistmantle."

There was a little laughter and a mischievous smile from Cedar.

"Since then," he said, "he has become Brother Fir's assistant and will soon be a priest. He, too, risked his life in the landslide. He has journeyed, not only over the sea, but under the earth to bring truth to you all, and I know he has made deeper and harder journeys within himself. Brother Juniper of the Journeyings, come forward. Receive the love and the honor of this island."

"Yes!" thought Urchin, for this was the way it should be, with

Juniper limping forward, calm and self-possessed, wearing a new tunic with its unfinished pattern, as Crispin settled the garland around his neck. And Urchin felt he was looking at Juniper the way Padra looked at Fingal. It really was like being brothers.

Crispin turned Juniper to face the islanders.

"When we gather here again," he announced, "it will be to see Juniper ordained priest, when he, too, will become a member of the Circle."

This time, there wasn't applause. The murmur of approval and smiles meant far more to Juniper.

"And now," said Crispin, "the rest of the day is celebration. There will be entertainment in the tower and on the rocks all day, and food will be served wherever our excellent tower animals find the space to lay a table. Evening prayer will be said at sundown."

There was a thank-you to the kitchen staff, followed by so much applause that Crispin had to call for quiet again before Fir could give a blessing, but Fir said that Juniper should do it. Then the feasting began.

Wine and cordial were served from silver trays; otters carried platters of fish and seaweed to the tables; squirrels dashed up and down the back stairs to fetch and carry. Every table in the tower was set with nuts, berries, walnut and hazelnut bread, cones, and all sorts of things that moles and hedgehogs ate and Urchin didn't like the look of at all. Then there were honey biscuits, raisins, and little fluffy creamy things which left white traces on fur and whiskers.

Acrobats leaped and balanced on the rocks, and music was played on the stairways. Choirs sang, small animals acted plays, there were jugglers, dancers, and singers on every landing, on rocks and turrets. Tightrope squirrels somersaulted from one turret to another so that animals stopped with biscuits halfway to their mouths and gasped. Dazzled with the day's excitement, they met at last in the Gathering Chamber for evening prayer as the sun set in gold and pink across a clear sky and a quiet sea. Prayers were said and sung; silences were kept; babies snored softly in their mothers' arms; Hope, smeared with cream and berry juice, fell asleep against Docken's shoulder; and the two smallest squirrels in the choir cuddled wearily against Sepia. Moth rocked Princess Catkin, who had fallen asleep clutching her blanket. Needle held Scufflen in her lap, discreetly slipping him raisins to keep him quiet until the final blessing was said, and the animals made their way home.

"Sepia," said the queen, "you can sleep in the nursery tonight if you like. I've moved Catkin's cradle into our own chamber, I can't bear to let her out of my sight."

"The only difficulty is keeping her in the cradle," said Crispin. "What are we going to do when she learns to climb out of windows?"

Sepia, yawning already, slipped to the nursery where she wrapped herself in a rug and curled up by the window, resting her chin on her paws. It was a beautiful night.

Urchin, leaving the Gathering Chamber, was about to go down to the Spring Gate to change when a furious pounding of paws up the stairs made him step aside just in time to avoid being knocked over by Fingal and Needle. Fingal dashed past him, turned around, seized him by the shoulders, and cried, "Come and see this!"

"It's wonderful!" said Needle. "It's . . ." Fingal clamped a paw over her mouth. "Ooboofoobooboo!" said Needle.

"Come and see!" said Fingal.

"I have to go down to the Spring Gate to change first," said Urchin.

"Meet you down there in a minute, then!" said Fingal.

Urchin turned toward the Spring Gate, but at the bottom of the stairs he caught sight of a squirrel so dashing and so elegant that he had to stop and look again. Then he stood quite still in surprise, looking at the very pale squirrel, garlanded and in a velvet cloak.

He was looking in a mirror.

There were brisk pawsteps behind him and he turned away quickly, not wanting anyone to think he was admiring himself. But then he heard Padra's voice, and Crispin's, and presently they appeared, talking as they walked down the stairs together.

"All right, Urchin?" asked Padra. "It's been a long day. Go to bed."

"I will soon," said Urchin, "but I have to go to the shore. Fingal wants me to see something."

There was a quick exchange of smiles between Crispin and Padra.

"Typical," said Padra. "As soon as you admit them to the Circle, they start disobeying orders."

"Then I command you to go and see what Fingal is making such a fuss about," said Crispin. "And get some fresh air into your lungs. Shall we put him on dawn patrol tomorrow, Padra?"

"Sir—Your Majesty—" said Urchin, knowing there were things he could say to Padra and Crispin that he'd never say to anyone else, "when I saw that mirror just now, I didn't know it was me. I look grown up, like a proper member of the Circle. But I don't feel any different inside."

"I know," said Padra gently, "that's what it's like, growing up. Off you go, and see what Fingal's getting so excited about."

Urchin laid his new cloak away carefully in a chest in the Spring Gate chamber and put on an old red one to go down to the shore. The fresh breeze was welcome after a day in the tower. In the darkness, the sea gently swished and hushed. There were lanterns at the jetty and an eager cry of "Over here, Urchin!" reached him as Fingal waved furiously with his free paw, holding up the lantern with the other. Needle and Juniper were there, too, with lanterns. More lights hung from a small boat with oars and and a furled sail, moored by the jetty. Even from a distance he could see how smooth and clean her lines were, and as he drew nearer he saw how her red and orange paint gleamed with its pattern of green leaves and the painting of a mole on the prow. He saw, too, the shining joy in Fingal's eyes.

"My *boat*!" he said breathlessly. "My new *boat*! Everyone's been helping to make it, Twigg's been working in secret, and Padra and Crispin had something to do with it, and I didn't know! Isn't it . . ." There was a catch in his voice and Urchin thought that, for the first time in his life, he would see Fingal moved to tears, but Fingal suddenly laughed and said, "Isn't it *wonderful*! Isn't she a beauty! Do you want to try her out? You'll all come, won't you?"

"Has she got a name?" asked Urchin.

"Only one name she could have, even though she's not a he," said Fingal. "*Captain Lugg*."

"Juniper," said Urchin, as Fingal untied the boat, "I'm really glad you were given a share of the honors. It was right."

Juniper smiled and shrugged. "It was very nice," he said, "But it wasn't really what matters."

"You'll be saying 'hm' next," observed Needle.

The boat rocked as they all stepped in. Smoothly, under a clear starry sky with a moon track on the water, Fingal rowed.

"What was the king saying to you when he gave you the garland?" asked Needle.

"Oh," said Fingal. "Um . . ."

"It's none of our business!" said Urchin.

"No, it's all right," said Fingal. "But he said he wouldn't be surprised if I end up in the Circle myself one of these days. I'd have to go all sensible, wouldn't I?"

"I don't think there's much danger of it," said Needle.

They rowed silently after that, apart from Needle remarking that with all the recent goings on, it was surprising that they hadn't had more riding stars, and Juniper replying that Fir hadn't said anything on the subject. When they reached the bay on the other side of the tower, Urchin said, "Here, please. Can you take me to the shallows? I don't mind getting my paws wet."

Fingal rowed until the boat settled softly in shallow water. "Don't wait for me," called Urchin as he sprang over the side. He stood alone as they rowed back to the jetty. Waves swished over his paws as he looked out to sea and up to the stars, taking time to let the day and the night sink into him.

This was the spot where Fir and Crispin had found him, newborn. Folding a paw over his bracelet, he hoped again that his mother could see him and was proud of him. As he watched, a single silver star twirled slowly down toward the sea.

Finally getting home to her burrow, Apple stopped to watch it float from the sky. Padra and Arran, emerging into the cool night air, saw it. So did Juniper, Fingal, and Needle, all turning in the boat to watch its progress. Sepia, wrapped in a quilt and wide-eyed with wonder, leaned forward at the nursery window to watch it.

"Good night, Captain Lugg," she thought, and looked down to see Urchin on the shore.

Crispin and Cedar at their window saw it and gasped in surprise, holding up Catkin to see it, too. Brother Fir smiled with joy, raised a paw in blessing and went to bed with peace and warmth in his heart.

Urchin, standing at the water's edge on the spot where he had been found, followed the star's slow, sure progress until it disappeared into the sea, and felt as if it were something to do with Lugg, and with himself. It was as if it came from the Heart and had somehow lodged in his own heart. A single star, merging into the sea at the end of its time.

He was one of the Circle now. As a child he had dreamed of such a thing, but never expected it to happen. But he still felt the same inside. He hoped he'd still have the chance to run up trees, to skim stones and splash about, to be young.

He wasn't surprised to find Crispin at his shoulder. It seemed like the most natural thing in the world that Crispin, who had made his dreams possible, should be here now.

"Find the king, find the queen, find the Heir of Mistmantle," said Crispin. "I think you've done your bit, Urchin. Have some fun before we expect you to start giving orders."

"Giving orders?" said Urchin, and Crispin laughed.

"Race you back to the tower?" said Crispin. He turned and pointed. "There's an open window onto the Gathering Chamber corridor, d'you see it?"

They leaped over sand, scrambled over rocks, sprang through bushes and treetops, recklessly jostling each other for the best branches and claw-holds until they launched themselves at the tower wall, skimmed up the stone, and tumbled side by side through the window.

"Ouch!" said Crispin.

"Guards!" yelled Needle, picking herself up. "Oh, Your Majesty, I didn't realize it was you. And Urchin. I might have known."

"Well guarded, Needle," said Crispin, and dusted himself down. "Sorry, did I knock you over?"

"I think that was a draw, Your Majesty," said Urchin.

"Good night, both of you," said Crispin, and turned toward the royal chambers.

Urchin leaned his paws on the window ledge and smiled gladly up at a sky full of stars that would ride and dance across the sky when their time came. There was joy in his heart, sea air in his breath, and a sky full of stars above him.

It was only starting.